LOVELY TORMENT

SAVAGE HEARTS SYNDICATE
BOOK 2

KIMBERLY QUINN

FOUR YEARS AGO

FINN

THE 9MM HIDDEN at my back was like an itch I couldn't scratch. Not only uncomfortable but troubling as hell. It didn't belong here.

I didn't belong here.

And yet…

"Do me a favor," Law rumbled through my earpiece. "Before you get us thrown off the job. Relax."

Relax? Tell that to my body. To my instincts screaming that something was off. With this crowd. This client. And the fact that I wasn't the only one carrying a gun in a sex club.

A goddamn sex club.

A place where people were at their most vulnerable and weapons were expressly forbidden. Where power was measured not by money or status but by submission.

Hell, tell it to the uptight part of me that refused to unbutton. The part whispering that the scene playing out in the center of the room wasn't meant for me. That I had no right to watch.

Still, I couldn't look away.

A naked woman was bound and gagged, her body slick with sweat and cum. She was wrung out but still being pushed past every limit by the three masked men surrounding her. With toys, hands, and cocks, they continued dragging shattered moans from her, even as her trussed body looked ready to break.

And I was fucking intrigued.

"Maybe if you'd given me a heads-up." I looked past the show to Law on the other side of the room.

Even in the shadows, with a spotlight stinging my eyes and the allure of rope biting into flesh vying for my attention, he was impossible to miss. A former semi-professional fighter, the man had to be at least six-five and easily had fifty pounds or more on me.

Formidable. Perfect for the job. And the only one of my new colleagues I trusted so far.

His massive shoulders rose and fell in a bored-looking shrug. "I told you, we go to some wild places." He tipped his head toward our client's wife, topless and draped across another man's lap. "Anything can happen."

He had warned me. And I still wasn't prepared. Not only for the place and the hardcore kink, but what it would do to me. How I'd feel.

The way I'd hunger.

Tiny shocks of electric sensation pulsed through me. My heart hammered and my ears rang with the bound woman's muffled screams. It was provocative. Exhilarating.

Scary as fuck.

"I know," Law said through a low chuckle. "Not what you expected."

Shaking my head, I glanced over my shoulder at our distracted client. The billionaire, big-pharma magnate was busy with two naked women. He casually held the legs of one over her head, while the other fucked her with a giant dildo.

"I expected wine and cheese." My gaze returned to Law. "Maybe some fancy cars and pretty women. The odd passing threat to manage. Sure as hell didn't expect a personal security gig to bring me here." *To a sexual goddamn awakening.*

"They serve wine here." He cocked his head with a grin. "And there's lots of pretty women. So, like I said…relax. Enjoy."

"I'm married, remember?"

He laughed again. "So are half the people in this room."

Maybe. But I'd bet none of them were wondering how or even if they should tell their partner about tonight. About their unexplored fantasies. Or the realization of how much of themselves they'd repressed over the years.

And just how fucking unhappy it had made them.

How would Emily react if I told her? If I asked to tie her up, what would she do?

Probably divorce my ass.

The dull thump of bass was momentarily amplified when the door leading to the rest of the club opened. Even with a private corridor separating the spaces, the sound echoed through the room. It vibrated through me, emphasizing the lack of control I had in this place. The lack of security anyone really had here.

A man sauntered into the room, an unlit cigar clenched between his teeth. And beside him, the most beautiful creature I'd ever seen.

Young, blonde, and delicate.

She was wrapped in a curve-hugging slip of white that made her look untouchable. Angelic, even. Too innocent for a place like this.

"You," our client barked from over my shoulder.

I turned to find him standing right behind me, adjusting his tie and smoothing his suit as though headed to a business meeting.

"Is there a problem, sir?"

"No." With an absent flick of his wrist, he sent the two naked women scurrying. Then, pointing at me, he ordered, "Stay here."

"But Mr. Alexander—"

His eyes flashed under the lights as he shot me a warning glare.

"Yes, sir." I stepped aside with a nod to his authority, despite my gnawing uneasiness.

Why bother hiring private security and dragging them to a place like this, only to leave them hanging in limbo?

But he was the client, and I was still too new in the

role to go against his wishes. Even if it did go against company protocol, all my training, and the feeling in my gut. I couldn't lose another job.

Alexander strode away, heading straight for the newcomers. My gaze followed him, my heart thudding harder as the gun dug into my back—a disturbing reminder of how easily shit could go wrong.

I scanned the crowd for possible threats, analyzing postures, wandering eyes, and unusual behavior. But nothing stood out.

Except her. The woman in white.

She stood so fucking still, like prey that knew it was cornered. Trapped.

Terrified.

She bit her pouty bottom lip, her hands balled together in front of her, every part of her body straining. Her wide-eyed stare kept darting from the scene at the center of the room to the man beside her. His arm was wrapped around her in a show of possession, his hand digging into her side.

Alexander reached them and the two men greeted each other, overlooking the woman in their exchange, before the three of them tucked into a booth together.

"Everything good over there?" Law's voice broke through the pulse pounding in my ears.

"Not sure." I flashed my gaze to him through the crowd. "Take a look at your ten o'clock. Alexander told me to stay put, but who's the guy with the cigar? Possible threat?"

Law only glanced at the trio before his eyes were

back on me, his head shaking. "That's Nikolai Rykov. And that's not your concern."

"You sure?" My heart continued hammering. "Because something seems off."

"Positive. Stop asking questions."

"Why? Will we lose the job if I ask questions?"

His gaze traveled toward our client's wife again, his hands curling to fists at his sides. "Maybe."

"Maybe?" What the hell was going on here?

"That's what I said." His voice dropped low like he was sharing a secret. "Or maybe you'll lose your fucking life. Now shut the fuck up and watch the show."

But his warning only raised more questions. Lose my life? Did he mean that literally? If so, who the hell was this Rykov guy? What did our client have to do with him? And the most important question of all...

"Who's the woman?"

"Yelena Markova. She's also not your concern."

Her name wasn't familiar, yet a tingle of recognition shot up my spine. "She doesn't look like she's here voluntarily."

"Finn, I'm serious. If you like breathing, forget about it. Forget her."

Forget her.

"Yeah, I can do that." But I wasn't going to.

CHAPTER
ONE
YELENA

"I KNOW YOU WANT ONE." His cruel smirk pulled wide as he shook the bottle of little white pills in his hand. "You've turned into quite the fiend, haven't you, darling?"

God, he was sadistic. Straight up evil. So heartless, he made the devil look kind.

Worse, he was right.

An endless riot of stinging tingles crawled under my skin. *Skittering. Scratching.* Thousands upon thousands of tiny pin pricks, slowly bleeding me dry.

And this was only the beginning.

Without those pills, I would feel everything, and after living so long with his horrors, it would all be too much. I needed those pills to survive in this hell.

Which was ironic, since I also needed them to escape it.

"Go ahead." His smoky rasp was like a knife to my

throat. "You can have it. All you need to do is take it from me."

He shook the bottle again, the contents clacking in a rhythm that made my nerves scream.

Was this some kind of test? Or just another way to keep me demoralized and desperate—stripped of autonomy to the point I was grateful if I remembered my own name?

"Come on." He moved closer, still holding the pills out of reach, the stench of old cigar coiling around me. "We both know what you want. Now take it."

When I didn't comply, the vicious smile he'd been wearing turned to an ugly sneer. "Why do you continue to provoke me?"

The familiar tang of copper filled my mouth, but I still didn't move. Didn't speak. Didn't release the skin of my inner lip, trapped between my teeth.

"I wonder what Anya would think of her mother defying my wishes?" Something sinister sparked in his gaze. "Maybe we should find out. Should I send a couple of my men to collect our daughter from your sister's cozy home?"

No! Dear God, no.

Frantically, I shook my heavy head, my stomach cramping and tears springing to my eyes.

"No? You don't want that?" he mocked. "Then take it."

Palm up and shaking, I offered him my hand. Seconds stretched to what felt like hours as I waited for his response, wondering what form his wrath would take and praying for something, or someone, to end him.

A sharp, violent boom split the air.

It hit out of nowhere—louder than thunder, and more jarring than Nik's fists—paralyzing me. My pulse faltered, and a cold shock of adrenaline rushed through my veins.

Was it an explosion? Were we under attack?

It echoed from somewhere outside, rattling the windows and drawing Nik's attention. But I kept my eyes on him, my body twitching as I waited to see what he'd do next.

For a moment, he only stared as beads of sweat formed at his hairline. Then, with a snarl, he slammed the pill bottle down on the counter and pointed a finger in my face. "Don't think you're getting out of this, you worthless bitch. I'll deal with you later."

Turning on his heel, he stalked from the room, leaving me alone at last.

Just me and the little white pills.

Thin breaths sawed through my lungs as I snatched the bottle, popped the top, and shook two pills into my trembling hand. Before I had time to think it through, I'd chewed, swallowed, and was pocketing the rest.

Shit, that was dumb.

He would remember leaving them. Punish me for taking them. Lock me in my empty room again with nothing but the clothes on my back, the gold pendant around my neck, and water from the adjoining bathroom tap. And maybe a broken bone or two to keep me company.

How long would it be this time? Days? Weeks? Or would he feed me just enough to keep me alive and hold me there indefinitely?

As I stood contemplating the peril I'd be in, the pills began working their magic. My body loosened and jitters subsided. Time expanded to a gauzy blur. The worries I'd been entertaining dulled to meaningless chatter, pushed farther and farther into the dim recesses of my mind.

With a euphoric haze washing over me, I shuffled through the kitchen in search of…something. A sound? Or an answer, maybe?

Only, I couldn't remember the question.

Head spinning, I turned my unfocused gaze to the sea of white cabinets and granite counters, scanning the room until I came face to face with someone I never expected.

My sister, Kira, stood in front of me with the hilt of a knife protruding from her arm and a look of fury etched on her face.

At least it all seemed real enough.

Blood trickled from the spot where the blade stuck in her skin, yet she looked stronger than I remembered. Her platinum hair was longer and wilder than I'd ever seen, her natural beauty more intimidating than I cared to admit.

It wasn't a drug-fueled hallucination—she was

really here. And despite her dreadful-looking injury, I was happy to see her.

But like a switch flipping off to protect a system from overloading, something inside me shut down as soon as that good feeling tried to take over. In a blink it was gone, replaced by a voice that gnawed at the back of my murky mind.

Wasn't she partly to blame for my prolonged imprisonment? After so much time and misery, should I be overjoyed or terrified she was finally here?

It was hard to know with the drugs coursing through my system, muddling my thoughts and turning my feelings to nothing but faded memories—diaphanous, fragile things that collapsed to gritty dust whenever I tried to pull them closer.

"Where is he?" She lunged, attempting to grab my arm.

I jerked away, her fingers brushing down my sleeve.

"Who?" I asked, forcing my voice to work after days of not speaking.

"Nikolai."

The leftover tingles that were still dancing under my flesh turned to fiery stabs as the echo of bruised ribs and broken bones rang to life like a chorus over my body.

Where was he? I had no idea, and—*oh, sweet hell*—he could come back at any time.

When I didn't answer, Kira lost her patience and stormed away in a huff, muttering under her breath. Unsure what else to do, I tagged along behind her like I had when we were kids, praying she knew what came next.

A bright burst of light stung my eyes as I followed her into the solarium. My favorite spot in the house, this was as close to the outdoors and freedom as I was allowed.

Sometimes, I'd lie on the sun-warmed tiles, stare at the sky beyond the glass ceiling, and imagine what it might feel like to break through. To fly away to some distant place where I didn't have to be on alert every second of every day, worrying if my next breath might be the thing to set Nik off. To be anywhere but here.

Other times, I closed my eyes and wished I could sleep through the misery. I wanted to wake and find it was all a dream, that my life was finally mine again.

But not now.

If I closed my eyes at this moment, everything might disappear. Kira and her stormy demeanor. The flicker of what might be hope, hidden beneath my breastbone. And the stranger who stepped through the doorway at the other end of the room.

The unexpected, dreamy, dazzling stranger.

His messy raven hair glinted in the sunlight, curled at the ends, and framed a face that rivaled the exquisite masculine splendor of mythological gods. Strong nose, squared jaw, expressive brow. He was built a bit like a god too, tall and broad with a quiet strength that seemed to radiate from somewhere deep within.

A man so handsome, it hurt to look at him.

No, I couldn't risk shutting any of it out, not even

for a fraction of a second. If I blinked, it might all prove to be a drug-induced fantasy after all.

This couldn't be real. Could it?

I dug my nails into my palms to test the theory. The dull bite of pain eventually registered, and a new sensation warmed my always chilled skin. A feeling both scary and enticing that made my heart beat like a steady drum instead of its usual delicate flutter of butterfly wings.

There was a man in the house. A man who was not Nik. A man with eyes so calm, so blue, yet so full of anguish, I wanted to drown in them.

Kira seemed furious with him—at least I wasn't the only one who made her angry. Although, her harsh tone might've been hiding what sounded a little like heartbreak. Or maybe it was fear.

Either was possible, since the stranger had a gun pointed at her.

Yet, despite his fierce expression and the weapon in his hand, his presence was comforting. His gaze hadn't met mine, still it soothed me, chasing away the torrent of insufferable pain I'd lived with for so long.

Maybe that's why I didn't panic when two more men joined the standoff from opposite ends of the room.

One of them was Sasha. I knew him because he worked for Nik. More than that, he'd once loved my sister, and I'd even considered him a friend. But that was all in the past. Now he was just another tool Nik could wield against me.

I didn't know the other man. Another stranger, he

looked nearly identical to the first. Only, he was covered in grime and blood, and he was bigger, scarier, and obviously wounded.

Their raised voices filled my ears with too much noise and confusion. Like trying to interpret radio static, I couldn't make sense of a single word. The buzzing in my brain intensified, and the annoying voice murmuring in my head told me this moment was big and important.

I should do something.

But what?

As I fought to piece together what was happening, Sasha grabbed Kira. She struggled in his grasp, and the second stranger didn't seem happy about it. He took the gun, turning his attention and aim toward them.

I really should've done something. Anything. But ocean eyes were now zeroed in on me, moving closer like the rise of a swelling tide.

Mesmerizing. Agonizing.

My broken soul cracked open, and I waited to be engulfed, sinking deeper and deeper to the bottom of his merciless gaze.

Until his arm encircled my shoulders.

I shouldn't have wanted his touch. Shouldn't have allowed anyone to get close. I definitely should not have leaned into his solid body or shuddered under the wall of protection his embrace instantly provided.

But how could I resist when I'd been deprived of this feeling for so long?

He nudged me forward with a noticeable hitch in his stride, moving me away from the deadly commotion.

And I went willingly.

Away from my sister and the danger she seemed to be in, out of the solarium, through the house, and to a side door that led to the yard. He closed his hand around the knob and turned it, pulling the door open as though it were as simple as breathing.

Except even the routine act of inhaling was suddenly insurmountable. The prickling, stabbing sensation returned, spiraling inward, and both my body and mind locked up tight.

"Let's go." He clasped my shoulder, making my bladder weak and my knees want to buckle.

"I can't." My throat tried to close around the words, turning them to a harsh whisper. But in my mind, I was screaming.

I can't. I can't. I can't.

If I did, Nik would find me. He would hurt me again, and then hurt me some more. Or worse, he'd hurt someone I loved. Maybe even kill them. And he'd do it to teach me a lesson. Just like he did with my grandfather.

Who would it be this time? Kira? Anya?

"Yes, you can." The stranger's hand moved from my shoulder, and I almost cried at the loss of connection.

But then his finger was under my chin, urging my gaze up to meet his, and those ocean blues tried to drown me in their calm again. "You have to."

I was shaking now, my leaden limbs cracking from the strain. "How?"

"Stop fighting your fear and work with it instead. Welcome it, like a friend."

"A friend? Is that what you are?"

An invisible wall shuttered his gorgeous gaze, and his lips hardened to a thin line as he staggered back a step, his hand falling to his side. "No. I'm just the man getting you the hell out of here."

Despite my drug-induced fog and bout of unforgiving dizziness, the meaning of his words was unmistakable. Rescuing me was only a courtesy. Either professional duty or personal obligation, it didn't matter.

He doesn't like me.

Why did that hurt so much? Hadn't the endless criticism from Nik reinforced all the ways in which I was lacking? Weren't his daily reminders of my inferiority enough to set me straight? He was the only man who'd ever claimed to love me, and still, he couldn't stand the sight of me most days.

So why did this stranger's rejection hit especially hard?

I shook myself from the chaotic, wounding thoughts circling my mind and swallowed back the bile that had crawled up my throat. Forget my twisting insides, stuttering heart, and the quiet ache his touch had elicited.

Forget friends.

All I needed was safety. For me and my daughter.

"That's fine." I ran my finger over the smooth plastic of the bottle in my pocket, my voice as dead as the hope he'd ignited. "I already have all the friends I need."

CHAPTER
TWO
FINN

The late summer breeze lifted the hair off the back of my neck, cooling my overheated skin and reminding me of all the ways this mission had hijacked my life.

I needed a haircut, but something so mundane, so trivial, felt like a waste of time.

Also, I'd forgotten.

Because this wasn't just a mission. It was a personal goddamn vendetta. A grudge match with Nikolai Rykov, the head of New York's biggest Russian crime syndicate and the deadliest adversary I'd ever known.

And I wouldn't rest until I'd finished it.

Unless he finished me first, which—let's be honest—he had an exceptional chance of accomplishing.

"Do you have eyes on it yet?" Robin's voice was a soothing presence in my ear.

My best friend and all-around fixer, she was a genius with code, a damn good strategist, and decent with people too. She had to be to keep up with me.

Especially at times like this, when I was running on fumes and our plan had gone to hell.

When I'd fucked up beyond measure.

"I'm at the edge of the property now." I scoped out the cottage in the distance. "It's quiet."

It looked like the perfect safehouse. Hell, it was damn near a postcard.

Situated at the end of a long and winding gravel road, just outside a small lakeside town in the Adirondacks, it was surrounded by tall trees and silence. Peaceful and pristine, there was a dried patch of wildflowers in the yard and a flowing creek nearby. There was even a porch swing.

"It's practically buried in trees," I added. "Decent visibility, no direct neighbors. Looks like the perfect spot to disappear."

"Exactly why I picked it," Robin said. "I've been holding on to it for a while now, in case we ever needed a way out. It's far enough from town to stay hidden, but close enough for easy supply runs. I've rerouted the utilities through dummy accounts, and there's no digital footprint tying it to you or anyone else. The title's buried under four layers of shell corporations. It's clean."

"Sounds expensive."

"Please," she scoffed. "Do you know how much I made off those crypto bros last year? You're lucky I didn't have it renovated to add a panic room and a wine cellar."

I huffed a quiet laugh. "Maybe next time."

"Don't tempt me."

This was why we worked. She never let me drown in darkness too long. She threw sarcasm like a lifeline, right when I needed it. And she was damn good at her job.

"And in case anyone gets nosy," she continued, "you're now Damon Cullen. Credit card and ID are on their way, and I've already scrubbed your real name from anything that might ping local records here in Manhattan. You're a ghost."

"Damon Cullen?" I arched a brow even though she couldn't see it. "Do I need to grow fangs and avoid sunlight?"

"The fact that you recognized the references says a hell of a lot more about you than it does me."

"Sure it does, fangirl."

"You're welcome," she deadpanned. "I also hired a local company to stock the place. Just standard stuff. But you'll need to swing by the post office in town to pick up the ID. This should keep you off the radar while we figure out a more permanent solution."

"You've outdone yourself. But don't get too comfortable. I don't plan on staying here long. All I need from you is Rykov. Once you find him—"

"Yeah, yeah. You'll handle the rest. I know the drill. And you should know I'm already working on it." Her fingers clicked over a keyboard in the background, punctuating her words. "Your brother's checked in, by the way. They all made it there in one piece and are waiting for you. Everything's good."

For now.

She didn't need to say it. I could hear it in her tone. Robin was brilliant and, despite her undying love for teen vampires, a shrewd professional. But she was still easy to read.

Then again, most people were.

"Did you talk to Bodhi directly?" I rubbed at the uncomfortable prickle running up the back of my neck, my unruly hair making it worse.

"No, he sent another message through our encrypted chat. He's still pretending to be you. Like I wouldn't know." Her light laughter floated over the phone line. "It's actually kind of cute he thinks the twin trick would fool me."

"It fooled everyone else for the last year. But I guess that's over now that Rykov knows the truth."

I'd rolled the dice by sharing an alias with my twin. Our plan—our long, brutal, beautifully reckless plan— was built on shadows and half-truths.

"You knew it was a risk," she said after a beat. "We both did. And we both knew it couldn't last forever. If Bodhi hadn't deviated from the mission…"

"It wasn't his fault." I swallowed hard. "It was mine."

It always was. Because I was a liar who twisted loyalty into leverage.

We'd spent a year tracking Rykov after he murdered my wife. A full fucking year of scheming, stalking, and careful maneuvers. I'd fed Bodhi the narrative, lined up the targets, and let him believe he was calling the shots. That it was his mission.

But it was always mine.

He was the weapon. A damn good one. And I just kept pulling the trigger.

We'd bled Rykov's operation dry, weakening him until revenge was finally in reach.

Then Bodhi went off-script.

Instead of playing his role as a hitman, he let his conscience get in the way. He decided to be a goddamn hero, forcing my hand and sending me on the run.

With her.

He had no idea the hell he'd unleashed on us. On me.

How could he? The secrets I'd been keeping were buried too deep. The web of lies I'd woven was so thick, even I wasn't sure how to get out from under it. If I even remembered the truth.

Hell, not even Robin knew the full extent of the fucked-up mess I was in now.

"Don't forget, I'm the one who leaked Bodhi's name to the enemy," I reminded her, my throat tightening. "If not for that, we might've finished the job."

"That was another calculated move. There's no point in playing a game of what-ifs," she shot back, cutting off any chance for remorse. "And I was the one who helped build that strategy. We made the call together."

"I know." I let out another frustrated sigh, running a hand over my too-long hair again. "I'm just pissed our operation is blown. Rykov knows everything—not only our names and our faces but our history. He'll have connected all the dots by now. He knows why we're after him."

Why I won't stop until one of us is dead.

"He doesn't know everything." She paused, giving weight to her words. "He doesn't know about me. I'm your secret weapon."

"True." No one knew the truth about Robin. Not even Bodhi.

But how much longer until Rykov figured it out? Until he knew every damn detail?

"And what about your guest?" Robin's tone softened. "How's she doing?"

My eyes darted to the stolen sedan and the fragile-looking woman who was passed out on the backseat. The soft curve of her exposed neck, her angelic face, and the slight part of her perfect, pouty lips. A woman who, up until three days ago, I'd done my best to shut out of my head.

Yelena Markova—Rykov's most prized possession, possibly his only weakness, and the most exquisite beauty I'd ever seen.

Also, the worst pain in my ass.

Not that she'd done anything to earn my annoyance. The minute I'd coaxed her into the car, she'd fallen asleep, only waking long enough to nibble greasy take-out and use the restroom a few times.

Hell, she hadn't spoken a word, and it should've been a relief. But her silence ate at me. It was too stark. Too wounded. Too goddamn deafening.

And like the singularity of a black hole, I was intrigued by the void it created. The mystery of it. The thought of how fucking easily I might fall in.

"She's fine." I pushed hard against the unwanted pull of attraction.

"Do you think she'll work with us against Rykov?"

"She won't have a choice. Willing or not, we need her to get to him. It's the only way."

Robin didn't respond, but I could tell she wasn't fully on board with my plan.

Not that it would stop me.

"Listen, I better go."

"Fine." She sighed. "Just do me a favor and take a beat to collect yourself, okay? You're no good to me or yourself if you're running on empty."

I let out a half-hearted noise of agreement and disconnected the call.

Slowing down wasn't an option, and I had no fucking intention of *taking a beat*. That was a luxury for someone without a score to settle. Without a nemesis to kill.

My focus shifted back to my surroundings, and I dragged in another breath, letting my mind unravel. It was quiet here. The type of place I could recalibrate, deconstruct the chaos of my failed objective, and finalize the details of my new plan. Figure out how to secure Yelena's cooperation—one way or another.

Maybe find a pair of clippers or a razor and shave my goddamn head.

Yet the longer I stared at the idyllic spot, the more

unease filled me, picking apart my already frayed nerves.

Peace didn't mean safety. Solitude wouldn't stop Rykov from seeking us out. It sure as hell wouldn't pacify his need for revenge. And with the forest offering not only seclusion but easy camouflage, there was a good chance I wouldn't see him or his men coming until it was too late.

Fuck. I'm so fucked.

No. Not just me. We.

Five people were already holed up here, including Yelena's sister, grandmother, and daughter. Once part of a powerful Russian crime family, they were now easy prey for Rykov, who'd murdered their patriarch, stolen control of the Bratva, and crushed their legacy.

But my concern wasn't them.

It was my family. My twin and our younger sister, Sunny, were also hiding here. She had no idea what I was tangled in. And even though Bodhi was more than capable of handling himself, he was in no shape to play protector.

I'd put them both in danger. Now it was up to me to get them out.

I knew what I needed to do. My only way forward was to use Yelena as a pawn to get to Rykov. There could be no hesitation, no second-guessing. She was my way in, and I'd be damned if I let that slip.

It didn't matter that she'd already been used by Rykov and the fucked-up world she was born into. It didn't matter that I was lining up to do the same. This situation was different. It was necessary.

This was fucking war.

Nikolai Rykov needed to be destroyed, and Yelena was how I'd do it.

And the fact that I wanted her? That I'd been obsessed with her from the first moment I saw her, four years ago? Didn't change a fucking thing.

She was the object of all my fantasies. And now the key to my revenge.

I stood with my gaze on the horizon, expelling another deep breath and appreciating the kind of peace I'd never get to keep. Peace I probably didn't deserve anyway.

"Where are we?" Her soft voice cut through the stillness.

And fuck me, it was more unsettling than her silence.

Exposed, raw emotion and vulnerability turned her words to weapons, carving a path over my skin that should've left me bloody. My body revolted, but I kept my composure, remaining focused on the treeline ahead of me.

"Somewhere you'll be safe."

She rustled around in the car before the door creaked open, her footsteps light as they moved toward me. "Where is that exactly?"

"Well, it's not Kansas, but it's the best I could do without a pair of ruby fucking slippers."

She didn't react to my bad attitude, just stepped up

beside me with her arms crossed in a way that enhanced the swell of her tits.

"We're upstate." I dragged my eyes away from her slender silhouette. "About an hour from the Canadian border. There's a town nearby and other cottages in the area, but this one's relatively isolated. It's where you'll be staying, for now."

She hesitated, her gaze flicking across the trees and the empty stretch of road, before settling back on me. "I'm not sure I like it."

You and me both. "Why not? Your family's here."

She turned, taking another step closer and making it impossible to avoid looking at her. "I don't know. Something about it doesn't feel right."

How could I argue with that? Even under duress, she knew her own mind and should've been free to make her own damn decisions. Wasn't that the whole point of rescuing her?

But freedom wasn't an option. Not for her. Not if I wanted Rykov dead.

"Your sister spent the last year working to get you out. Sacrifices were made. I know it's not ideal, but it's a hell of a lot better than the alternative."

Her eyes roamed my face as though searching for something, and her pouty lips turned down at the corners. "It's not that I'm ungrateful. But do you really think this will be enough to keep Nik from finding me?"

Nik. The casual way she said his name made my skin crawl. Blood rushed in my ears, my teeth ground together, and every cell in my body urged me to lash out. But I held it back.

Anger wouldn't get me what I needed from her.

And she wasn't the enemy.

She was a victim. Conditioned through years of untold violence. Coerced into not only tolerating but maybe even loving him.

"There's no way he'll find you here," I lied.

"How do you know we weren't followed?"

"If his men had tracked us, they would've acted by now. They'd have tried to kill me. Maybe even succeeded. And you…"

"I'd be back with him." Her body shook, hands gripping her arms like she was holding herself together.

"Come here."

Without question, she stumbled forward as though on instinct. As if the idea of being near me made her feel safe.

A warning blared in my head—*too close, too much temptation*. But I ignored it and pulled her in. My arm slipped over her shoulders, drawing her closer until her uncontrolled shaking quieted to a mild shiver.

Despite the hostility, the guilt, and the goddamn war raging inside me, the second we touched, my world shifted. Heat licked up my spine, and every nerve sparked to life at the electric friction between us.

Her slight curves pressed up against me, her shallow breath heated the space between us, and she leaned into me like I was something solid in an unpredictable world of cruelty and despair.

It was a dangerous illusion.

For her, and for me.

Because her scent, her delicate body, and the quiet way she exhaled against my chest all fed something dark and restless inside me. Something that had been simmering for four fucking years.

Something with no place in this mission.

Fuck, I should've listened to the warning I was given the first night I saw her. I should've walked away, forgotten Yelena Markova.

Now it was way too late.

"You're safe." Another lie. But fuck, I needed her to believe it. "My sister's here. She's a nurse and can take care of you. And my brother's here. Kira, too. You'll be well guarded."

She tilted her head up, her wide eyes locking with mine. "And you?"

I swallowed the truth without hesitation. The only answer that mattered was the one she needed to hear. "I'm right here."

"Good." She shivered, setting off sparks along my skin. "You're the only one I trust."

Trust. It hit like a punch to the gut, nearly knocking the wind from me.

Her trust was misplaced.

And I was going to use it anyway.

CHAPTER
THREE
YELENA

"You trust me?" His rough voice was a mixture of irritation and accusation, and it probably should've scared me.

Honestly, I should've run from him the first chance I found. He was a stranger, after all, and I had no idea what he wanted. No clue why he'd pulled me from the monster's clutches.

Instead, I clung to him in a way that was no doubt irrational and unhealthy. Because despite all the things I feared at that moment, he wasn't one of them.

"I do." I shook off the urge to say more. To relax into him. To call him my hero.

The arm he'd wrapped around me tensed, but he continued staring into the distance, the look on his face unreadable. "What about your sister? Don't you trust her?"

"I want to trust Kira." Except I'd always seen her as

more of a competitor than a friend, and my deep-rooted resentment didn't leave much room for things like trust. "But our relationship is complicated."

He hummed his understanding. Still, the hard set of his jaw and furrow of his brow were as immovable as granite.

My body cramped with spasms, the relentless tremors returning, and I struggled to stay upright through the discomfort. The high of the drugs was long gone, my memory was spotty, and I'd taken an immeasurable risk by escaping with this man.

But more than the pain, more than the risk, it was the possibility he might leave that was freaking me out. He was solid. Strong. Demanding, even. Yet somehow, his presence soothed me. He made me feel not only safe but bold enough to defy Nik's orders. Heck, he was touching me, and it felt good.

It was illogical. Incomprehensible. It could get us both killed.

And none of it mattered. Not if he planned to leave.

Sure, he said he was here, but that didn't mean he was staying. And despite our physical contact, I could feel him pulling away. Could sense he already had one foot out the door.

I needed him to stick around. Anya's life was on the line. I'd survived a year in captivity with a madman for her. Now this stranger was my best shot, maybe my only hope, of keeping her safe.

"Rykov will be looking for us. For you." He interrupted my tangled thoughts and the silence that had stretched between us.

My arms were still crossed over my chest, my spine still stiff, and the clawing under my skin was more relentless than ever. But I leaned closer, drawn to his warmth as if it alone could shield me from the storm closing in.

His grip tightened on my shoulder. "This won't be over until I stop him. For good."

"For good?" A shock ripped through me, sending my heart into an unsteady gallop. "You're going to kill him?"

"Fucking right, I am. That's always been my plan."

My pulse was racing now, but for once it wasn't fueled by fear.

How many times had I wished for Nik's death?

I'd imagined it in countless ways—quick, slow, violent, quiet. I'd dreamed of being free. Free of the next terrible thing he might say or do. Free of the punishments he dealt out for his own amusement. Free of the threat he posed to Anya and everyone else I loved.

Too many times to count.

But there was a difference between wishing for someone's death and making it happen. A disturbingly dark and vicious deviance.

And yet…

The idea of this man killing Nik was vibrant, exciting, and sent something electric pulsing through me. It wasn't fear. It wasn't guilt. It was something else entirely.

Something wicked that felt deliciously right.

The invisible chokehold of my neck finally loosened, and for the first time in years, I could breathe.

"Good. He deserves to die. Only, do me a favor?" My lips curved into an impossible smile. "Make it painful. Torture him first."

A short, low sound rumbled from my hero, and his gaze collided with mine.

Was that a laugh?

His expression hadn't changed, but there was something about his stormy blue stare that felt untamed. Maybe even slightly unhinged.

I studied him. My gaze lingered over the severe cut of his jaw and the subtle tension in his shoulders. Fine lines fanned from the corners of his eyes, suggesting he'd smiled a lot in life, maybe even laughed often.

But he wasn't laughing now.

He was watching me. And as I peered into the depths of his gaze, I wondered what was running through his mind. Did he think I was disturbed and savage for making such a malicious request?

Does the idea of torturing Nik make him want to smile again, too?

Before I could find the courage to ask, he shook his head, breaking whatever connection had settled between us. He dropped his arm from my shoulders and turned away, scanning through the trees again.

And just like that, the moment was gone, leaving me

with a slew of unanswered questions and a man I barely knew. Beyond his sharp features, ability to play rescuer, and lethal fixation on Nik, I didn't know a thing about him.

Not his past. Not his motives. Not even the most basic thing.

"What's your name?"

"Finn." He rubbed the back of his neck, his hand moving over his thick hair, and I had the sudden urge to run my fingers through those messy locks. "Finn Decker."

"Well, Finn Decker…" I forced confidence into my voice. "It sounds like maybe this is more than just a job for you. It sounds almost personal."

"It's about as personal as it fucking gets."

I waited for him to elaborate, but his jaw only clenched harder, his lips forming a tight line.

"So your plan is to kill Nik. But until then, are you staying? Will you keep us safe until it's done?"

"Us?"

"Me and my daughter." It was bold of me to ask. Maybe even selfish. But the tiny flame burning inside me, the one I'd thought was long dead, urged me to take the chance.

Make fear my friend. Wasn't that what he'd told me to do?

"Right. Your daughter." He cleared his throat and shifted farther away, as though having caught himself in a compromising position.

But what did it mean?

If I knew him better, I might have been able to read him. Might have been able to decipher the meaning behind the slight shift in his posture and the brief flash of his gaze.

Instead, all I could do was grasp at the one thing that kept me from unraveling. "Her name's Anya, and keeping her safe is all I care about. She's the most important thing in the world to me."

"Okay." He gave a subtle nod.

My hopes soared, and I hugged my arms harder to myself to keep from throwing them around his neck. "Okay?"

"Yes. But if I'm doing this, we do it my way." His calm gaze met mine again, his beautiful blues reassuring, yet rousing. "There'll be no leaving the property. No unescorted walks. You don't even sit on the porch alone. We're on lockdown."

I swallowed hard, my throat suddenly dry.

"Will that be too much for you?" His voice was calm, unwavering. "After everything?"

The real question burned beneath his words. *Can you handle being trapped again?*

I wasn't sure, but I nodded anyway. Because absolutely anything was better than being caged alone with Nik.

"You sure?"

"I'll be fine." And it almost sounded like I believed it.

"Good. Follow my rules, and you'll be safe." He

turned his back on me, rubbing at his neck again. "We should get our asses moving and get you out of sight."

Terror was creeping over me, but I shook it off, forcing my body to obey as I climbed back into the car.

Don't think about the danger. Not now. Not when I was about to see my family again. Not when what I needed most was courage.

As Finn backed the car out of the trees, gravel crunching under the tires, my gaze drifted to the landscape around us. It was beautiful here, with nothing but nature and blue sky for miles. The air was fresh, birds were singing, and the mountains in the distance were like a painting.

This was the freedom I'd dreamed of. The moment I'd endured all of Nik's punishments for. The reason I'd swallowed down every threat, every humiliation, every ounce of pain. My chance to finally step into the light with my daughter.

But the brilliance of the sun didn't warm or comfort me. It only exposed the truth.

I still wasn't free.

Years under Nik's thumb had left me a cracked and nervous casualty of his madness. A fool who once believed love could conquer all. That devotion could tame a monster.

Now, without his rules and the suffocating weight of his control, I wasn't sure what to do. Who I was. Or how to act.

And instead of finding my own way, I was clinging to a stranger, trusting him to keep us safe.

My chest tightened and thoughts spiraled as a cold, familiar ache twisted inside me. I shoved my hand into my pocket, seeking the reassurance of the bottle I'd hidden there.

But just that one touch sent my skin crawling with need, and the incessant urge crashed through me with a roar.

No. I was anything but free.

Finn's head tilted my way. "Are you planning to take one of those?"

"What?" My heart stuttered. For a moment, it might've stopped.

Instead of shifting the car into drive, he put it back into park and turned to me. "I saw you eyeing them at the last service station."

Pain laced my chest, slithering around my heart. *Crushing. Clawing.*

For the first time since meeting him, I wanted his gaze anywhere but on me. "I have no idea what you're talking about."

"No?" He leaned toward me, his broad upper body easily devouring most of the space between us. "Then tell me, if it's not the pills making you so damn jittery, is it me?"

Another convulsion rolled through me. I tried to rein it in, but it was next to impossible when my banging heart felt ready to burst from my chest. "Why would it be you?"

"So you admit it's the drugs."

"If I admit to that, will it change your mind about staying to protect us?"

He shifted even closer, the fresh scent of mint lighting up my senses and the cool blue of his gaze pinning me in place. "No, Lena. It doesn't change a goddamn thing."

Lena? Le-na. Lena.

The uninvited nickname circled my mind, and the rough edge of his seductive voice turned my insides liquid. It was a penetrating sensation that pulsed through me, distressing yet alluring all the same.

"Well, maybe it's both. Maybe it's the drugs and it's you."

Inching a hand toward me, he grasped a stray lock of my hair and tucked it behind my ear. But he didn't stop there. His light touch moved down, tracing over my jaw, lighting sparks along the way.

How did something so sweet feel so sinful? And why on earth did I like it so much?

"Don't worry." The rough pads of his fingers slid over the thrumming pulse in my neck. "I'm not in the habit of giving away secrets. Mine, yours, or anyone else's. You're not the only one with demons to hide."

Air caught in my lungs, and my head swam.

"But you better get control of that secret." His fingers moved like lightning, scoring a heated path up my throat and flicking off the end of my chin. "Or those demons will eat you alive."

A shudder rushed through me, and my teeth sank into the raw, tender flesh of my inner lip.

Swallowing hard, I tried to pull myself together. "It's under control."

"I don't believe you." His thumb swiped the corner of my mouth, coming away bloody.

The glossy spot of red was a visceral display of evidence against me. He held it out, circling his finger through the mess, examining it. Examining me.

Was he judging me?

"That's not fair."

"Fair or not, it's still a fucking problem." His gaze locked with mine as he brought his blood-streaked finger to his mouth, running it between his lips before pulling it out clean. Then he repeated the motion with his thumb.

Oh. *Sweet hell.*

Why did something so vulgar, so vile, ignite an ache deep in my core? It wasn't just fascination, it was need. A raw, searing desire that tangled with my darkest cravings, blurring the lines between fear and want.

Something was wrong with me. Deeply, irreparably wrong.

"You don't know me." Better to deny the problem than let him see the truth. It was the smarter choice. The safer choice. "You have no idea what I can handle."

"Maybe not." Finally giving me space, he turned back toward the wheel. "But I guess we'll find out soon enough."

"I guess so."

He cast a final, challenging look my way, then shifted the car into drive.

Despite his attention now being elsewhere, the unrelenting, crawling itch under my skin returned, and my thoughts drifted back to the bottle in my pocket.

Only seconds had passed, and I was already proving him right. Proving myself a liar.

I was not in control. Not even a little bit.

We pulled up beside the cottage, and without a word, Finn shut off the engine and opened his door. But all I wanted to do was hide. From the fear, the truth, and myself—the unstable person I'd become, the dark thoughts inhabiting my brain, and the even darker cravings flooding my body. All the mistakes I'd made.

If only I could redo all the choices that had led up to this moment.

There'd be no pills. No pressure. No regrets.

No Nik.

Only, without him, there'd be no Anya. And even though it had been over a year since I'd last seen her, she was more precious to me than anything.

Finn unfolded himself from the car, leaving me alone with my thoughts and the stupid damn pills. I stared at his vacated seat, allowing the cold to seep back into my bones, and then reached into my pocket again. The bottle still fit perfectly in my hand, yet it felt heavier than before. The lid was harder to remove, but the contents were more appealing than ever.

Demons indeed.

But compared to the other monsters lurking in my head, the drugs seemed the lesser evil. At least if I were medicated, I wouldn't feel the need to hide or escape.

Before I could change my mind, and before Finn had the chance to see, I took a pill from the bottle and bit it in half.

Just a little something to take off the edge.

He leaned down to my open window just as I was returning it to my pocket. "You ready?"

"I am now." Meeting his calm ocean gaze, I swallowed the crushed pill and tried not to choke on my fear. "Are you?"

CHAPTER
FOUR
FINN

WAS I READY?

Hell no.

That hadn't stopped me from diving in headfirst though, had it?

Her proximity made me reckless. Revenge should've been the only thing on my mind. Yet one brave request from those pouty lips had me right back at her side, playing savior.

I could call it strategy. Tell myself I was testing her limits, twisting her vulnerability, feeding off her trust. And maybe some part of me was.

But it felt a hell of a lot more like instinct.

I told her she'd be safe, but how was I supposed to keep that promise when she was the key to my operation? When the thing I needed most meant putting her right back in harm's way?

Yelena stared at me through the car's open passenger window, her brown eyes wide and brimming with trust. It was a look that clawed at my insides, taking aim at my soul. And I hated her for it.

At least I wanted to.

I wanted to hold her in contempt for all the ways my life had been torn apart since the first night I'd watched her. For the feelings she evoked. The memories she stirred.

The all but forgotten urges she continued to unearth.

"Let's go." I yanked her door open, the car rocking slightly from the unnecessary force.

As though on command, she swung her legs out and stood. The wave of her hair fell like a veil, the gold pendant around her neck glinted in the sun, and her breezy red skirt floated around her ankles.

Hands clasped, head bowed, and gaze cast to the ground, she was a beautiful picture of submission. So stunning, I was nearly hard just from looking at her.

Except her response to me—hell, to everything— was either born of trauma or an effect of the drugs. Her compliance was a result of the pain and fear Rykov had created, not something I'd earned through care and respect.

And it still turned me on. Every little move she made. Every fluttery breath she took. Every pleading goddamn look she cast in my direction.

Gritting my teeth, I pushed past the mix of discomfort and lust lodged in my throat and moved the hell out of her way. Out of the path of my own goddamn destruction.

"You should go inside," I growled in warning. "I'll be there in a minute."

Before she could take a step, the cottage door opened, and her sister rushed out.

Kira raced forward, flinging her arms around Yelena, catching her off guard and crushing them together. "I can't believe you're finally here. I was so worried."

Yelena only nodded, her expression tight, and her gaze seeking mine again.

I refused to meet it.

She was the only leverage I had against Rykov. And if I let myself get distracted—if I let her wide-eyed trust mean something it shouldn't—I'd lose sight of what really mattered.

Ending him.

"Let's take this inside." My gruff voice matched my mood, and I wasn't sorry for it. "We haven't had a proper rest or meal in three days."

Kira pulled back with tears running down her cheeks, but she didn't acknowledge me. Didn't even spare me a glance.

Not that I could blame her—I had shoved a gun in her face.

"Come on." She flipped her long hair in my direction and ushered Yelena toward the cottage. "Let's get you inside and cleaned up."

The two of them walked ahead of me, moving awkwardly around each other, and the annoying prickle at the back of my neck returned with a vengeance.

Despite their obvious bond and Kira's show of concern, something stood between them. Something more than the traumatic events we'd run from, or even the danger we were still facing. Whatever the problem was, it wedged between them like a splinter, growing more tender with every word they didn't say.

And it was all a bit too close to home.

Without thought, I moved up behind Yelena, placing my hand at the small of her back, and whispered in her ear, "Remember to use the adrenaline. It's your friend."

But fuck, it was a mistake.

Too close, my lip grazed the shell of her ear. Every nerve ending in my body crackled and fizzed. Her silky hair snagged against the rough stubble along my jaw, and her scent overwhelmed me.

Lavender. Citrus. And her.

A smell so divine, I wanted to drown in it. To lap it up until she was screaming for more.

And Yelena—*lovely, tempting little Lena*—melted at my inadvertent touch. A shaky sigh escaped her lips. It was soft and uncertain but laced with something intoxicating.

Something that sounded like an invitation.

I jerked away before my traitorous body decided to take up the offer, regardless of the consequences.

She turned to me with her eyes narrowed. "Right, I almost forgot. I can be friends with fear, just not with you."

Fuck me. She was devastating. A contradiction I

couldn't afford. The key to taking Rykov down, yet the one temptation that could ruin me.

I wanted her in ways I had no right to. Craved things that would only unravel her further. Things I hadn't let myself need in…hell, it felt like forever.

Fists clenched and heart racing, I bared my teeth like a feral animal before storming past her. I bounded up the porch steps and stalked inside the cottage, not bothering to take off my boots or even hold open the door.

And almost ran headlong into the tiny child that greeted me.

She had fuzzy chestnut curls, round cheeks, and the sweetest big brown eyes. Anya stared up at me, not in shock or fear, but with open curiosity. It was a look of pure innocence, even if there was a hint of mischief to it. And it punched past all my defenses.

Instantly, all my anger and frustration drained, leaving me deflated. Stomach clenched and throat tight, I stared back into eyes that were too much like her mother's, trying to remember how to breathe.

The cottage door opened again, and the little girl's attention shifted to the women entering behind me.

"Mama." She ran forward, her small legs carrying her faster than I expected.

I turned to watch the reunion, despite the pain building behind my eyes.

Yelena waited, practically glowing from her stunning smile and the absolute joy she radiated.

Until Anya threw her arms around Kira's leg.

It was like watching glass break. Yelena's smile

didn't just dissolve, it fucking shattered. Her hand flew up, covering her mouth to hide it. Too late. I'd seen the damage—the weight of loss and longing. The obliteration of her heart.

Turning my back on the carnage, I caught the concerned glower of my sister. But the minute our gazes collided, she broke into a wide grin.

"Hey, big brother," she called. "Took you long enough to get here."

The irritation at the back of my neck finally eased as my feet ate the distance between us. "Who invited you to our secret getaway? Now the whole vacation's ruined."

Rolling her eyes, she came in for a hug, clinging to me like she was afraid to let go. "This is a vacation? I'd hate to see what happens when you're on the job."

"I'm happy to see you, too." I hugged her harder, ignoring her obvious attempt to dig for information. I trusted her with my life, but I'd still never tell her the truth about it—all the illegal, dangerous shit I'd fallen into. "Where's Bodhi?"

"In here," he called from a room ahead of me. "I'd come out there to see you, but the warden won't let me get out of bed on my own."

"Worst patient ever," Sunny grumbled.

I detached from her snug hold, but I didn't move to look in on our brother. Instead, I scanned the interior of the cottage, looking for weak points and the best spots to hide, mentally sketching a plan for the worst-case scenario.

The place was what I'd expected. The solid beams overhead were dark with age, and the floor was scuffed from years of use. A dining table separated the kitchen and the open living room, where a stone fireplace dominated the outer wall. There were two bedrooms with a bathroom tucked between them, and a narrow staircase led to a loft that overlooked the main floor.

It was clean, cozy, and despite its ruggedness, would've made a decent vacation spot. Hell, if it weren't for the threat of death stalking us, I might've even liked it.

My gaze landed on the couch where Yelena and Kira sat with an elderly woman I assumed was their grandmother. The three of them huddled together, whispering and crying, while Anya played on the floor at their feet.

It was the picture of a loving family.

And yet Yelena still seemed out of place.

She glanced up, our eyes locking momentarily, and I had the sudden urge to sweep her out of the room. To save her. To keep her all to myself.

Just like the very first time she'd caught my eye.

But that was the past—even if I was still living with its consequences—and this was her family. Whatever discomfort might've been between them was none of my business. Or my fucking concern.

Pulling my attention away from the golden-haired beauty and the annoying cavern of need that had split open inside me, I turned back to my sister. "Has there been any trouble?"

"You mean, besides your twin being in the worst

shape I've ever seen him?" Sunny's concerned gaze darted toward the women before returning to me. "No. Why? Are we expecting some?"

"Hope not. But do me a favor and keep an eye on Yelena." I leaned closer, dropping my voice to a whisper. "A very close eye."

The faint lines between Sunny's eyebrows deepened. "Any specific reason?"

"Nothing I can say."

She looked ready to argue, but I cut her off before she had the chance. "I promised her I wouldn't. But you're smart and probably too observant for your own good. I'm sure you'll figure it out."

"Okay." She gave a sharp nod, understanding clear in her expression. "Whatever it is, I can handle it."

"I know you can." Resisting the urge to ruffle her hair, I opted for a quick squeeze of her shoulder and tipped my head toward Bodhi's door. "Give us a few minutes alone?"

"You've got five, then I want both of you resting. He's got a nasty concussion, and you look like you haven't slept."

Body sore and mind weary, I lingered outside his bedroom, ignoring my little sister's stare as I tried to figure out what to say.

How the hell was I supposed to bridge the gap I'd created?

"You gonna stand out there all day?" His voice was hoarse, but at least it held some strength.

Swallowing the last of my reluctance, I entered the

room, moving to the foot of his bed. "You look like hell."

That was putting it mildly. One eye was swollen shut, his lip was split, and bruises painted his skin sick shades of blue and purple. Multiple cuts and burns only made it worse. He looked small. Broken and defenseless. The opposite of everything I knew him to be.

"You should see the other guy." His lips curved into a crooked smile.

A wave of nausea hit, nearly doubling me over, and it wasn't because of the lame, out-of-character joke.

I almost lost him.

I forced the sick feeling down, acid still swirling in my gut. "I'm so fucking sorry. For everything."

"You should be, asshole. You almost got Kira killed."

"Almost got her killed? Fuck, Bodhi, I nearly did it myself. I thought she was working against us." I swallowed thickly. "You have no idea how close I was to pulling that trigger."

"Yeah, well, you didn't."

But I could've. Hell, part of me was still wondering if I should have.

And if I was willing to do that to her—not to mention what I'd already done to my own fucking twin—what did it say about me? What did it say about how far I was willing to go for revenge?

I nodded, shoving the doubts down. "Robin wiped our data, and she's searching for Rykov now. We'll find him and end this thing."

"Find both of them." Bodhi shifted, wincing as he tried to sit up.

"Both? You mean Sasha Novikoff?"

"Who the hell else? I thought Kira had done him in when she shot him. Hell, we left him in a pool of his own blood. But he's like fucking Houdini and disappeared practically right in front of us."

"I feel like I've missed something," I admitted. "I know he's Rykov's right hand, but why's he so important to you?"

A dark, lethal glint flashed in his eyes, and for a moment I could see the killer I'd turned him into. The hitman he'd convinced himself he was meant to be. All in the name of my dead wife.

"Because not only is he in love with my woman, he thinks she belongs to him."

His woman?

Fuck, my brother hadn't just fallen for Kira's pretty face and her lies—he'd gotten attached, maybe even fallen in love. With someone other than a ghost.

It should've been a good thing. But in our world, love made you weak. Love made you blind. And when it came to lowlifes like Rykov, we had to keep our eyes wide open.

Love would only make him an easy target.

"I'm guessing you're not okay with that." I stretched my neck from side to side, trying to relieve the unforgiving strain.

"Fuck you, Finn. Would you have been okay if some

asshole had decided Emily was his property and tried to take her away from you?"

Pain ripped through my chest, all my poorly hidden scars tearing open as I struggled to keep my breath.

Bodhi stiffened. His expression shifted, his eyes widening as the weight of his words crashed down. As he realized that was exactly what had happened.

Emily, the girl we'd grown up with, the woman I'd married and ultimately fucking failed, had been taken by Nikolai Rykov. He'd abducted her, held her for days, then murdered her in cold blood. Without any fucking remorse.

Bodhi's expression fell. "Fucking hell, Finn. I'm sor—"

"Don't." My fists clenched as I fought off the urge to drive them through the wall.

What good would it do? She'd still be dead. And it would still be my fault.

The truth of it festered, rotting me from the inside out. Guilt clawed through me, sharp and merciless, but I swallowed it like broken glass. Like I deserved.

And Bodhi? Hell, he'd loved her too. Maybe more than I ever did. Maybe more than I ever could. Except I wasn't supposed to know that. I was supposed to pretend she wasn't the first wedge that had been driven between us.

"We've both said and done enough regrettable shit to last a lifetime." My voice turned rough. "And I'm sure neither of us feels great about it."

"Yeah, I'd say that's a fair assessment."

"Good, then let's focus on what counts—bringing Rykov down."

He shifted in the bed again, exhaling a pained groan. "Fuck, I can't."

"What?" I tensed, my body preparing for the blow I sensed coming.

He scrubbed a hand down his face, refusing to meet my eyes. "I'm out."

The words hit harder than they should have, and the sick feeling returned, rolling in my gut. "Out? You think Rykov and Novikoff are just going to forget about you? About Kira?"

"Of course not." His gaze snapped to mine. "If either of those bastards shows his ugly mug, I'll knock it clean off his body. But the rest of it—the paid hits, dismantling the Bratva, purposely looking for trouble—I promised Kira I was done."

"What about the promise you made to me?"

He started to shake his head but stopped short with a wince. "A hit list didn't solve our problems. It only created more."

Our problems. He had no idea.

The mess I was tangled in wasn't his to fix. Never had been. But that hadn't stopped me from using him to get this far.

"It's okay." I scratched at the back of my aching neck again, my fingers snagging in my hair. "You've done more than enough. This was always my fight."

"Since when? I'm the one who started it. It was my idea to go after him."

A smirk tugged at my lips. "No, brother. I fed you the breadcrumbs and let you believe you came up with it. But going after Rykov, setting you up as a hitman so we could get inside his twisted organization, killing off his crew and associates—it was my plan all along."

His face went slack. "You sneaky asshole."

"I pointed. You shot." I shrugged.

"You've been playing me this whole fucking time?"

"Not really playing you, no. You wanted it too. Vengeance for Emily."

"You're right." He sighed, the quiet sound weighted with old, familiar grief. "But only because I thought you needed it."

"I did. Fuck, I still do. For Emily. For myself." *And for Yelena, too.*

"It's a bad fucking idea." His voice dropped, tension threading every word. "Rykov's got more connections than we realized. You can't beat him on your own, Finn. He'll kill you."

"Then I die," I said, already aware of the danger. "But if it happens, I promise I'll do my best to take that fucker with me."

"Guess the twin bond's all in my head. I really thought you'd want to stick around with me a little longer."

"The bond's still there. Promise."

But would it be once he figured out how much of a lie I'd been living? When he finally learned the truth about Emily's death and how she'd died to pay for my sins?

"Good, 'cause there's no way I'm letting Sunshine take my spot." His busted lips pulled to another wide smile.

"I heard my name," Sunny called from behind me. "What spot of yours am I absolutely taking?"

Her laughter filled the tiny room, and just like that, our conversation about crime and punishment was over.

But the problem remained. Rykov needed to die, and I needed to be the one to kill him. With or without Bodhi's support. And there was only one way that would happen.

Yelena.

I needed her. Not only because she could get me in front of Rykov, but because she was the catalyst to it all. And because taking her from him was the single most satisfying thing I'd ever done in my life.

Yes, I needed her. I fucking wanted her too.

But I'd just have to find a way to work around that.

CHAPTER
FIVE
YELENA

"Please, Yelena." Kira's amber eyes glossed with unshed tears.

It had only been forty-three hours since we'd arrived. Not even two whole days.

But they'd been the longest, hardest hours of my life. Days almost as bad as the ones spent locked away by Nik in that empty room.

Only here, I couldn't get a moment to myself. My sister constantly wanted something from me.

Get out of bed. Eat a meal. Take a shower.

"You need to talk to me. Tell me how I can help."

Talk.

It was all so exhausting.

"You can help by leaving me alone." I pulled my legs toward my chin, dragging the bedsheets with them and curling myself into a ball. It was the only position that offered my body relief from the utter agony of trying to rip it apart.

I hadn't taken a pill, and the effects of the drugs had worn off again. Every nerve ending in my body was on fire. My skin felt raw, the lights were too bright, and every sound was amplified.

It all felt too…real.

"Leave you alone?" She didn't raise her voice, but she didn't need to.

It was the same tone she'd used since we were kids —the one she'd whip out when our grandmother, Babka, left her in charge. The one I always pretended to respect but ultimately ignored. Sometimes even mocked behind her back.

"Are you kidding me?" Her brow pinched. "Do you have any idea how much guilt I have for doing just that? For leaving you alone with that monster? For letting Nikolai take you?"

And now she wanted me to carry the burden of her guilt.

"He didn't take me. I went willingly. Besides, you couldn't have stopped him."

It was the truth. No one could've stopped him when he was holding all the cards. Yet, deep down, didn't part of me still blame her? Not that she'd known what she was doing. She'd simply pushed him too far. She'd tried to steal the thing he wanted most.

Power.

Over everything and everyone. Including me.

"Maybe not. But I didn't really try. I could've bargained to get you away from him."

I rolled my neck, burying my face in the pillow. "He

wouldn't have accepted any deal but his own. And I wouldn't have let you make one anyway."

"What?" She pulled the pillow out from under me, my head flopping to the mattress like a wet noodle. "Did you just say you wouldn't have let me?"

"Yes. And if I had to do it all again, I'd do it exactly the same. Now give me back my pillow."

"Fuck, no. Not until you explain yourself."

I already felt like death, and still she wanted more.

But what was the point? There was no possible way for her to understand. She hadn't lived in constant fear or been cut off from the world. Hadn't mourned the loss of herself, her child, and her connection to the people and things around her.

"I didn't mean it." Sweat rolled over my forehead, and I squeezed my eyes shut.

"You did, and that scares me. This"—she motioned to the bed and my prone body—"all scares me. What will Anya think if she sees you this way?"

"Don't let her." My voice cracked, but it was only a shadow of what had already happened to my heart. It broke the moment Anya ran to Kira instead of me. The instant she called her *Mama*.

My baby didn't recognize me. Didn't know me.

And I couldn't deny, maybe it was for the better.

"I know that's not what you really want," Kira insisted. "Just talk to me."

But there were no words.

Kira had cared for Anya like she was her own. Kept

her from fear, pain, and the horrors of her own father. And I should be grateful. I was grateful.

But now?

Now she'd have to protect Anya from me because I was unfit to be around my own daughter.

"Please give me back my pillow or go away," I said, my voice tight with unshed tears.

The pillow landed on my head, but I did nothing to move it. If I lay motionless for long enough, maybe the oversized square of cotton could block out the world around me. Hide me from not only Kira but the ruthless, gnawing ache of my soul.

"You can't ignore me forever, you know."

When I didn't respond, she let out a huff. "Fine. I give up."

I waited, listening as she went down the stairs. When she was finally gone, I tossed the pillow to the other side of the mattress with a heavy sigh. But when I opened my eyes, I wasn't alone.

Sunny stood at the foot of the bed with a glass of water in hand and a concerned look masking her pretty face.

She'd been sweet to me, and even though we were sharing the loft, she'd been respectful of my privacy. I appreciated her for it. But right now, her blue eyes weren't the ones I wanted to see.

I searched the top of the stairs behind her but came up empty.

Finn had been avoiding me. From the moment we'd walked through the cottage door, he'd done a complete about-face. No more drowning glances. No more warm touches. Not even a challenging damn word.

Not that I blamed him. I was a mess, and we both knew it. And after everything—getting me away from Nik, promising to keep my secret, and agreeing to keep me and Anya safe—he didn't owe me a thing.

But I missed him.

Which was ridiculous, considering I didn't really know him.

"She's worried about you." Sunny came to the side of the bed, filling the spot Kira had vacated. "And I realize we just met, but I can't say I blame her. You don't look like you're feeling too well."

"Is that your professional opinion, Nurse?"

Ignoring my snarky attitude, she smiled and set the water on the bedside table, along with two pills.

My heart raced and my skin crawled. "Take it away. No drugs."

Her knowing gaze darted over me. "It's aceta-minophen. Were you expecting something else?"

"No." I groaned. "Maybe. I don't know what to expect anymore."

"You've barely left this bed since you got here, and I heard you getting sick last night. I figured you could use this. But if there's something else going on, something you want to tell me about, I might be able to help."

Sweat was pouring off me in buckets now, despite still feeling cold. "I'm fine." I forced my denial from between gritted, chattering teeth.

"Look." Palms up, she moved closer. "I'm not going

to bullshit you. I know you're not fine, and I'm ninety-nine point nine percent sure I know the reason. Why don't you just tell me the truth so we can quit the games and move on with getting you better?"

She knows.

I couldn't hide it anymore. Truth was, I'd never hidden it well. But admitting it made it real. It meant facing not only what Nik had done to me, but my own weakness.

The fact that he'd turned me into an addict.

And I'd let him.

"Okay. You want the truth?" A cold knot pulled at my insides.

Her hands dropped, fingers lacing together as she waited me out. She knew—of course she knew—but she'd make me say it anyway. Resentment burned through me, tangled with a grudging respect.

"It's pain pills," I mumbled. "The truth is, I'm...I have a problem with them."

"That's what I thought." Her expression softened.

The ball of dread crawled up my throat, closing off my airway and making my eyes water. God, I didn't want to cry. Not in front of her. Not in front of anyone. But the pillow was too far away, so I covered my face with my arm instead.

Unfortunately, my arm couldn't block out her voice. "You're in withdrawal."

"I know. It's not the first time." I bristled as a painful spasm ran through the muscles in my shoulders and back.

"How many times have you tried to detox?"

Tried? There'd never been a choice. When Nik deemed me worthy, he fed the addiction. When he didn't, he'd strip me down to a writhing, puking mess.

"It was never intentional. Sometimes, I just didn't have access to the drugs."

"And this time?"

Tired of her questions, I flung my arm away from my face with a huffed sigh. "What about it?"

Her jaw clenched, but her soft blue gaze remained open and honest. "If it's a decision you're making, I can help you. If it's a matter of supply, there's not much I can do."

"So you're only willing to help if I want to stop?"

"That's not what I said." Her tone hardened, but she kept calm and professional. "But if I help, are you willing to try?"

Didn't she start this whole conversation with an offer of help? And what the hell did she think I was doing? Did it look like I was having fun?

A scream built inside me, begging to break free.

But that reaction wasn't me. That was the addiction trying to take over. It still had all the control.

God, I'm sick of that.

I'd given enough of my life to the pills, to Nik, and the power they had over me. This was the only hold he had left. Physically, at least.

And I didn't want to give him a single second more.

"Yes." Uncurling my stiff limbs, I moved to sit on the edge of the bed. "Whatever it takes."

I could be a good patient. A better me. The real me, maybe.

Whoever that was.

But most of all, I could learn to be a good mother.

Digging into the pocket of my borrowed sweatpants, I retrieved the bottle I'd stolen from Nik and offered it to Sunny like a prize.

With a dazzling smile, she wrapped her hands around mine. "Good. There's a doctor who owes me a favor. He can set up a treatment plan, as long as you're willing to talk to him."

My stomach turned again at the thought of telling a stranger anything at all. And again, at the realization I didn't have a penny to my name. "I can't afford a doctor."

"Don't worry about the cost." Sunny squeezed my hands, the pill bottle still trapped between them. "We can work that out later. Right now, you only need to worry about getting healthy."

I tried to smile back, but it was impossible when my insides were still swirling.

"You can do this," she said. "And I'm going to be right here, supporting you."

When she pulled away, she took my precious pills with her, and my entire body howled in protest. What had I done? How would I cope?

Make fear my friend.

Yes. I could do that. I had to do that.

Breathing through the panic, I took the aceta-minophen Sunny offered before grabbing for the glass of water and gulping down the entire thing.

She smiled again. "Good job."

It seemed ridiculous to receive praise for such a simple, silly thing. Still, it made me feel better. Like I'd accomplished something. Even if it was a simple necessity of life.

"I think I'll get some more." The minute I stood, the room went black, my legs gave out, and I crashed to the floor.

"Shit, Yelena." Sunny's voice was muffled and distant, like it was traveling through a tunnel to reach me. "Are you hurt?"

Black spots floated in my vision, further upsetting my balance and making me feel like I was glued to the hardwood. "I'm okay. Just dizzy."

"What happened?" Finn's deep voice wrapped around me, steadying my senses and bringing me back into my body.

I blinked away the shadows to find him hunched down next to me. He stared, his calm ocean blues filled with something that resembled concern.

But that couldn't be right. He had no reason to worry about me—someone he wouldn't even consider a friend.

"I think she tried to stand too quickly." Sunny hovered over us. "Likely dehydration causing low blood pressure."

"You okay?" His voice was soothing, almost tender,

and it sent another wave of dizziness washing over me. "It sounded like you crashed pretty hard."

"The floor hit my ass. But it's okay, I've been spanked harder."

Heat flooded my cheeks. *Ass? Spanked harder?* What was wrong with me? I wanted to hide, but the bed and blankets were too far away, and there was nowhere else to go.

Not that Finn was letting me escape. He drew nearer, lulling my anxiety before sweeping me off the floor and into his arms like I weighed nothing at all.

And didn't let go.

He held me tight against him, his thick arms locked around me and his gaze penetrating as my heart tried to burst from my chest.

This connection. This feeling of security. This was what I'd been longing for. The thing that made the pain ease.

The only feeling I wanted from now until eternity.

"Better?" Sunny asked, and I almost jumped out of my skin.

Finn's grasp on me loosened enough for me to breathe, but he didn't set me down.

"Y-yes. Thank you." I forced air through my lungs, trying to keep my voice even. "And I'm sorry. I didn't mean to cause a scene."

"You didn't." Sunny waved me off with a small smile. "Now let's move you down to the couch, and I'll get you another glass of water."

She looked at Finn in silent question, and he gave her a nod before shifting me higher in his arms.

I clutched at his broad shoulders, wanting—no, *craving*—his touch.

Something this innocent shouldn't have made such a difference. Shouldn't have made me feel anything at all. But it did.

God, did it ever.

By the time he carried me down the stairs and into the living room, I was near breathless. Like I'd run a marathon instead of being cradled against him.

Strong hands helped lower me to the couch, and cool blue eyes assessed my every move. "You good?"

"I'm fine." I sank back into the cushions, wishing I could bring him with me.

Sunny returned, sitting in the chair beside me, and handed me the refilled glass. I sipped at it, no longer thirsty. Heck, I was no longer anything other than tired and mildly embarrassed.

"You can talk to me about other things, you know." She shot a pointed look at Finn. "Privately."

Without another word, he turned his back on us and strode to the other side of the room, hovering near the doorway as though waiting to be called on again. As though standing guard.

"I'm not a therapist." Sunny pulled my attention back to the conversation she clearly wasn't going to let me avoid. "And I'm going to insist on finding you one. But for now, I'm happy to listen. I've met lots of women who've come from similar situations."

Similar situations? I tilted my head, examining her solemn expression and trying to gauge how much she already knew. "What kind of situation do you think that is?"

She leaned forward, grasping my hand again. "An abusive one."

Abuse. That's exactly what it was. Yet the word felt too small. Too easy. Too simple to describe the hell I'd endured.

And I couldn't say it. Not out loud. My throat tightened, like the word had wedged itself there, too heavy to speak.

Finn shifted on the other side of the room, his silence thick and suffocating.

But I didn't look at him. I couldn't. If I met his gaze, I might see something I couldn't handle. Like pity or judgment.

Or worse, nothing at all.

Instead, I kept my eyes on the floor, my insides twisting. "It was my own fault. All of it."

"Fucking hell." Finn's voice was sharp enough to make me flinch.

He stormed away, his unsteady gait not slowing him. Without explanation or even a passing glance, he stalked straight outside, slamming the cottage door behind him.

Kira poked her head out of the room she was sharing with Bodhi. "What's his problem now?"

"Sorry." Sunny's brow furrowed. "I have no idea. He's not normally like that."

Heart racing, I flopped back in my seat. "I think it's me."

"What?" Kira sputtered, just as Sunny blurted, "Why?"

"I think I made him feel obligated to stay and help me when he didn't want to."

The corner of Sunny's mouth quirked. "Oh, I think it's more than that."

Kira made a choked sound of protest, drawing Sunny's gaze.

The two shared a look that I had no hope of comprehending before Sunny turned back to me with a soft smile. "We're going to come back to that thing you said before he left. But first, are you hungry?"

The thought of food was revolting, and my empty stomach cramped. But it was time to try harder. "Sure." I grabbed the water from the table where I'd set it, gulping it down.

With another big smile, Sunny rose to her feet. "Great. I'll make us some lunch."

Kira came to sit across from me, the concern clear in her expression. "I'm sorry."

"For what?"

"Everything." Her eyes brimmed with tears, and she looked away. "I thought I'd get you away from him and life would go back to normal. I should've known better."

"It's not your fault." I swallowed hard, the water I'd just chugged threatening to make a reappearance. "I'm the one who fell for a monster."

Kira shook her head, her soft platinum hair falling over her shoulders. "You didn't know, and I should've been paying closer attention. I would've never let you get involved with Nikolai in the first place."

She was right. And yet, she was so very, very wrong. "I might not have known exactly what he'd do or what he would become, but I knew he was capable. And I chose him anyway."

Sniffling, she swiped away the single tear that was trailing down her cheek. "Why?"

Why? I'd asked myself that same question so many times.

"He was handsome, and he paid attention to me." I shrugged. "It was flattering. But there was more to it than that. More than I can really explain." More than I wanted to admit out loud.

The truth was childish. Disgraceful, even.

Truth was, I'd been tired of being overlooked. Tired of being small. And Nik carried the promise of greatness. I thought if I stood beside a man like that, maybe I could carve out a piece of the empire for myself.

Or maybe it was something darker. A sickness. A part of me that didn't just tolerate the danger he carried but craved it. That lusted after the power he held, even when he turned it on me.

Especially then.

Until it turned violent.

"I guess I don't know why." I bit at the inside of my lip, wincing when I drew blood again. "And I don't want to talk about it anymore. Please don't be mad."

"I'm not. All that matters is that you're here and you're safe."

"I am happy to be here." The words were meant to appease her, but as I said them, I almost felt it.

Happy.

It was there—a faint memory, buried under the shame. Beneath layers of terror, sorrow, and pain. I could sense it, like a sprouting seed pushing through the dark, reaching for light.

A groan came from Bodhi's bedroom, followed by Anya's tiny giggles.

"Shit." Kira jumped to her feet. "Don't worry, I've got her."

My stomach turned again, and all the progress we'd just made crumpled to dust. "Of course," I mumbled to her back as she hurried away. "You've still got it all."

CHAPTER
SIX
FINN

WITH MY SENSES ON ALERT, I stalked the perimeter of the large property for a third time, looking for anything suspicious, stealing glances at the cottage and trying not to think about what was happening inside. Or more accurately, about who was inside.

It was my own fault. All of it.

Yelena's words had hammered at my skull for days, replaying in my head until hatred and rage echoed through me. And fuck, I couldn't handle another second.

It wasn't just her misplaced guilt, the tears she kept hidden, or the goddamn distress she was still drowning in. It was her vulnerability—fragile, exposed, and fucking dangerous.

It clawed at me, digging deep, shredding my restraint the same way shrapnel had torn through my leg.

I needed her. Needed to use her to get to Rykov.

But one thought of his filthy fucking hands on her

shattered my plan. Strategy, caution, and consequences all ceased to exist. All I wanted was to find the bastard and rip him apart, make him pay for every minute of fear he'd created and every sick moment of gratification he'd taken from her pain.

Not only because I loathed him, but because she deserved vengeance.

And I wanted to give it to her. I needed to see the look on her beautiful face when I told her I'd made him suffer. Would it bring her peace? Satisfaction? The same twisted sense of pleasure I got every time I thought about spilling his blood?

Breathing hard, I staggered over a tree root and nearly dropped to my knees. Savage fury surged, but I shoved it back. I wouldn't feed the chaos tearing through my head. If I succumbed to my wounds, old or new, I'd never make it out alive.

I won't be able to protect them.

A loud crack sounded behind me, and I whirled, my bad leg protesting the move. Pain slashed from knee to hip, and my steps faltered again. This time I went down hard, pulse racing.

Instinct and training kicked in, and I rolled to a crouch.

Coming face to face with a goddamn squirrel.

Relief flooded my system, and I sat back to dig my fist into the spasming muscle in my thigh. The rodent only stood, mocking me with its beady eyes.

"What are you looking at?"

It flicked its fuzzy tail, as though giving me the

middle finger, and blinked twice before scampering off in the other direction.

"That's right, run, you little asshole."

Shit. I was arguing with the wildlife. Not even a full week here, and the place was already getting the better of me.

Except it wasn't the place, and I fucking knew it.

It was her. *Lovely little Lena.*

She wasn't just impossible to forget, she was impossible to avoid. No matter which way I turned, she was there. Only feet away. All day and all goddamn night.

Every room I entered smelled like her. The delicious temptation of lavender and citrus. My downfall waiting to happen.

Even now, when she wasn't right in front of me, I couldn't get her out of my head. On repeat, my thoughts wandered to the silky feel of her hair, the fluttering pulse at the base of her neck, and the hitch of her sweet breath whenever she looked me in the eye.

It was the best and worst kind of torment. And I was helpless to stop it, as evidenced by my current situation —flat on my ass, cock half-hard from nothing but thoughts of her, despite the pain I was in.

"Finn. Are you hurt?" Her voice broke through the snarl in my head as though I'd conjured it.

My heart leapt to my throat. I twisted to find Yelena standing behind me, her brows pinched and one hand clutching the necklace at her throat as though it were a lifeline.

Fucking stunning. And reckless beyond reason.

"What the hell are you doing out here?" I shot to my feet, the pain in my leg forgotten. Grabbing her arm, I scanned the area for possible threats, pulling her close. "And how the hell did you sneak up on me like that?"

She flinched, her big doe eyes going wide, but she didn't back away.

"I thought you understood the rules. The danger." My voice was too rough, too loud, too fucking desperate. "You can't be wandering alone."

"But I'm not alone. I'm with you."

Her words landed hard—blunt, unexpected, and disarming. My chest seared, my gut knotted, and I forgot how to breathe for a second.

"Did you ever think, maybe you shouldn't be alone with me either?"

"W-what?" She blinked up at me, not in fear, but with trust. Like she truly believed she was safe here. With me.

I didn't let go. Didn't even loosen my grip. Hell, I couldn't let her go now that she was right in front of me, flustered and wounded-looking. And maybe, if I wasn't imagining it, a little turned on.

Fuck me. I was treading into dangerous territory here. Because I needed her, not just for my plan, and not just to lure Rykov to his death.

I needed her in a way that had nothing to do with revenge.

"You heard me," I growled, fighting the pull between instinct and strategy.

The pulse at her wrist raced under my thumb.

"Sunny wanted…" She shook her head, her bottom lip disappearing between her teeth.

Goddammit. Now all I could think about was biting it myself. Licking the wound she'd created. Soothing her tender flesh with my mouth. Drawing in whatever whimpers she'd make, along with the sweet, metallic tang of her blood.

I tugged her arm, coaxing her toward me.

She surrendered to my silent demand, each hesitant step pulling her closer. A blush bloomed at the base of her neck and spread like wildfire, betraying her nerves. Then the toe of her shoe nudged my boot, and she froze.

We were both breathing hard now.

The rapid rise and fall of her chest, the glint in her wide eyes, and the pure lust that seemed to radiate off her sent my blood pressure soaring.

"Never mind my sister. I'm only interested in what you want, Lena."

Her dark lashes fluttered, and another tremor rippled through her.

Did she want this as much as I did?

Fuck, I wanted to hear her say it. For her to open those perfect, pouty lips that I'd had one too many filthy dreams about and tell me she felt this too.

The hunger. The brutal, aching need that was demanding to be fed.

Just one more step, one sound of consent, and I'd have crossed a line there was no coming back from. A line that would satisfy the feral beast inside me but ruin everything else.

This wasn't just lust. It was a threat to the mission. To the lies I'd built around us. To everything.

But I still didn't let her go.

The gravity of the moment tipped, pulling us together. Her breath mingled with mine, her pulse hammered under my fingers, and her gaze burrowed into my fucking soul.

Movement in the trees snapped me back to reality. My body tensed as I glanced over her shoulder, the moment between us shattering.

"What is it?" she whispered, her voice edged with panic.

I raised a hand to silence her. Scanning the trees, I caught another flicker—this time a solid form.

A person. Lurking? Stalking us?

They moved fast, but they were sloppy. Either they didn't realize we were here, or they were trying to stay hidden and failing miserably.

My stomach clenched. It could be one of Rykov's men. Maybe a spy who would lead a larger team to our doorstep. Or a decoy, sent to lure us into a trap.

"Stay close," I murmured, pushing Yelena behind me. "And keep quiet."

She nodded, her hand sliding into mine—warm, trembling, but holding firm.

It was probably a mistake to drag her into this. To pull her further into danger. But what other choice did I have? Leave her unprotected?

No fucking way.

I moved forward, keeping low, slipping through the

trees with silent, practiced steps. And Yelena followed. Just as cautious. Just as quiet.

I expected hesitation. Maybe even questions. For her to slow me down, force me to shield her at every turn. I thought she'd be a liability.

But she wasn't.

She moved when I moved. Stopped when I stopped. Shadowed me with a precision that was surprising for someone so raw, so wrecked.

It wasn't just obedience. It was something deeper. Sharper. Maybe even instinctual.

She was still vulnerable, fractured, and fragile. But she was a hell of a lot stronger than I'd given her credit for.

With time, healing, or maybe just the same burning hatred for Rykov that had kept me alive this long, she could be unstoppable.

The figure ahead moved with purpose, gliding between the thick trunks like they knew exactly where they were going.

Were they leading us somewhere? Or were they running?

Either way, I needed to know who the hell they were. What kind of threat they posed.

I tightened my grip on Yelena's hand, leading her deeper into the forest. The trees grew denser, the scent of damp earth thickened around us, and somewhere close was the soft, rhythmic sound of water trickling over rocks.

The creek came into view, and the figure moved

toward it with their shoulders slightly hunched beneath the weight of a large backpack.

I slowed, crouching behind a thick tangle of underbrush, pulling Yelena down with me. She was vibrating with tension, but she didn't make a sound. With her hand still in mine, we watched and waited.

The person stepped into a clearing where the creek snaked through the forest, its surface dappled with shifting sunlight.

It was a man—tall, lean, and dressed in hiking gear. He adjusted his pack, rolled his shoulders, then let out a low whistle.

A child's laugh rang out, and a girl, no older than six or seven, came bounding from the opposite bank, her small hiking boots splashing through the water as she ran toward him.

Behind her, a second figure emerged. A woman, a little older than Yelena, with her own pack strapped to her back and a walking stick in hand, moved toward them. She smiled, brushing sweat from her brow as she watched the girl throw herself at the man's legs.

Not a Bratva soldier. Not a threat.

He was a father. A husband. Just a man with his family.

The breath rushed out of me as I turned to Yelena, but her gaze stayed locked on the scene in front of us. She took it all in—the man lifting his daughter, spinning her in the air, and the woman laughing as she scolded them both for making a mess. The change in Yelena's expression was devastating. It was a look of exposed, unspoken grief. And it settled in my gut like a stone, heavy and unmoving.

It should have been a relief. The threat was nothing, just a false alarm.

Yet a slow, creeping dread settled over me. Not from the adrenaline still burning through my veins. Not even from the unsettling ease with which a civilian had gotten this close.

No. It was her. *Lena.*

As I looked at her—broken but unyielding, fragile yet fierce—I wondered if a part of me had wanted the fight. Needed it.

Maybe facing a real enemy would've been easier than facing what was standing right in front of me. Easier than facing the truth of how I really felt about Yelena Markova. And how those wild, undefined, and unfathomable feelings had created this entire mess in the first place.

How they were threatening to upend my entire goddamn plan.

"Come on," I tugged her hand, pulling her away from the man and his family.

We left them laughing and playing in the creek, unaware of the danger they'd stirred and untouched by darkness. The perfect picture of a happy, white picket life.

The kind of life I'd never have.

But Yelena still could, if she wanted it. And judging by the way her gaze lingered on them, something aching and wistful in her eyes, she absolutely did.

The walk back to the cottage was less deliberate. We didn't have to be careful anymore. Didn't have to move like shadows through the trees. Yet neither of us said a word.

She didn't stop when we hit the edge of the clearing, just kept trudging forward. Like she could slip back inside and pretend nothing had happened.

But I caught her wrist before she could leave, my grip brutal. "What the hell were you thinking?"

She stiffened, but she didn't pull away. She also didn't answer me.

"You left the cottage. Alone."

"Nothing bad happened." Her words were brave. Defiant, even. But her tone told an entirely different story.

She was rattled. Maybe even scared.

Good. She fucking should be.

"Nothing bad happened this time." I moved closer, my voice laced with venom. "But what happens next time? When, instead of an innocent family, it's one of Rykov's men?"

Her jaw tightened, but she kept quiet.

"You know the rules. They're there for a reason—to keep you alive. But you broke them. Why?"

She looked away. Anywhere and everywhere but at me. "I didn't go far."

"That's not good enough." I released her wrist and crossed my arms, caging my temper behind clenched fists. "You don't just get to wander into danger because you're restless."

"That's not…" Her lip trembled before she caught it between her teeth, as if holding back tears.

Fuck, had I pushed her too far?

But then she squared her shoulders. "I was looking for you."

"Why?" I asked again, quieter this time but no less sharp. "What did you want, Yelena?"

"I just…" She swallowed hard. "I needed to know you were still here." Her voice was soft, barely audible. Almost pitiful.

And it fucking gutted me. Something shifted in my chest, a feeling I refused to name. Hell, maybe I couldn't. Maybe giving it a name would make it real.

But I couldn't let her see it. Couldn't let her know that her vulnerability pressed on a fracture I'd spent years pretending wasn't there. So instead, I shoved that feeling down.

"Now's not the time to fall apart," I said coldly. "Not after everything you've already overcome."

Her shoulders tensed, and she blinked as if I'd startled her. "I'm not falling apart."

I didn't argue. Didn't need to. We both knew it was a lie. Her red-rimmed eyes and jerky, shaking limbs were giving her away.

Still, I needed her to be strong. I needed her clearheaded. Most of all, I needed her alive.

Without her, the plan unraveled. Without her, Rykov walked free.

"I'm still here." I stepped in close again. Close enough to feel her tremble. "I'm not going anywhere.

But don't confuse that with safety, Yelena. I'm not safe. I'm just the man standing between you and everything that's worse."

Her eyes flicked up to meet mine, glossy and filled with something that poked at the fissure in my chest. "I'm not asking you to be anything you're not."

"Good. Because I'm not changing the rules or the way I fucking operate just for you." My low voice was nearly a growl. "I've got my own demons to battle. I can't keep worrying about yours and whether it's going to get you killed."

The silence that followed twisted between us like barbed wire. Her gaze dropped again, her breath catching in her throat.

I should've walked away. Should've turned my back and let her vanish inside to lick her wounds in peace.

Instead, I reached out, my fingers trailing over the soft skin of her arm before curling around her wrist. Not forceful. Not cruel. But dominant and possessive all the same.

"You want me to keep you safe?" I leaned even closer, the scent of her hair catching in my throat. "Then don't make my job harder. Don't pretend this wasn't self-destructive. I can protect you from Rykov, but I can't protect you from yourself."

She went still. No argument or bravado. Just the weight of everything unsaid, everything she didn't know, pressing down between us.

And I still didn't let her go.

Truth was, I wasn't ready to be done. Not with her.

Not with this moment. Not when some weak, selfish, traitorous part of me wanted her to be more than just a pawn. More than a means to an end.

Fuck, I wanted her to be mine.

Finally coming back to my senses, I released her, my fingers dragging against her skin like a warning. Or maybe it was a confession.

Or a goddamn prayer.

"Go inside," I ordered, even as every part of me screamed to keep her close.

Without a word, she turned and walked away.

This time, I let her. But I didn't stop watching. Didn't stop thinking about how the most dangerous part of this mission wasn't Rykov.

It was her. *Lovely little Lena.*

The way she made me question which part of this was about my revenge…

And which part was for her.

CHAPTER
SEVEN
YELENA

"Thank you, Doctor Mercer."

My voice was clear, and for the first time in a long time, so was my head. No more crawling skin. No more wicked headaches. The sickness had gone. Heck, I was even starting to feel energetic.

It was amazing what consistency and healthy habits could accomplish once the weight of an abusive narcissist was gone. And it hadn't even taken long.

"I'm glad the plan is on track. Just remember to continue following those directions precisely." Despite his firm tone, he radiated a kindness that was detectable even over a phone line.

"I will," I promised, and after thanking him again, disconnected the call.

Sunny smiled up at me as I skipped down the stairs to the kitchen, with her borrowed cellphone in hand. "How'd it go?" She pushed a plate of raw veggies and hummus in my direction, and my stomach growled in response.

That was new. When was the last time I'd been hungry for anything beyond the drugs?

"So good. Doctor Mercer is fantastic, and I was going to…" All words escaped me as Finn stalked through the door.

Oh, right. Finn.

I'd been greedy for him from the beginning. Even though it made no sense. Regardless of whether it was right or wrong. Whether or not he even liked me. And despite still not knowing much about him.

He made a beeline toward the kitchen sink, passing us with a grunt and a gruff nod.

"Well, hello to you too." Sunny huffed beside him, crossing her arms and leaning a hip against the counter.

Instead of responding, he turned the tap on full and stuck his head under it. Water streamed over his face as he drank, his movements unhurried. Like nothing in the world could rattle him.

That control had me flashing back to the woods. Almost a week later, and I was still replaying the moment like a waking dream.

He'd been unwavering and steady. I'd watched him, crouched low in the brush, his focus locked on the man and his family at the creek, and for the first time in as long as I could remember, I'd felt safe.

Not because the world was suddenly less dangerous. Not because the threats had disappeared. But simply because he'd been there.

I might've taken his hand, but he was the one who'd refused to let go. Even as he chastised me, his grip had said everything—he cared about keeping me safe. Maybe more than anyone ever had before.

And now, as he rinsed the sweat from his face and ran a hand through his damp hair, that same steadiness was in him. He was effortless and strong in a way that had nothing to do with muscle.

Of course, that didn't stop my eyes from tracing every inch of his body.

His hair was slicked back, water dripping from the stubble along his sharply angled jaw. The scowl he wore should've sent me running. Instead, it rooted me to the spot. He was beyond handsome. Dangerous in a way that didn't require warning.

Yet I couldn't look away.

A single droplet slid down the side of his neck, disappearing into the collar of his T-shirt—tight, black, and clinging to every inch of muscle like it had been stitched in place. It left nothing to the imagination.

My imagination ran wild anyway.

I pictured him shirtless. Sunlight catching on slick skin, muscles taut and glistening. I imagined water sliding over those broad shoulders, across sculpted pecs, down the ridges of his abs, flowing over the groove of his hips...then lower.

Heat flashed through me as an ache pulsed to life between my legs. It was sharp and insistent. More demanding than the addiction.

Sweet hell, it scared me. But not enough to break the craving.

"Yelena?"

I jumped as Sunny's voice infiltrated my daydream. Face flaming, my attention flew back to her. "Y-yes?"

She smirked, amusement sparkling in her eyes. "You were telling me about your conversation with Doctor Mercer."

"Right. I was…"

From the corner of my eye, I caught Finn's movement. My gaze drifted back his way, only to find him staring, his ocean blues studying me with an intensity that set me on fire all over again.

I cleared my throat. "…telling you about Doctor Mercer?"

"Pease. Story." Anya's sweet little voice chirped from behind me.

Instantly, the lust-filled heat drained from my body, replaced by a new kind of warmth that bloomed in my chest. With a smile and a hopeful heart, I turned to my daughter, willing to do whatever she asked.

But she wasn't asking me at all. Kira had come into the room beside her, their hands linked, and Anya's innocent face tilted up toward hers.

My hope withered, and along with it, my heart.

"Pease," Anya repeated, hopping from toe to toe as she pleaded with my sister.

Kira ignored her, looking at me instead. "Come join us?"

Hesitant, I looked for Finn's gaze, needing his

steadiness. But all I got was the rigid line of his back—silent, unreadable, and deliberate. Like he knew I was looking and chose to shut me out.

"Go on," Sunny whispered, giving my shoulder a nudge.

With a deep breath and a nervous smile, I moved toward the living room, where my family was waiting.

Babka was already there, sunk into the same chair she'd been dozing off in every day around this time. Kira sat on the couch, her arm stretched over the back and her legs tucked under her. Anya was busy sorting through a small pile of books on the coffee table.

For a moment, I stood there, watching my precious girl in her deliberation, marveling at her beauty. It was still hard to believe I was here with her, that she was more than just a memory, when less than two weeks ago I wasn't sure if I'd ever see her again.

"Yelena," Kira called, catching my attention and waving me over.

Each step sent my stomach into a slow, tumbling flip. My nerves buzzed, and the cruel little voice in the back of my mind whispered that I wasn't good enough.

You're too broken for something this good.

But I knew that voice. It wasn't mine. It was Nik's. It coursed through me like poison, threading through every doubt and every wound he'd carved into me. He'd filled my life with pain and chaos, making me question my worth until there was practically nothing left.

But not today.

I pushed past the fear, shoved through the weight of

uncertainty, and smothered every last whisper of the self-hatred his words had fed.

I wouldn't let him take this from me. Not this moment. Not my chance at something real.

Limbs stiff and mind buzzing, I sat on the edge of the cushions and waited to see what would come next.

"Dis one." Anya raised a book from the pile, waving it like a prize. "Dis one, dis one."

Her enthusiasm was directed at Kira, but she crawled up on the couch between us, her chubby leg only inches from mine. It was the closest we'd gotten to contact so far, and although it wasn't nearly enough, I'd take whatever I could get.

Anya squirmed in the seat, moving just a fraction closer. "Story. Pease." Her request was still aimed at my sister.

Kira feigned a yawn. "My eyes are tired. You should ask someone else."

I glanced up to catch the sly wink she sent my way.

"Pease?" Anya persisted, her feet kicking the couch cushions.

"Hmm…" Kira placed a finger over her chin. "Yelena, do you know anybody who could read a story?"

Anya twisted to look at me, her expression alight with excitement and hope.

God, this was what I'd been praying for. The chance to make a connection. To have my daughter see me as someone other than a stranger.

But my throat had closed, and all I could do was nod.

"Ask nicely, and your mama Yelena will read it to you." Kira motioned from Anya to me.

My heart squeezed a mangled beat as two little hands slid a book into my lap. "Pease? You read."

I stared at the story of Rapunzel, trying to keep my imminent meltdown at bay.

Babka squinted at us from her chair. "Read your baby the book, Yelena."

Chest tightening, I smiled at my beautiful grandmother. She'd lived through so much, but she still put on a happy face. Every damn day.

Taking strength from her example, I nodded again. "Yes. I would like that very much."

Anya was close enough to see the pictures, but I leaned toward her anyway, holding the storybook between us. The smell of baby powder enveloped me, and I fought back tears as I opened the worn cover.

How many times had my own mother read this to me? It was hard to remember. Heck, it was difficult to remember anything about her at all.

After our parents died, it had been Kira who helped me with books. Not bedtime stories but spelling and math. Those memories formed a much clearer image in my head. Along with my grandparents, it had been my big sister who'd taken care of me.

She'd taken care of my daughter for me, too.

Even before Nik had locked me away, she'd been there for us. She'd been the one at my bedside when I'd given birth. The only one, other than Babka, who'd bothered to check in when I didn't come home.

How was I still holding a grudge?

With my voice strained and eyes stinging, and despite stumbling over most of the words, I somehow made it to the end of the story.

"Again." Anya tapped the book and wiggled closer, her eyes drooping.

The warmth in my chest expanded, and I relaxed into the moment. I felt lighter. More centered. Like a lost part of me was finally clicking back into place.

And I couldn't hold back my smile. "Yes, again. Anything for you, my angel."

Heck, I'd read Rapunzel a million times if she asked.

I flipped back to the beginning and started the story over. Halfway through, a soft head of curls was resting against my arm, and I peeked down to find Anya fast asleep.

The moment stretched and blurred as I studied her, memorizing every dimple, every dark lash that brushed across her round cheeks.

A pang squeezed my chest. I'd missed so much. But I was here now, and I was never leaving her again.

At least not willingly.

With my smile still firmly in place, I looked up to find Kira was gone. I'd been so immersed in my baby, I hadn't even noticed her leave.

I turned to my grandmother, but she'd drifted off too.

"Need a hand getting her to bed?" Finn asked from over my shoulder.

Neck straining, I tilted my head to find him staring down at me. How long had he been there?

"That's okay. I've got her."

Intent on carrying my sleeping beauty to the room she was sharing with Babka, I carefully extracted myself from beside her and stood. But when I bent to lift her, a wave of unforgiving dizziness hit.

"Hey." Finn was suddenly beside me, his hand sliding across my back, steadying me as I straightened.

He lingered longer than he needed to, but I didn't mind. I soaked in the heat radiating off his body, the clean scent of mint, and something deeper—earthy, warm, and unmistakably male.

"You good?" His warm breath skated across my cheek.

"Yes." But it was a lie.

I wasn't sure I'd ever be good again. Not on my own. Not without him this close.

The thought unsettled me, catching low in my stomach like a warning I couldn't quite name.

Was I mistaking comfort for something else? Trading one kind of craving for another?

Something shifted in his gaze, turning it dark. Dangerous. And I took a step back, seeking the balance I'd found only moments ago but had somehow lost again.

His jaw hardened, and he broke our stare to retrieve Anya. He lifted her easily, settling her head over his shoulder with a single arm. Without a word, he turned and walked away with my daughter.

Drawn like a magnet, I followed him to the bedroom, where he placed her on top of the covers.

The twin bed was scattered with books and stuffed animals—each one chosen by someone else. Not me.

Was there any trace of me in her memories? Any part of her that still knew me as her mother?

The ache in my chest was sharp, hollow. I had to do better. Be better.

But how was I supposed to do that on my own? Especially when it felt so good to have Finn beside me. When his presence was the only thing keeping the emptiness from swallowing me whole.

"Thanks for this," I whispered, clearing space to tuck Anya in.

He didn't respond.

I turned to find him only steps away, a dark look still shrouding his handsome features.

"For all of it." The jitters tried to take hold again, but I refused to let them take over. My gaze travelled back to my baby. "She's safer because of you."

"I'm not the one who's kept her safe." His voice was low, almost menacing, and it sent a chill running down my spine.

Why did he sound so angry?

"Yes, Kira's done a lot for her too. For both of us."

"What about you?" He moved closer, his big body blocking my path to the door. "Have you forgotten everything you've done to protect her?"

"What?" Heart pounding, I kept my eyes on Anya. "I'm the reason she's in danger in the first place."

I caught the motion of his shaking head from the corner of my eye, but I didn't dare look at him. Didn't dare acknowledge the desire his proximity stirred.

Instead, I leaned over my angel, brushing her curls from her forehead. "She shouldn't have to live like this—hiding from her own father. She doesn't deserve any of it."

"Neither do you." He moved even closer, angling his body toward me, arms crossing over his hard chest.

"You don't understand." Bracing a hand against the headboard, I straightened to face him. "I created this situation."

"No." The muscles in his arms hardened and flexed, drawing my attention despite my resistance. "Rykov created it, not you. He forced you into an impossible scenario."

He really didn't understand. But how could I explain it without uncovering all my secrets—the dark parts of me no one had ever seen, except Nik?

"But that's the thing, Finn…he didn't force me."

"For fuck's sake." His voice dropped even lower. "Do you think I haven't noticed the bruises? The scars? How many more would I find if I stripped you right now?"

Sweet hell. My heart raced, the ache between my legs climbed out of control, and I bit the inside of my already bloodied lip to keep from begging him to do it.

Strip me bare. Explore my body. Touch me. Please, please, touch me everywhere.

But we were standing less than a foot away from my sleeping daughter. I couldn't let my irrational need for him take over.

"I deserved what I got." I forced the words out, unsure if I even meant them. "All of it."

The line of Finn's shoulders and neck went rigid, a muscle ticked at his jaw, and the look on his face was unforgiving. He stared at me, his ocean blues turning downright glacial.

And I still wasn't afraid of him.

If anything, his rigid stance and barely restrained fury only made me want him more.

With a sudden sound that could only be described as a growl, he closed in on me. In an instant, there was nothing but a breath between us.

Slowly, he leaned in. His lips hovered beside my ear, my entire body thrumming with need.

He lingered there a moment, radiating raw power and control, before whispering, "And I'm going to fucking kill him for it."

And just like that, he turned and walked out the door.

CHAPTER
EIGHT
FINN

THE DAY'S suffocating heat had faded with the sun, but there was still no relief. The pressure at the base of my neck refused to let go.

How could it, when every moment spent near Yelena dragged me closer to the edge?

She was supposed to be leverage. A pawn. But every day, the line between using her and wanting her blurred a little more.

Damp from sweat and limping harder than usual, I crept inside the shadowed cottage. Silence greeted me, along with the soft yellow glow of a single dim light.

And Yelena.

She was lying at the end of the couch—*my goddamn bed*—like she belonged there. Her head was on the armrest, legs were curled to her chest, and her hands were tucked under her chin. Eyes closed. Lips parted. Perfectly still, except for her breathing.

Devastating, even in her sleep. Alone, even in a house full of people.

With a lump in my throat and staggering pain under my ribs, I moved toward her, drawn to her beauty the same way gravity pulls the moon. Each step was inescapable. Inevitable.

I knocked the edge of the coffee table with my bad leg, nearly pitching into her. She still didn't stir. Even when I loomed over her, catching my balance and studying the messy pile of hair at her crown, she didn't move.

Not even when I crouched down next to her, waiting and watching as she dozed.

She looked peaceful. Like this quiet moment was exactly what she needed. And fuck, after everything she'd been through—the pain, the struggle, the constant uncertainty—any shred of stillness she found was hard-earned.

I should've backed off. Let her rest. Left the room and found another place to lay my head like any decent man would've done.

But I wasn't that man, and I was sick of pretending.

Sleep was the last thing on my mind when the woman I'd been dreaming about, fucking obsessing over, was only inches away. Exposed. Unguarded. Achingly beautiful.

I reached out, my fingers ghosting over the tops of her bare feet. Just a touch. Just enough to solidify her presence.

She stirred, unfurling like a flower—back arching,

legs stretching, and shoulders rolling. For a moment, she went rigid before relaxing again, her hands falling to the cushion as if reaching for me. Her head shifted, breath brushing across my face like a whisper.

It undid me.

Everything I'd been holding back surged to the surface. The anger, longing, frustration, and need. Every dark, compulsive thought I'd buried came screaming forward.

With claws and goddamn teeth.

I reached for her again. Slower this time, but more daring. With a single finger, I brushed back the hair that had fallen over her cheek. Marveled at her silken skin. Traced the contours of her face, skimming the arc of her brow, following the curve of her jaw, and outlining the bow of her lips.

Lips I'd been aching to taste since the moment I pulled her from that hell.

No, it was long before that. I'd been obsessed with Yelena Markova from the start.

She wasn't just a distraction. She was the reason I was here. Maybe the reason we were all here. And if I wasn't careful, she'd be the reason we all ended up dead.

Fuck me. I pulled my hand away. "What are you doing to me?"

Her eyes snapped open on a gasp. Frozen, she held my stare for what felt like forever, until her breath rushed out and she finally blinked. "Finn?"

"I didn't mean to wake you." I shifted backward, putting space between us.

It still wasn't enough. Not when her scent was still in my lungs. Not when the image of her, pliant and dreaming, was carved into my skull like a brand.

I needed to go. Hell, I shouldn't have hung around in the first place.

But as I stood, she bolted upright, her hand grasping hold of mine. "No. Stay. I was waiting for you."

Now I was the one struggling to breathe.

Fingers squeezing, she pinned me with her big doe eyes. "Please."

"You were waiting for me?" I leaned back toward her, towering over her, and turning her hand in mine.

She nodded, with her eyes focused on our entwined fingers. "Y-yes."

"Why? Was there something you needed? Something you want?"

Eyes still impossibly wide, her breath hitched and body wound tight again.

Fuck, this was reckless. Possibly the most dangerous thing I'd ever done. But self-preservation had always been my weakness. And right now, with all my blood rushing south, I wasn't sure I cared.

"I wanted…" Her whole body seemed to vibrate with a shiver.

"What?" I urged, my muscles straining and cock growing hard. "Tell me."

"I…I want to talk."

Talk. She wanted to talk. Of course she did. What

else would she be looking for from a man like me? Protection, maybe. Safety. But anything more? Anything real? That was dangerous ground.

For both of us.

"What do you want to talk about?" I forced the words out.

"You."

"Me?" Now both legs felt useless, so I dropped onto the couch beside her.

Close. *Too close.*

My hip crowded her outstretched legs, claiming more space than I should've. It might've seemed like an intrusion, yet she simply made room for me, her knee pressed to my side, and her thigh snug against mine.

We sat face to face, her open, innocent expression eating at my resolve.

"I know you don't really want to be here." Her voice was soft and tentative, making her statement sound more like a question.

"What makes you think that?"

Her brow pinched. "Just a feeling, I guess."

"I already told you, I'm here. I'm not going anywhere."

"You did." She nodded, and a lock of golden hair slipped over her shoulder, tempting my fingers to follow. "But something's bothering you, and I just…feel like maybe it's me. Like I've upset you somehow."

My lungs pinched, my breath growing ragged as I fought back a low growl. "You've done nothing wrong."

"But you were angry." Something flickered across

her face. Something that looked a hell of a lot like uncertainty. Doubt.

And fuck, I'd put it there. Not Rykov. Me.

A quiet ache pulled tight in my chest. I'd wanted to protect her. Shield her from the part of me that couldn't be trusted. Instead, I'd made her question herself.

What kind of monster was I?

"You've been angry from the beginning," she said, her voice low. "And you've been avoiding me. Always outside. Always gone."

Her eyes dropped, fixed on the floor like she couldn't bear to look at me.

"Hey." I reached for her chin, coaxing her gaze back to mine. "Eyes up here."

She resisted, lashes squeezing like she could shut me out with willpower alone.

That small act of defiance? It shouldn't have gotten to me. Shouldn't have turned me on.

But fuck me, it did.

"Look at me." The request came out rough, urgent, and closer to a command than I intended.

She gasped, her eyes snapping open, and the jolt that tore through me was instant. Electric.

I forced myself to stay grounded, to push back the need clawing at my insides, and searched her pretty, too-trusting eyes. "I'm not angry with you."

Her brows drew together, but she didn't look away. "Then why have you been acting like it?"

Because I crave you, even knowing I'll ruin you.

"Rykov."

"Nik?"

Fuck, I hated the way his name rolled off her tongue. So familiar. Too goddamn intimate.

She shook her head, her breath shuddering. "I don't understand."

I scoffed. "I know you're not that naïve."

The look on her face was a mix of shock and disbelief. Her mouth opened, then closed again, and she kept quiet.

"That wasn't an insult." I tapped her chin. "It was a compliment."

She didn't look convinced.

Hell, maybe she really didn't know. My hatred for the bastard had clouded not only my thoughts but my actions and my fucking judgment. Maybe it had hidden my respect for her, too.

And along with it, the brutal truth of my unmitigated and disastrous obsession.

"I thought it was obvious." The infuriating, crawling burn crept up the back of my neck. "I can't fucking stand that he touched you. That he hurt you."

"Oh." A faint blush bloomed across her cheeks.

Fuck, it was sexy.

Without thinking, I pulled our entwined hands to my chest. Right over my hammering heart. "And you talk about it like it was your fault. Like you asked for the trauma. Like there's any fucking version of this that can justify the horrible shit he did to you."

"I know it's not all my fault. Not really. And there are things I've never said out loud. Things I haven't been ready to face. But…" Uncertainty caught in her throat as the tension between us pulled tight, almost painful.

"But what?"

"Maybe it's time I did."

Her hushed words brushed my skin, and a sharp, crackling heat licked down my spine. "I'm listening."

She caught her bottom lip between her teeth, and my jaw tensed. Fuck, she had no idea what that did to me. She held it there, tormenting me, before finally letting it slip free—glistening and inviting. Goddamn irresistible.

She lifted her free hand and pressed it to my chest, just beside our entwined fingers. Her grip tightened in my shirt as if she couldn't bring herself to let go. "I told you I trusted you. And I do. At least I want to."

Her trust should've scared me. Because fuck, I could've so easily corrupted it. Twisted it into something dark and selfish. Hell, part of me still thought I should. That it was the smartest move. The surest path to revenge.

But in that moment, with need coiling inside me, I felt nothing but greedy anticipation. The urge to take her deepest fears and darkest secrets and claim them for myself. Just like the rest of her. "You still can. Whatever you want to say stays right here, between us."

"Okay," she said in a rush. "The reason I talked about Nik hurting me like I asked for it? It's because I did. Not the cruelty. But the control." She swallowed hard. "I was drawn to the way he influenced others. The power he wielded. God, I encouraged it. Because I liked…"

Her head shook, and the flush crept down her neck, deepening the color in her cheeks. "He was always domineering. And part of me wanted that. Needed it. I just didn't realize how far he'd take it."

My pulse pounded, but the rest of me went still. "Are you talking about sex?"

She pulled her hands away, folding them tightly around her middle, and her big doe eyes peeked at me through thick lashes. "In part. But there was a lot more to it than that."

"It doesn't matter how much more there was or wasn't. There's a line between a consensually explored kink and what he did to you. One's built on trust. The other exploits it."

Goddammit, just saying it made my gut sink. Wasn't that exactly what I'd been planning on doing? Exploiting her trust and triggers—purposely manipulating her for my own benefit?

She only blinked, her luscious lip disappearing between her teeth again.

"Liking something unconventional isn't shameful." My voice was low and measured, despite my cock straining behind my zipper. Despite this being the worst goddamn time. "And it doesn't give your partner an open door to abuse you."

"It wasn't abuse." Her fingers clenched tight against her ribs. "It was fucking torture. Punishment for every little thing I ever did wrong. For things that had nothing to do with me at all."

Suddenly, she was seething. Rage simmered beneath her resolve, quiet but smoldering, buried so deep for so long it was only a matter of time before it boiled over. And damn it was beautiful.

Stunning.

Still, her voice was barely more than a whisper. "He used his power to lure me in. Teased me with promises of—" She faltered, her voice cracking.

Pain burrowed into her expression, a sorrow so sharp it echoed in my bones. But she cleared her throat and pushed on. "I guess it doesn't matter, because after Anya, something shifted. He started using obedience like a leash, then starved me of everything—touch, attention, kindness—until it was like I didn't have a voice. Didn't even exist."

She paused, swallowing hard. "Until he got bored or something set him off. Then he'd explode…"

"Nothing you said or did could legitimize—"

"I've done some very bad things, Finn." Her words cut me off, but the anguish in her voice cut through me. "Things I regret. He's a monster. I know that. But I'm the one who invited him in. I opened the door. He simply walked through."

I was going to kill the fucker. Hunt him down and bleed him dry.

"We've all done bad things." I forced my voice to remain steady.

Her gaze flicked back to mine. "You really don't think less of me for it?"

Fuck, I had no right to touch her, but that didn't stop me. I reached out, my fingers sliding to the back of her neck and tugging her close enough for our breath to mingle. For her eyes to widen. For my will to crack.

She was fragile, yes. But there was something raw and unfinished about her. It was a hunger that stirred deep inside her. A fire that hadn't gone out, only waited to be fed. The promise of something savage and stunning.

Something I wanted. Not only for myself, but for her.

"We never know what kind of mark someone's going to leave." My voice was low, almost gentle. "Some sear their names into our souls. Others leave us bleeding. There's no way to know which it will be until we open the door. Why would I think less of you for that?"

She held my gaze, but there was something hesitant about it. "I stayed," she admitted, her voice raw. "When I still had a choice. Even though I knew what he was, I stayed."

I dragged my thumb along the curve of her jaw. "And you survived."

"Did I?" She shook her head, her eyes glistening. "There's not much left of me, Finn. Just pieces I barely recognize. And I don't know if I'm strong enough to pull myself back together on my own."

Her words hung between us, seeping into my

marrow. Eating me alive. Because this? This was the moment I had to choose. Lift her up until she found her own strength, until she could join my fight freely. Or drag her into my darkness, despite knowing it could be the thing to ruin her for good.

"You might be a little broken. Fuck, we all are. But you're not alone."

Her breath stuttered.

"You're strong enough to do this. I know you are." My fingers pressed the silken flesh at the back of her neck, my thumb at her throat. "And I promise you, one day soon, you'll believe it."

But it was more than a promise. It was a fucking vow.

And I was going to be the one to get her there. I'd raise her up. Reinforce her. Show her she'd been the one with strength and power all along. Until she believed in herself again—steady, fearless, and completely in control.

A long silence stretched between us. It was filled with her lingering uncertainty and my growing hunger.

I eased back, my hand sliding down her arm until I was holding her hand again.

"Finn?" Her voice was soft and sleep-tinted. Delicate and fucking delectable.

I stroked my thumb over hers, relishing the way my touch seemed to settle her. "Hmm?"

"Does this mean we're friends now?"

"Friends?" I echoed, a quiet, humorless laugh slipping free. "No, Yelena. That's not what this is."

She blinked up at me, her fingers twitching in mine like she wasn't sure if she should pull away or hold on tighter.

"What is it then?" she whispered, her pulse visible at the base of her throat.

Fuck, I wanted nothing more than to lean in, take that fluttering vein between my teeth, and show her all the dark and depraved ways we could be so much more than friends.

But I couldn't. Not here. Not now.

Maybe not ever.

"I told you I'd keep you safe." My voice was smooth and soothing. "That's what matters."

A fucking lie. Because I knew exactly what this was. For me at least.

And exactly how dangerous that was for her.

CHAPTER
NINE
YELENA

I JOLTED AWAKE, the tail end of a dream chasing me.

No, not a dream. A chilling nightmare. One that left my throat raw as if I'd been screaming, my muscles aching like I'd been fighting, and my heart pounding like it wanted out of my chest. My body was strung so tight I thought I might snap.

The memory of the dream blurred at the edges, slipping from my grasp, mixing with reality and leaving nothing but lingering dread.

It wasn't real. I repeated the mantra, dragging in slow, steady breaths. *Just a dream.*

But the tension wouldn't let go.

I lay still, eyes wide and breath ragged, searching the darkened ceiling for answers that weren't there. But as my eyes adjusted to the low light, I realized the ceiling above me was unfamiliar. Panic flooded my system, and I bolted upright, my head whipping around to search my surroundings.

I was in the cottage. Downstairs. On the couch.

My pulse slowed as the memory washed over me—waiting here for Finn, sitting beside him, talking for hours. His voice had steadied me, even as he pushed me, challenged me. And eventually, exhaustion had dragged me under.

Where was he now?

I strained, searching the darkness for signs of him. But there was no trace. Only silence.

A sickening thought slithered into my mind, cold and merciless.

Nik.

It had been weeks, but he was still out there somewhere. Probably looking for me. Plotting to capture me. Or worse, punish me in the most gruesome ways he could find.

Had he found us? Sent his men to collect me? Taken Finn first, leaving me exposed and vulnerable? Alone.

My stomach twisted violently, bile rising in my throat. I pushed to my feet, legs shaky and fists tight as I scanned the darkened room.

Every corner was filled with shadows. The walls closed in, and silence loomed.

I'm safe. Just breathe.

Swallowing hard, I forced myself forward, one step and then another. Nothing seemed out of place. The room was untouched, undisturbed. But that didn't mean we were safe.

A dull thud echoed from somewhere outside.

I sucked in a sharp breath, my body turning rigid as my heart slammed.

Was this real? Or was it all in my head? A paranoid spiral, born from the wreckage of abuse and addiction?

Another noise registered from outside. This time, closer. And it wiped any hope that it was just a hallucination from my mind, leaving only the cold certainty of danger.

I crept forward, my muscles taut, my ears straining, and my bare feet padding softly over the wood-planked floor.

Get a weapon. Find Finn.

But every step felt clumsy. Every breath was deafening. And my pulse was too wild, like the fear invading my senses would somehow give me away.

The kitchen was bathed in faint moonlight, and like the rest of the space, it was empty. No sign of a struggle.

But that didn't settle the fear still clawing at my insides.

At the sink, I twisted the faucet just enough to let a trickle of cold water run over my wrists. The shock centered me, dragging me back to my senses. My breath slowed. My heart steadied. And instead of reacting to an invisible, likely imaginary threat, I forced myself to stop and think.

If Nik's men had taken Finn, there'd have been a fight. Noise. Maybe even gunshots. Finn would not have gone willingly. And wouldn't they have taken me too?

Unless they caught him off guard. Unless he fought and lost. Unless—

A floorboard creaked behind me.

Air trapped in my lungs as my adrenaline spiked and fight, flight, or freeze took over.

Freeze. Why did I always freeze?

Use the adrenaline. Make it your friend.

Another floorboard moaned, this one much closer.

I summoned every ounce of courage I could find and moved to spin around, ready to face down my attacker. But a large hand grabbed me, circling my waist and locking me in place. Before I could scream, another rough hand cupped over my mouth.

My whole body went rigid. Fear overloaded my senses. But I fought against the paralysis, sending an elbow backward into a solid form.

A masculine grunt sounded at the contact, sending a chill down my spine, and the arm around my middle squeezed. A charge of heat pulsed through me as I was pulled hard against a sturdy male body, my fear mixing with something that felt far too much like pleasure.

"Hey." Finn's low voice rumbled against my ear. "It's just me."

All my breath let out in a shaky rush, leaving me wilting and wanting in his arms.

"Sorry." He dropped his hand from my mouth but didn't let me go. He turned me in his arms, his hold firm but careful. "I didn't mean to scare you, but I also didn't want to wake the whole house."

"You could've just called my name, instead of sneaking up."

A crooked smirk tilted his lips. "Where's the fun in that?"

Oh. *Sweet hell.*

Shadowed against the moonlight, the angles of his face seemed sharper. His eyes more piercing. His intentions far more devious.

Sparks skittered over my skin as the sudden urge to run took hold.

Not to escape. No. Some dark, primal part of me wanted him to chase me. Catch me. Pin me down and do unspeakable, dirty things to me.

"You think an elbow to the ribs is fun?" I challenged, forcing myself to stay put.

His laughter was a low rumble that did nothing to curb my craving.

"Don't worry, it didn't hurt." His gaze dragged over me, his jaw working and hands gripping tight around my waist.

Desire, stronger than should've been possible, wound its way through my body. I drank in his heated stare, my nipples pebbling against the thin fabric of my borrowed tank top. As if caught in a spell, my back arched and chin lifted in an unspoken surrender.

A silent offering of my body to his unyielding command.

His hands flexed at my middle, his restraint tangible. The air between us was thick and heavy with something unspoken. Something inevitable.

With a sharp inhale, he released me. Taking a step

back, his hands curled into fists at his sides, and his eyes snapped away from me.

The loss of his touch was immediate and jarring. I crossed my arms over my chest in a pathetic attempt to shield myself from his rejection.

This situation was ridiculous. I was ridiculous. The man didn't even want my friendship. What on earth made me think he'd want something more?

And yet the hunger in his gaze was all-consuming.

I took a shaky step back, watching him and trying to ignore the part of me that still burned for his touch.

"Where were you?" My lower back hit the counter as I shifted away, fighting to keep the damage to my battered pride from bleeding into my voice. "I woke up on the couch and you were gone."

"Perimeter sweep," he said, as if it were the most ordinary thing in the world. Like assessing the security of our surroundings in the dead of night was simply routine.

"Did you just wake up and decide to check things out?"

"Nah, I haven't gone to bed yet."

That didn't sound right. According to the microwave clock, it was almost three in the morning.

"Where is your bed?" My cheeks heated, the question sounding far more like a come-on than I'd intended.

He didn't seem to notice. Hitching a thumb over his shoulder, he motioned to the living room. "The couch."

"What? That's not built for a man your size." And he'd let me fall asleep there. How needy was I?

"I don't mind. Trust me, I've slept in much worse places."

Me too. "Like where?"

"In the back seat of a Humvee. On the ground in the desert. In a VA hospital. All of them much worse than that plush sectional over there."

"You served?" How did I not know that? Heck, I still didn't know a thing about him.

This man had risked his life for me. He was still risking it. And the only real thing I knew about him was how good I felt in his presence. How I wanted not only his attention and protection, but so much more.

"Yeah. Afghanistan." He ran a hand over the back of his neck, the motion stiff and uneasy. "But why are you awake?"

"I had a bad dream."

His gaze sharpened. "Want to talk about it?"

I hesitated before shaking my head. "It's the same as always. Just fragments of memories, disjointed and jumbled. It never makes sense." A shiver ran through me as my skin cooled, and the remnants of my nightmare crawled back in. "The only thing I ever remember is being alone. But it feels like someone's watching me. And I'm always afraid."

His voice was quiet. "And that feeling lingers. Even after you wake up."

I sucked in a breath. "Always. I heard you outside and immediately assumed the worst. I started to panic before I realized it was you."

He studied me, his voice careful. "After everything

you've been through, I'm not surprised. And I'm sorry if I made it worse."

"You didn't." But pressure built in my chest, working its way up my throat—the edges of panic still trying to suffocate me.

Desperate for a distraction, my mouth moved before I could stop it. "Will you tell me about Bodhi?"

His expression fell, and the fine lines that gave his face so much character drew tight. "What about him?"

"Did he serve too?"

"We served together." His voice was still low and rough, but there was something uneasy about the way he answered.

He probably thought my line of questioning was invasive. Maybe it didn't even make sense. But it was too late to take it back. And right now, any information related to Finn was valuable. Anything to rationalize the way I felt about him. The way I craved his proximity.

Anything to feel like I wasn't falling for a complete stranger.

"Together?" I prompted, hoping he wouldn't shut me out again.

"Yeah. Until I was medically discharged."

"Because of your leg?"

His nod was slight. "Hit by shrapnel from an IED. I was lucky, I wasn't that close to the blast. We lost a man that day, and two others were badly injured. It was a fucking mess. Those men deserved better…" His voice faded, lost to whatever hold the memory still had on him.

"That sounds awful." It was nothing like the events I'd lived through. Yet I could easily picture it—the blood and gore, men hurt and dying, and the feeling of terror in that moment. Those things were all too familiar.

"It was especially bad for Bodhi." He scratched absently at the back of his neck, his gaze still far away. "I almost bled out right there on the desert floor. Bodhi saved my life. I think it still haunts him."

"What about you? Doesn't it still haunt you?"

"Nah." His jaw hardened as a look of agony crossed his face.

It was intense. Unbearable. But in an instant, it was gone, leaving me to wonder if it was all in my head.

"Honestly," he said, his tone even and expression blank. "I don't remember most of it. With the blood loss and shock, it all blurred together."

"Still." I moved back toward him, my fingers brushing his chest before settling there. "It sounds like a living nightmare."

His hand landed over mine, strong and steady. "Guess you'd know a little something about that."

I frowned up at him. "It's not the same."

"Maybe not exactly, but I'm willing to bet it sums up the last four years of your life with Rykov pretty damn well."

My heart lurched, and I was seized by a cold jolt of panic. I tried to pull away, but his grip was unyielding, his hand a steel vise over mine.

Four years.

No one knew I'd been with Nik that long. Not even Kira. We'd kept the relationship hidden. Right up until I got pregnant. Until I was in too deep, and it was too damn late.

How the hell did Finn know?

"The last year," I corrected, my voice thin and brittle. "Singular. That's how long he kept me locked up."

"Yeah, that's what I said."

But it wasn't. And now my mind ran in circles. Was it coincidence, a slip of the tongue, or something Finn was keeping from me?

"I don't want to talk about that anymore." The uneasiness spread outward, moving down my neck and over my skin. "No offense."

The craving hit hard and fast, like a punch to the gut. *A pill. Just one.* Something to smooth out the jagged edges of this moment.

"None taken. But maybe talking to a therapist would be a good idea. Because you can't bury that shit and hope to get better."

"I'm already getting better." I forced the words out, hoping that saying them would make them true. Even though the gnawing at the back of my brain said otherwise. "Your sister's helped a lot with that."

"Maybe." He lifted our joined hands to his mouth, his lips brushing against my knuckles in a featherlight kiss. "But I can hear those demons nipping at your heels, Lena. I'd hate to see them catch you."

There it was again—that oddly shortened version of my name that no one else had ever used. The one that made my insides buzz. The one that sounded like a treasure, even though his voice was rough and his words were harsh.

"Me?" The craving twisted, sharp and demanding. But which did I want more, the pills or him? "What about you?"

His brow creased, but he didn't pull away. "My demons caught up with me a long time ago."

Something in the way he said it made my stomach drop. "But I thought Nik was part of that. Isn't he one of your demons?"

His expression darkened. A slow, terrifying shift—hard, merciless, menacing. "Not exactly."

"Then why do you want to kill him?"

Finn buried his nose against the inside of my wrist, inhaling deeply, his eyes closing like he was memorizing my scent. It was primal. Possessive. And it sent a violent shudder through me.

He landed another kiss there, this one slower and more purposeful.

Like he was marking me, binding me to him. Making me his.

And God, despite the voice in my head warning that he was hiding something—something that could change the trajectory of everything—I wished it were true. Wished this intense, heated thing between us could be real. Not just a delusion or yearning for something I'd never had.

His lips ghosted over my skin before he finally lifted his gaze to mine.

"Retribution." His voice was a whisper, low and edged with something lethal.

Retribution.

Now that was a pretty word. Dark, raw, and dripping with promise. I wanted to hear it again. To feel it roll off his tongue. Wanted his hands on me, his body pressing that word into my skin like a vow he'd never break.

The craving for a pill still lingered, razor sharp and insatiable. But that word dulled its edges, offering me something else to cling to. A purpose beyond the hollow ache in my veins.

"Tell me more." I was desperate now. "Please, Finn. Tell me you won't just make him bleed. Tell me I can be part of it."

CHAPTER
TEN
FINN

Fuck, she was devastating.

Drenched in darkness, she stood with moonlight tangled in her hair, begging for vengeance like it was foreplay. Begging me to give it to her.

"You want to be part of it?" I challenged, my voice rough and my cock growing hard.

A glint of something raw and hungry sparked in her gaze. "I need it. Retribution."

She didn't just want revenge. She craved it. And hell, after everything, she deserved it.

But as our fingers stayed locked together, my last threads of restraint fraying fast, doubt crept in. Did she understand what it meant?

"What exactly are you asking for, Lena?" My voice was low, laced with violence and something darker. Something that had nothing to do with bloodshed and everything to do with her.

She shook her head, her golden hair slipping over

her shoulders like silk. "I-I'm not sure. To not feel so lost, I guess. To take back what he stole from me."

She'd mentioned torture, and she was open to the idea of Rykov's death, but it was a big fucking leap from letting it happen to wanting to take part.

And yet there was something fierce and untamed flaring to life inside her. Something that called to all my darkest parts. A fire that, once stoked, could threaten to burn our world.

And us along with it.

"You want power? Control?" I scored my teeth along the tender flesh of her inner wrist—not marking her, just testing.

How far was she willing to go? How far would she let me push her?

She sucked in a sharp, audible breath, and goddammit, I almost lost it. Holding back the growl clawing up my throat, I leaned in, crowding her against the kitchen counter, leaving her nowhere to hide.

No way to run.

"Well, Lena?" I brought our joined hands back to my chest, allowing her to feel the erratic tempo of my heart. "Is that what you want? To prove he's not as untouchable as he thinks?"

"Yes." Her words whispered over my skin. "Do you think it's possible?"

"Maybe." I braced a hand against the counter beside her hip, blocking her in tighter. "But revenge isn't clean. It never is. It would change you in ways you won't see coming."

"I don't want clean. I want to see him suffer."

I exhaled slowly, tightening my grip on her hand. She needed to know what she was inviting. What I was willing to become.

The lengths I was willing to go to get what I wanted.

"You want to be there when he dies?"

"I-I think so." She faltered, her gaze dropping from mine. Then she returned the pressure on my hand, her voice stronger. "Yes. I do."

"What if things go sideways? What if he kills one or both of us instead?"

"I'm not afraid to die. Anything to protect Anya." Her chest rose and fell in deep, shuddering breaths, contradicting her words. "Besides, I trust you to make sure that doesn't happen."

Trust. If only it were that simple.

Her words settled around me. She was asking for a decision that couldn't be undone, and an instinct screamed at me to stop this. To pull her back before she stepped too far into the dark.

But another part of me—the selfish part I kept buried beneath duty, guilt, and rage, the part that craved more than simple control—wanted her to take that step. Wanted to watch her cross the line. To see what she'd become when she stopped holding back. When she shed the skin of the insecure, anxious victim he'd turned her into and emerged as something bolder. Deadlier.

A goddess, even more stunning than she was before.

"Good," I murmured, a thrill hitting fast and hot beneath my skin. "Because I need you."

Her mouth dropped open, eyes blowing wide, and her body wound tight as she swayed toward me.

"The only way I'm getting close to him is with you at my side."

She blinked, the heat in her gaze dimming. "So what does that make me? A bargaining chip? Bait?"

"Do you want me to lie?" I dipped my head, catching her gaze again. "Should I feed you something sweet and meaningless? Tell you you're not the leverage I need to draw him out?"

She made a strangled sound of protest, but said nothing more.

"I could've done that," I admitted, my eyes locked on hers. "Fuck, I almost did. But I don't want to lie to you."

I moved even closer. Let the heat wind between us, one breath away from combustion. "And I don't want to use you." My voice dropped to something rough and honest. "Unless you're willing."

Doubt shadowed her beautiful face, but I could still see the spark of desire in her.

I lifted her hand, brushing my mouth over the back of it again. "I don't want you to be a pawn, Lena. I want you to be a fucking queen."

Her lips curled into a breathtaking smile—dangerous, seductive, and begging for sin.

The annoying prickle at the back of my neck took a backseat as a gnawing urgency built at the base of my spine. An appetite I'd denied for too long.

But the sun would be up in a few short hours. And

our families were sound asleep, only feet away, blissfully unaware that we were out here plotting murder.

"For now, you should go get some sleep." I shifted backward, giving us both space to cool off. "Nothing happens until you're better. I need you strong."

She held my gaze for a beat too long, as if weighing my words, taking my measure. Then, with some silent decision made, she turned and disappeared up the stairs.

She left behind the smell of lavender and citrus, and the echo of something unspoken.

Something that threatened to ruin not only my plans but me.

I ran a hand through my shaggy hair, exhaling sharply.

The night stretched on, thick with thoughts of her. Thoughts I had no goddamn right entertaining. Desires I couldn't fucking afford. And by the time morning came, I still hadn't found sleep, only the cold clarity that last night had changed everything.

Everything.

I dragged myself into the kitchen where sunlight was creeping through the windows, soft and warm and completely at odds with the chaos in my head. I opened the fridge, intent on making breakfast to help keep my mind off her. Anything to outrun the memory of Yelena standing there, barely contained, like a live wire ready to snap, danger and desperation radiating off her in waves.

The fabric of her shirt hadn't hidden much. Her nipples had been tight against the thin cotton, taunting, daring me to lose control. It had taken everything in me not to stare. Not to give in to the primal urge to tear that flimsy barrier away. To touch her. Taste her. Brand every inch of her with my need.

"Everything okay?" Sunny asked from the other side of the fridge door, and I nearly dropped the carton of eggs.

I shoved the filthy images out of my head, closed the door, and turned to her with a forced smile. "All good, little sis. Just figured you might like a break from cooking. Thought I'd help out."

She cocked her head, analyzing me with her clinical stare. "That's nice, I guess. But you know Kira's vegan, right? And Yelena's on a clean diet to help with her recovery."

"Clean diet? I'm not sure I even know what that is."

"That's what I'm here for." She shot me a wink. "Why don't you leave this to me? Maybe you can find some other way to be useful."

As though on cue, a high-pitched giggle sounded behind me, and the pitter-pat of little feet came running across the hardwood.

I set the eggs down just in time to turn and catch Anya as she launched herself at my legs. Bending low, I scooped the wiggling toddler into my arms, tickling her middle in the process.

"Look, Sunny," I said with a straight face. "I found a wild animal in the house."

"No, I not," Anya protested, her bouncing knees catching my ribs.

"Did you hear that?" I wrangled her into the crook of my arm, pretending to examine her mouth and nose. "I think this wild animal can talk."

"No. No aminal," she exclaimed between giggles. "Anya."

"Well, hey there, Anya. I didn't recognize you." I gave her another round of tickles, throwing in a few exaggerated faces just to hear her laugh some more.

She kept squirming, kicking frantically and squealing at a pitch only dogs and other hellions could hear.

It was so fucking adorable I couldn't stop the uninhibited smile that tugged at my mouth. A surge of joy hit me, uninvited and unstoppable.

"Anya," Kira called. "Come on, little dove, let's get you cleaned up before breakfast."

Breathless, I placed the wriggling toddler back on the ground and tousled her soft brown curls. "Guess you better go do what she says, little animal."

Her nose scrunched, and, with one last giggle, she ran back the way she'd come.

When I turned, Sunny was watching me, her eyes glistening and a bittersweet smile on her lips.

"You're good with her," she said, her voice thick.

I looked away, the sudden ache in my chest threatening to hollow me out. "Gotta keep her busy somehow."

Dish towel in hand, I started wiping down the already clean counter. Anything to avoid thinking about what I'd lost. About what could've been. The future Emily had begged me for. The one I'd denied her.

The one Rykov had stolen.

"Why don't I cook?" I offered, steering the conversation away before it could spiral. "You can boss me around. Tell me everything I'm doing wrong."

"Boss you around?" She sniffed, the corners of her eyes still damp.

"Don't even pretend to be offended. We both know you love it."

She let out a soft laugh, brushing at her face with the back of her hand. "I do kind of like being in charge."

"Pretty sure it runs in the family."

Shoulder to shoulder, we fell into an easy rhythm, just like we had when we were younger. It was odd, but I had more memories of times like this with my almost ten years younger sister than I did with my twin. But Bodhi had always been the adventurer, trying to drag me along for the ride, and I'd always been content staying close to home.

Fuck, how times had changed.

As I followed Sunny's instructions, a sense of bitter melancholy crept in. *Comfort. Home. Family.* When had I lost sight of those things?

My phone buzzed in my back pocket, slicing through the moment. Unwelcome, but inevitable. Because as long as Rykov was alive, calm like this could only ever be temporary.

Sunny's head snapped up, our eyes locking. There

was tension in her gaze. Fearful anticipation. And it made my gut sink.

No matter how much I wanted to keep her away from my dark, twisted world, her reaction told me it was already too late. She might not have known the details, but she understood enough. More than was safe for her.

Fuck, I'd have to do something about that. Later.

"I'll be right back," I muttered before striding out to the porch.

The screen door banged shut behind me as I stepped into the early morning light, pulling my phone from my pocket.

One new text from Robin. The message I'd been waiting for.

My grip tightened around the phone, my jaw clenching as everything else fell away.

Rykov spotted in Manhattan.

Manhattan was good news. For now. It meant he wasn't breathing down our necks. Wasn't waiting in the shadows of the forest to strike at any minute. Still, it was a bold move for a wanted criminal. Too bold. Especially for someone with a list of enemies a mile long.

Did he want to be seen? Was this an intentional ploy to draw us out and lead us into a trap? Something designed to make us feel safe just long enough to fuck us over?

A faint creak sounded behind me. On instinct, my hand shot toward the gun I usually carried.

Only it wasn't there. It was locked up. Out of reach.

Goddammit. Why had I thought that was the safer choice?

"It's just me." Yelena's voice was quiet, cautious, like she feared I was close to snapping.

She wasn't wrong.

"What the hell are you doing out here alone?" The tightness in my body didn't ease, it just shifted. Still coiled. Still dangerous. But now threaded with something sharper. Something protective. Possessive.

And almost completely out of my control.

I moved toward her, the rising sun casting long shadows across the worn wooden boards of the porch.

She sat curled on the swing, legs tucked tight to her chest, arms wound around them, her face buried in her knees. Small. Fragile. Nothing like the strong, revenge-driven woman I'd spoken to last night. She looked more like the broken shell of a person I'd rescued weeks ago.

"Lena." I eased down onto the swing beside her, the wood groaning under my weight. "What's wrong?"

She shook her head, letting her legs slide back to the porch as she tilted her face to the pale morning sky. "Nothing. I'm fine." But the waver in her voice told me otherwise. "It was still early when I snuck out here. Even you didn't notice. No one did."

Against my better judgment, I trailed a finger over her jaw, urging her to look at me.

The second her tearstained face turned my way, I was done for. My thumb brushed over her delicate cheek, cutting a path through the wetness. The dark pools of her eyes pulled me in, holding me there as another tear slipped free.

I wanted to touch her. *Everywhere.*

Not just to wipe away her tears, but to taste the salt on her skin. To feel her pain, understand her torment, and soak in her sorrow.

To take it all from her and leave her in ecstasy.

She drew in a ragged breath—a quiet, fragile sound that tore through me. And fuck, I couldn't stand another minute of the torture. Pulling away before I did something I couldn't take back, I braced my arm over the back of the swing and forced my gaze to meet the sun.

"Did I upset you?" My voice was still too raw. Too rough. "Just now. Or last night?"

"No," she whispered.

"Then why are you out here crying?"

Silence stretched between us until she finally gestured toward the open cottage window. "I heard you in there."

Through the glass, I caught a glimpse of Sunny bustling around in the kitchen, unaware of the turmoil unraveling outside.

I frowned. "So it is me?"

She shook her head again, a heavy sigh escaping her lips. "Not you. It's Anya."

Anya. *Shit.*

"She's so easy with you. With everyone. Everyone but me."

"There's nothing easy about kids." The lump in my throat made the words hard, more hostile than I'd intended. I swallowed, forcing a softer tone. "I think she just needs time to get to know you."

She nodded, another tear coursing down her cheek. "I'm sure you're right. It's just…"

Before I could stop myself, my arm dropped from the back of the swing, pulling her against me.

The moment our bodies touched, she melted into me, relaxing in a way that made my blood run hot. I held her tighter—*too fucking tight*—savoring the way she fit against me, the way she exhaled into the curve of my neck like she belonged there.

"I was so desperate to see her. She was the only thing that kept me going for so long." Her voice cracked again, more tears spilling over. "But she doesn't even know I'm her mother."

She swiped at her face with shaking hands, as if fighting back the flood of emotion. "I've always wanted what's best for her. But with everything that's happened —with all those demons you keep talking about—I'm not sure I fit that description."

Her tear-filled gaze locked with mine, and fuck, I wanted so badly to kiss her. Needed it more than sanity. More than air.

Almost as much as I needed Rykov to die.

My hand cupped the back of her head, guiding her even closer. "How can you say that?" I leaned in, tempting my control. Tempting fucking fate.

She opened her mouth to argue, but I stopped her— not with my mouth like I wanted, but with a finger to her lips. Those perfect, pouty fucking lips that made my cock hard and my mind short-circuit.

"Things might be fucked up right now. You might feel like you're too broken to be fixed. But I promise you, Lena, you're not."

My finger slid from her chin to her throat, pausing over the frantic beat of her heart. "You'll find yourself again. And in the process, your daughter will find you too."

She snuggled into me, her head against my chest and her alluring scent wrapping around me. "What about Nik?"

The bastard's name twisted like a knife in my gut. "What about him?"

Her head lifted, her eyes cutting straight to mine. "We're still going to kill him, right?"

She didn't waver. Just stared at me, lips parted, breath shallow. Like the thought of it thrilled her.

My grip tightened around her, my fingers threading through her golden hair. Fuck, I was barely holding myself back.

The sharp edge of her need and the dark promise in her voice fed something primitive inside me.

"He's going to die." My words were rough, almost guttural. "Slowly."

A shudder ran through her, and it was the most beautiful thing I'd ever seen.

She wasn't afraid of the violence. Wasn't recoiling from the darkness in me. She was leaning into it.

Leaning into me.

Her body pressed tight against mine, her fingers tracing up my chest, nails dragging hard enough that I felt them through my shirt.

"Good," she murmured. "I need to see him buried. To know he's gone forever."

I wanted to say something, to tell her she didn't have to go down this road, that there was still time to turn back.

But I didn't. Because at that moment, I saw the truth.

She wasn't looking for a way out. Hell, she wasn't even keeping pace with me. She was leading the goddamn way, pulling us both deeper into darkness.

And I was ready to follow.

CHAPTER
ELEVEN
YELENA

I woke to the smell of freshly brewed coffee—rich, enticing, and laced with something sweet. Pancakes, maybe. With syrup.

It was the kind of smell that wrapped around my senses, whispering of comfort, innocence, childhood, and everything I'd lost.

For a moment, memories tried to pull me under. To suffocate me with thoughts of what could have been. What should have been.

But then Anya's laughter bubbled up from below. It was wild and free, bouncing off the walls and spilling into the room like sunlight.

It tugged at something tender in my chest, bringing a smile to my lips and happy tears to my eyes.

I dressed quickly, putting on a clean T-shirt and shorts, my usual necklace, and a wide, foolish grin. I didn't bother brushing out my hair or even looking in a mirror. The only thing that mattered was getting to Anya as fast as possible.

My feet carried me down the stairs with a kind of urgency I hadn't felt in years.

I had a mission now. More than just hiding. Greater than survival. Not only to protect my daughter from the nightmare that was her father, but to erase the threat of him completely.

To ensure he could never touch Anya or anyone I cared about ever again.

My eyes found her the moment I hit the bottom of the stairs. She sat in a battered old highchair, her legs swinging against the footrest, a pink spoon clenched in one hand while the other dripped syrup. Her mouth was full, her face alight with mischief and her whole body wiggling with joy.

She was the most beautiful thing on this earth.

"Your daughter's a menace." Kira grinned as I took a seat beside them. "An adorable menace, but still."

"She's a little devil," Bodhi added, a cocky, lopsided smirk breaking across his face like it had a mind of its own.

It was the kind of grin that had probably gotten him out of trouble many times, and I could see how it had worked on my sister. But even though they were twins, Bodhi's smile didn't carry the same heat that Finn's did. It didn't make my breath catch or my pulse skip.

No, Bodhi's smile only brought relief that he was healing from his injuries.

"She's just spirited. Like her mother," Sunny said,

flipping something on the griddle. "Isn't that right, Yelena?"

Oh. She meant me. The words landed like a soft weight in my chest, warm and unexpected.

"I guess so." I swallowed hard, blinking back fresh tears as I turned to Anya. "Do you take after me, angel?"

She only glanced at me. It was brief, maybe uncertain. Just a quiet, sticky-cheeked acknowledgment of my presence. Her curls were matted to her forehead, and her chin gleamed with sugar. Still, she was perfect.

And yet so far away.

Babka watched from her usual chair, a cup of coffee in hand, but her eyes were on me—quiet and knowing. The pride glowing in her gaze was like a blessing I hadn't known I was waiting for.

A smile quirked the corners of my mouth as I looked around the room at the strangers who'd become fast friends and the family I was finally reconnecting with. For once, I felt safe. Happy.

Even without Finn.

Kira scraped her chair back from the table and stood. "Do you want some coffee?"

Sunny turned. "She's—"

"I'm not allowed," I said, finishing the sentence before she could.

"Oh." Kira's gaze bounced between us.

"All stimulants are off limits as part of my recovery. Even caffeine," I explained without hesitation. There was no need to hide it anymore, and no shame attached to the truth.

Kira nodded. "Well, it sounds like you've got things under control."

I returned the brilliant smile Sunny shot my way, a glow of satisfaction and confidence lighting me up.

Because I did have it under control.

Not that I was delusional enough to believe there wouldn't still be moments of weakness. Moments of wondering if I could keep it under control. But for now, I was on top of my game. And that was enough.

Anya dropped her spoon with a clatter. It bounced on her tray before landing on the table, just out of her reach. Her brows drew together and, for a moment, I wasn't sure if she would laugh, cry, or give it a scolding.

"I've got it." Grabbing the spoon, I wiped it clean before holding it out to her.

She studied me, like she was taking my measure. Then, after coming to some silent decision, she slowly reached for it. Her fingers brushed mine—small, warm, and sticky.

She didn't react to the contact, just turned back to her food and resumed eating like nothing had happened. But something had.

She'd let me help.

It was small. Insignificant, maybe. But it was real. A million times more real than any of the self-doubt or insecurities Nik had beaten into my head.

And I wanted more.

I reached for a napkin to wipe her syrup-covered

hand, laughing softly as she yanked it away with a muttered *no* and smeared more syrup across her cheek instead.

"Savage," Kira said with admiration. "She's going to rule the world someday."

"I think maybe she already does." Bodhi laughed.

Amid the laughter, I caught the faint creak of the front door opening.

No one else took notice, but I felt it—a shift in the air. It was subtle, quiet, and like the calm before a storm. Or the silence before the next beat of my heart.

I turned, and he was there. Just as I'd expected.

Finn stood in the doorway, with his boots dusty, shoulders squared, and hair mussed like he'd run his fingers through it too many times. He was dressed in black, the sleeves of his T-shirt stretched tight across his biceps as he lingered at the edge of the room.

Calm. Collected. Dangerous as hell.

His eyes scanned the room once before landing on me. There were no words. Just a look. But that look was filled with something potent that stalled my breath and quickened my blood.

His eyes dragged over me, sending a ripple of heat surging through my veins. But when his gaze settled, it wasn't on my face. It was on my hand that hovered near Anya's curls, brushing back a strand of sticky hair with more courage than I knew I had in me.

I turned back to my daughter, but I could still feel him. He watched as I smoothed the hair from her face and tickled a finger over her cheek, drawing a small smile in return.

When I looked back at Finn, his expression had shifted. Now it was filled with softness. Longing, maybe? Something that made him seem a little lost and a lot sad.

Then I blinked, and it was gone.

With his gaze locked on mine, he gave the barest of nods and turned, vanishing back out the door as silently as he'd come.

No explanation. No real disruption. Just that familiar coil of tension winding tighter in my core.

It wasn't until later—after my daughter had eaten her fill and clambered down from her highchair with syrup still crusted in her hair—that I found my moment. Anya had nestled herself beside Babka with a tangle of plastic animals, chattering in her toddler language while Babka nodded along like she understood every single word. The others were busy clearing dishes and joking about how many pancakes it took to feed a two-year-old tornado.

No one noticed when I slipped out.

But my heart was already racing. I knew he'd be waiting for me. And I knew he wouldn't have bothered making an appearance the way he did unless something was on his mind.

Unless something was wrong.

The screen door creaked softly behind me as I stepped onto the porch. Mid-morning light spilled across the clearing, golden and deceptive. The air was thick with heat and humidity, birds called from deep within the forest, and the mountains in the distance shimmered under the sun's unrelenting glare.

And then I saw him. Finn stood just past the treeline, one hand braced against a trunk, his head bowed as though to steady himself, and his shirt pulled taut across the muscles of his back.

His body drew tighter with each step I took, like he could sense me before he saw me. A predator waiting to strike.

"What's going on?" The words slipped out before I reached him, sounding more anxious than I wanted. "Why didn't you join us for breakfast?"

He didn't answer, but his back and shoulders expanded on a heavy breath.

The air cooled as the shadows of the trees swallowed me, the harsh sunlight cut off by the dense canopy overhead. Pine needles and soft grass blanketed the forest floor, muffling the sound of my steps.

It was beautiful here, but there was something almost eerie about it. The wilderness seemed so vast. So untamed. Like a person could walk into it and disappear forever.

And it was right here, at our doorstep.

I held back a shiver, pushing aside the skittish feeling that was trying to overcome me, and moved up beside Finn, close enough to touch him.

Dear God, I wanted to touch him. To run my hands down the tight line of his back, trace the sharp edge of his jaw, and bury my face in the warmth of his neck.

But he still hadn't even acknowledged me.

My stomach swirled. "You gave me that look, then left. Do you want to tell me what it was about?"

Finally, he turned, his ocean blues pinning me with an unavoidable intensity. "I didn't want to ruin the moment."

"That's not an answer." My arms folded on instinct, bracing for whatever was coming. "If there's something I need to know, please just tell me."

"It's nothing urgent. Nothing that changes today." But the way he ran a hand over the back of his neck told a different story.

I kept quiet, waiting.

With a nod of understanding, he shifted toward me. "My contact, Robin, picked up some intel. She was able to confirm there's been movement."

"Movement? What does that mean?"

"Sasha Novikoff was spotted at the Red Hook docks. Overseeing a shipment."

A sense of dread settled over me, squeezing around my middle, crushing my lungs, and making my limbs feel weak.

"So Nik's still running business as usual." The words tasted bitter.

But why was I surprised?

"Looks that way. Robin says Sasha's running a crew for Rykov like nothing's changed. Like they aren't both wanted criminals, and we didn't wipe out half his men."

"What kind of shipment?"

Finn's gaze darted away, scanning through the trees

as though Sasha or Nik might materialize from the shadows at any moment. "Could be anything. Weapons. Girls. Drugs. Who the hell knows? The dockworkers were paid to look the other way."

I swallowed hard. "And we're sure it was Sasha?"

"Confirmed. No one approached him, but we got eyes on him. He was calm. Comfortable." A muscle ticked in his jaw. "And that tells me he's not worried. At all."

"Because Nik's still in control."

"Because he thinks we're done. That we're not a threat." His rough voice was edged with tension. "Or they're planning to make sure we're not."

We stood in silence for a moment, the woods seeming to press in on us from all sides.

"So what's our plan?"

Finn was steady and controlled as always, but underneath his calm exterior, something dangerous simmered. "For now, we wait. We gather as much intel as we can. If Sasha's taking the lead, maybe we just watch and see. Or maybe we get someone inside his circle. Someone who can tell us what's being moved and where it's going."

"And if it's women?"

"Then the objective changes." His expression turned to stone. "We don't just kill Rykov, we burn him and his entire operation to the fucking ground."

A wild idea sparked to life in the back of my mind, too dangerous to ignore, but too thrilling to resist. "Do you think I could get inside his circle?"

"I think you might be the only one who could."

My body quaked as I held his gaze. "Then use me."

"It's risky as hell. Sasha's not going to be easily fooled. The whole thing could backfire and then…"

"And then nothing. I can do this."

He shook his head like the idea was pure madness. Every rough breath, every clench of his fists carried a volatile energy that pressed against me, daring me to get closer.

"No," he said, shutting me down. "This is more than we talked about. I don't want you to feel like it's the only way. We can get to Rykov without this move."

"But finding another opportunity will take longer."

"Lena." He leaned in, towering over me in a way that should've felt threatening. But all it did was turn me on. "As much as I want the bastard dead, it's not worth sacrificing your safety to do it."

I swayed toward him, my hand landing on his chest as if it had a mind of its own.

A crease formed between his brows, and his heart thundered beneath my palm. "I don't want you to feel obligated to do anything you're not ready for."

"But I want to do it. I'm ready," I insisted. Because it was true.

At least it felt true in that moment—with Finn's strength holding me up and the seclusion of the forest as a shield.

"You're not." His expression didn't shift, but his voice held a note of regret. Maybe guilt. "But you will be."

His eyes moved over my face, lingering on my mouth before gliding down my neck. And sweet hell, he didn't need to touch me, his gaze alone set me on fire.

"Then it's a plan." My voice cracked, and I took a step away from him, letting my hand drop before I did something embarrassing.

Like kiss him.

"It's only the beginning of a plan." His firm grip caught my wrist before I could retreat any further. "We've got a lot of ground to cover before we make a move."

I nodded, but my body betrayed me. My pulse kicked hard, my hands were unsteady, and my breath caught somewhere between a gasp and a moan.

Was this fear or anticipation?

Or maybe it was just the way Finn looked at me, like he couldn't decide if he wanted to protect me or consume me.

The air between us sparked with something electric.

Fingers locked, he drew me in until I could feel the tension humming beneath his skin. Close enough to fall, if I let myself.

"I know this isn't what you wanted." His voice was low and edged with gravel. "Any of it. But you're stronger than he ever let you believe, and I need you to remember that. Not just when things get bad. Always."

I nodded, my eyes misting over.

"I see the way you look at Anya." His hand slid to the side of my neck, fingers grazing the underside of my jaw. "It's like you're trying to memorize her in case you lose her again."

I swallowed hard, the growing lump in my throat making a response impossible.

"You won't. Not this time. Not while I'm still breathing."

The promise struck deep. Maybe because he'd offered it so freely. So fiercely. Or maybe because of the way it tethered us together. An oath only broken by death.

I didn't know what to say. So I didn't say anything at all. I just leaned into him, my forehead brushing the line of his shoulder and his arms wrapping around me like they belonged there.

His steadiness surrounded me. And beneath it, something darker lurked.

Fury.

Even contained, it pulsed through him, bleeding into his every move—the way he stayed tight, controlled, and ready for a fight. It lived in the harsh edges of his voice. And it fueled his ruthless commitment to the only thing that mattered now.

Justice. Or maybe just vengeance.

Either way, it was ours.

Because whether it was right or wrong, whether it changed me for better or worse, I was going to help take down Nikolai Rykov.

And I was going to do it with Finn Decker at my side.

CHAPTER
TWELVE
FINN

As suffocating as the cottage had felt, coming to town was somehow worse.

Nestled against the mountains and surrounded by nature, the place had a quaint, picturesque charm. Designed for tourists, its main street leaned into the appeal, lined with shops catering to vacationing adventurers while still offering everyday necessities.

It was scenic. Almost too perfect. Idyllic in a way that felt manufactured.

And it was bustling. Much busier than I'd anticipated for a town this size, setting me on edge.

The buildings seemed to close in around us like a trap. The air was thick with an unidentifiable tension. And every person we passed looked like a potential threat.

What the hell had I been thinking?

Beside me, Yelena was a fucking goddess with her

golden hair tied back, wearing a simple white T-shirt tucked into her long, flowing red skirt. But she was just as anxious as I was.

Her posture was rigid, her movements stilted. Every shift she made pulled my focus, demanding my attention in a way that made it impossible to properly scan our surroundings. Impossible to stay sharp.

And that?

That was fucking dangerous.

But if we were going to follow through on our plan—if we were going to find Rykov and finish him for good—we couldn't stay cooped up forever. This first step out of hiding was only the beginning.

A test of our partnership. And my fucking control.

It was also a chance for her to get out in the world again. To be in a public setting after a year of captivity. To do something normal.

At least we could pretend it was our average Saturday.

The new ID and credit card Robin had sent were now safely tucked into my wallet, along with a few hundred dollars.

"Let's get the shit we need and get the hell out of here," I murmured in Yelena's ear as we walked into the pharmacy.

She gave a curt nod, moving toward the prescription window with her eyes stuck on the floor.

Goddammit, she'd never be safe if she wasn't watching her surroundings. Anyone could come up from behind and jam a gun to her ribs. She wouldn't even see it coming.

Frustration coiled in my gut. Without thinking, I grabbed her arm and yanked her back toward me. Not rough, but forceful enough to make my point.

Her breath caught. Her head snapped up. And fuck, those lips—parted, perfect, and begging to be kissed.

I forced my grip to loosen and my thoughts back on track. "Keep your head up and eyes open."

She swallowed and nodded again, but I caught the flicker of something else in her gaze. More than fear. More than understanding.

It was something that made my cock stir.

I let her go. If I didn't, I'd have a hard time stopping myself. And the sooner we were out of here, the better.

The place looked a bit odd for a pharmacy, its shelves crammed with an eclectic mix of goods. All part of its small-town charm, no doubt. Front and center stood a display packed with sunscreen, first aid kits, kids' bubble wands, and bug spray. Strange at first glance, but the more I thought about it, the more it made sense. Every item was something we could probably use.

The bubbles, especially. Anya would love them.

And shit, just thinking about making her happy put a smile on my face.

She was a wild little firecracker with more energy than seemed humanly possible, but she'd grown on me. Hell, I looked forward to our interactions. To the way her whole face lit up when she laughed. To the sound of her giggles echoing through me like they belonged there.

Who'd have guessed I could form a bond with Nikolai Rykov's kid?

My smile stretched wider at the thought. She liked me. Came to me without hesitation. But she didn't even know he existed. He was a stranger to her, but I was a trusted friend.

I grabbed a bigger bottle of the bubbles from the shelf and turned, looking for Yelena. Except she was nowhere in sight.

The air sucked from my lungs, my heart slamming hard, and a dull, pulsing pain spread through me.

Where the fuck was she?

Like a wild man, I stalked from one end of the store to the other, scanning every aisle. Each step grew sharper. Faster. Each empty row tightened something deep in my chest.

Immediately, my mind leapt to the places I usually kept locked away. The dark, disturbing corners I never allowed myself to linger in. Where all my worst memories prowled, clawing at the walls of my brain like the dead refusing to stay buried.

Violence came first. Always. The bright burst of muzzle flash. The loud crack of gunfire. The stench of something sterile, and beneath it, copper, mud, and death.

And then her.

Emily.

Skin too pale, lips tinged blue, and hair stiff with

blood. Lifeless, glassy eyes that somehow stared through me. *Blamed me. Condemned me.*

As the image flickered through my mind, it shifted and blurred. Until I was no longer haunted by Emily's cold face.

Now it was Yelena's features in front of me, beautiful but lifeless.

Same empty stare. Same crimson halo.

My insides twisted, and my lungs screamed for air, like the weight of her death was pressing down on me. This wasn't just a memory—it was a fucking warning. A glimpse of my greatest fear.

And the most likely outcome if I failed.

I rounded a corner too fast, blinded by the frantic need to find her. And ran straight into her.

She gasped, catching herself with splayed hands against my chest.

The bottle of bubbles hit the floor as I threw my arms around her, pulling her to me, burying my face in her hair, and breathing her in. *Lavender and citrus.* Grounding myself in the feel of her and the evidence she was still here. Still alive.

"Holy crap, Finn." Her hands ran circles over my shoulders. "Are you okay? What happened?"

I couldn't answer. My throat was too tight, still choked by senseless dread and memories I didn't want but couldn't fucking let go of. So I held her tighter, brushed my lips over her hair and across her forehead, and waited for my nerves to settle the fuck down.

"It's okay," she whispered. "I'm fine. You're fine."

She pulled back, searching my face and soothing my goddamn soul. "I got everything I came for. What about you?"

I bent, grabbing the bubbles that had rolled to a stop at her feet. "I found a treat for Anya."

When I straightened with the bubbles in hand, I was greeted by her devastating smile. Bright, gorgeous, and so fucking genuine.

Suddenly, I felt like a fool.

I'd had a breakdown in the middle of a store, all because I'd lost sight of her. Because even after warning her to stay alert, I'd let my own guard down. And for what? A cheap plastic wand in a bottle of liquid soap.

I pulled away, clearing my throat and smoothing my shirt.

"Should we check out?" She was still wearing that blinding smile, but it didn't hide the concern in her eyes.

I wasn't supposed to be the one falling apart. How could I be her protector if she was the one looking after me?

"Actually, I need a few more things. Walk with me?" I swallowed down my discomfort and offered her my arm.

With a nod, she looped her arm through mine, like she understood my need to keep her close.

Twenty minutes and almost two hundred dollars on my new credit card later, we were leaving the store. *Thank you, Damon Cullen.*

"Here," I said, reaching for her bag. "Give me this."

She handed it over without argument, but there was

a flicker of something unreadable in her expression, like she was complying just to keep the peace. To soothe me.

But that wasn't what this was.

I didn't need comfort. I needed purpose. Something solid in my hands. Something that made me useful again. This wasn't about power, and it sure as hell wasn't about control. It was about anchoring myself in the present. About standing on steady ground after the spiral.

"Listen." I hoisted the bags over my shoulder. "About what happened back there—"

She laced her fingers with mine, stopping me dead in my tracks. "You don't need to explain. Heck, if anyone understands what it's like to have a panic attack, it's me."

A panic attack. Is that what it was?

I'd never put a name to it. Never thought of it as anything other than my fucking failure to cope. But maybe she was right—the shit in my head was panic-inducing.

"Thanks." I brought her hand up to my mouth, brushing my lips over her knuckles.

Her skin heated with a pretty pink blush, and I was mesmerized. I wanted to trace the light pattern over her cheeks and follow it with my fingers. With my tongue. Down, down, down…

Pulling my gaze away from her, I tugged on her hand. "Come on, let's get back to the car."

She didn't move. My heart lurched as I turned back

to see the color had all drained from her beautiful face, replaced by a mask of fear.

"What's wrong?" I hissed, darting a glance around.

She inched toward me, and her eyes locked on something over my shoulder. "Two of Nik's men," she whispered, her body trembling. "They're on the other side of the street. And they look like they're searching for someone."

A slow, burning rage curled through me.

"Okay." I gripped the bags tighter. "We're just going to pretend they're not there. I want you to stay right next to me and keep your face hidden." I wrapped an arm around her, pulling her to my side. Shielding her. Protecting her.

From the corner of my eye, I watched the two men. They weren't browsing. They weren't killing time.

They were hunting.

And there was no doubt, it was Yelena they were looking to put in their crosshairs.

"Just keep walking," I murmured. "You're doing so good."

At my praise, she practically melted into me, and despite the danger, despite the chaos, my body took notice. But now was definitely not the fucking time.

Right now, we might only be one step away from death. Now it was time to survive.

A woman's high-pitched cry split the air.

I glanced over my shoulder to find that one of the two goons had pulled a gun. He'd spotted us and was shoving past people, eyes locked on Yelena.

I didn't wait. Didn't fucking think twice.

"Run!" I shoved her forward.

Not hard, just enough to get her moving, but it was still too much.

She stumbled, and my stomach dropped. For a split second, I was sure she'd hit the ground, but at the last minute, she steadied herself. Then, shaky as a newborn deer, she broke into a sprint.

I faltered, torn between taking on the men or staying by Yelena's side.

As much as I wanted to make those bastards regret all their life choices—especially the choice to come after her—this wouldn't end in a simple fistfight.

And leaving her unprotected? That wasn't an option.

Catching up with her, I grabbed her hand to keep us together and moved ahead, my body a battering ram.

Then my leg cramped. The muscles seized from hip to knee, and keeping pace became next to impossible. The limp I usually managed with ease now made me an obvious target. Like a wounded animal, I was easy to track. Easy to kill.

Fuck, why hadn't I listened to Robin and taken a goddamn rest?

"In here." I yanked Yelena through an open doorway, into an indoor flea market.

Slow down. Blend in. Disappear.

If we were smart, we might be able to hide in plain sight.

Breathing deep, I pushed past the pain in my leg,

trying to keep my gait even. I pulled Yelena past shops and vendors, searching for another exit.

The moment our pursuers breached the entrance, the shift in the air was palpable. A ripple of unease spread through the small crowd, a collective murmur rising like a warning bell.

I snatched a hat off a nearby rack, pulling the brim low to cover my face, and dropped our shopping bags in the middle of the aisle—a two-hundred-dollar distraction I hoped would buy us time.

At the next juncture, I cut a hard right. Then, again at the next one. And again, at the one after that. It was a sharp maze of turns leading us back the way we came.

Through the gaps between vendors, I caught glimpses of movement—shadows stalking us from the next aisle over. The urge to run clawed at me, and I felt it in Yelena too. Her body tensed, ready to bolt, and her grip on my hand was crushing.

But we couldn't afford to panic. So I kept our pace steady, even as the walls seemed to close in.

The moment we hit the sidewalk, I pulled her into a sprint, weaving through the afternoon foot traffic as fast as my bad leg allowed.

She pressed close, her small frame glued to my side like she knew our lives depended on it.

Because they fucking did.

The echo of pounding boots behind us confirmed Rykov's men were gaining. I didn't dare look back. Couldn't afford to. Every second mattered. Every step had to be forward.

"Left," I barked, steering her between two brick buildings off the main street and into the narrow alley behind them. A dumpster, some old crates, and a stack of folded patio chairs cluttered the path, but it was better than an open road.

She gasped as she stumbled over a crack in the pavement, but I caught her, hauling her upright and pushing her forward.

"Keep going." My voice was harsh. But fuck, there was no time to be gentle.

A gunshot rang out.

Grit and stone hit the back of my neck as the bullet cracked against the brick only inches behind my head.

"Fuck," I hissed. How the hell was I going to get us out of this?

Yelena flinched, but she didn't stop running. Her red skirt flowed behind her as her strappy sandals smacked against the pavement.

We burst out onto a quiet side street, far from the bustle of downtown. A few parked trucks. A gas station on the corner. And an old man rocking on a porch, watching us with a slow blink like he was just enjoying the show.

That's when I spotted it. An old, dark blue pickup sat at the side of the road, engine still running, and no one inside.

With one last burst of speed, I dragged Yelena toward it.

"Keep watch," I ordered, pressing her against the side of the truck.

"What—"

She didn't get to finish. I wrenched open the unlocked door—*thank fuck for small town trust*—and shoved her inside.

"Get down," I demanded, just in time for another shot to ring out. I ducked, and the bullet clipped the driver's side mirror with a sickening crack.

"Finn!"

Shards of broken mirror crunched underfoot as I dove into the driver's seat, slammed the door shut, and jerked the shifter into drive. Gravel spat from the tires as I tore down the road, leaving two pissed-off Russians in the dust.

"They shot at us." She braced an arm against the dashboard as she twisted to look behind us. "In public. They actually took a shot."

"They don't give a fuck about bystanders."

"I know. I just can't believe we got away." She sank back in her seat with a nervous laugh. "That was really close."

I should have been focused on the road. On putting as much distance as possible between us and the men who wanted us dead. On getting us the hell out of town before their backup arrived.

But I could still hear her crying my name, the sound burrowed deep in my skull. Still feel the press of her body against mine as we ran, her heat searing into me, her pulse pounding against my grip like she belonged there.

Even now, she was still breathing hard, her body

coiled tight and hands gripping her seat. She was scared. But she was alive.

And it wasn't just fear that sparked in her eyes—it was exhilaration. The sharp, dynamic kind that came from standing on the edge of something precarious. One step from the abyss.

And just like me, she reveled in it.

CHAPTER
THIRTEEN
YELENA

FINN'S GAZE burned through me. Wild and chaotic. An inferno that should have terrified me, but instead, made me euphoric.

Higher than I'd ever been on the drugs.

And when you climb that high, the only way down is fast and hard. One wrong move, and I could lose everything I'd fought for. Every bit of progress. Every ounce of control.

I could slip right back into the addiction I swore I'd escaped.

Yet somehow, I knew if I fell apart, even if I shattered, he'd be right there to rebuild me. It wasn't just a feeling or a fleeting hope, it was instinct. A deep, unwavering certainty.

As dangerous as Finn might be, he was nothing like Nik.

Clearing his throat, he tore his gaze from mine as he

pulled his phone from his pocket. With a few taps, the line started ringing.

"What's wrong?" Bodhi answered through the speaker.

"We've been made." Finn's voice was steady and sharp. "Two of Rykov's men were in town. They took a couple shots at us."

"Fucking hell," Bodhi swore.

"What's wrong? What's happening?" Kira's voice cut in from the background.

"You need to leave. Now." Finn's tone left no room for argument, even over the commotion happening on the other end of the line. "I'll alert Robin, but don't wait. Just go."

"We're on it," Kira confirmed.

"Good. I'll check in once we're settled."

"Be safe, brother," Bodhi called before disconnecting.

Finn lowered the phone, tension still etched across his face, his thumb hovering like he was about to make another call.

"What did you mean, once we're settled?" My breath was still too fast, and now my chest felt way too tight. "Won't we meet up with them?"

Instead of answering, his mouth pressed into a thin line, stubborn and unreadable.

"Finn? Tell me."

"No." His ocean-blue gaze flicked to mine, then away again.

Silence stretched, thick and suffocating. I waited for

a deeper explanation—*something, anything*—to ease the tight grip of dread closing around my heart.

"Pull over." My voice wavered, my throat clogging with unshed tears.

But he said nothing and kept driving.

"Please," I begged, sounding weak and helpless.

His gaze shot to the rearview mirror, scanning the road behind us. Without warning, he tossed his phone onto the console, yanked the wheel, and slammed on the brakes.

The truck jerked to a violent stop, throwing me forward into the dash. Pain shot through my palms as I braced against the dashboard, my breath hitching.

"What the hell, Finn?" My voice shook, but it wasn't just from the sudden stop. It was the sick feeling coiling in my stomach, the one that started building the second he said *no*.

He didn't look at me right away. His hands gripped the wheel like a vise, knuckles white and chest rising and falling with deep, measured breaths.

"Why aren't we going to them?" My voice pitched higher, cracking with panic. "Why are we separating?"

He still said nothing.

"Finn," I choked, the tears I'd been holding back spilling free. "Kira has Anya. My daughter." Terror wrapped around my ribs, and I hung on the edge, ready to fall. To snap. "I need to get to her. I can't leave her again. I need to know she's okay."

"She's safer without us." His words hit harder than Nik's fists ever had.

When he finally turned, his expression was cold. Unyielding. And it ripped the ground out from under me.

"You don't know that. You don't—"

"Yes, I do." There might've been a flicker of guilt in his eyes, but his tone was all steely resolve.

My stomach twisted violently. "No. No, you don't get to make that choice for me."

"Yelena…" He dragged a hand through his hair, his jaw locking tight.

"Take me to her." My nails bit into my palms. "I swear to God, Finn, if you don't turn this truck around—"

He shot forward, shocking me as the space between us vanished in a blink.

"Think, Lena," he murmured. "Rykov's men weren't there by accident. They were waiting. And if we go back to the cottage, we lead them straight to Kira, straight to Anya. What happens then?"

I swallowed hard, trying to push past the fear. To put sense and reason ahead of the panic that was threatening to undo me completely.

"They weren't just waiting," I whispered, the words tumbling out like a revelation. And maybe that's exactly what it was, because with a single breath, the truth cut clear and sharp. "They were looking for us."

His silence was all the confirmation I needed. It hadn't been my imagination. They were searching as if they'd known exactly where to find us.

A cold certainty seeped into my bones, stripping away my denial, my hope.

He was right. We couldn't go back to our families. Not yet. Not with a target on our backs. But that didn't make it hurt any less.

When Finn finally spoke again, his voice had softened, but only a bit. "I promised I'd keep you safe."

I lifted my chin, my body still trembling from the weight of it all. "No. You promised to keep us both safe. Me and Anya."

His intense gaze locked with mine before he gave a single nod. "And that's exactly what I plan to do."

Without another word, he shifted the truck into gear and pulled onto the road. There was no turning back now. He was right.

Despite the anguish, fear, and crushing despair, the harsh truth was undeniable. Right now, the biggest threat to Anya's safety was me.

"I need to get a hold of Robin." His voice was clipped, his features tight. "You should try to get some rest."

I turned toward the window with a lump in my throat and fresh tears flowing.

I had no intention of falling asleep, but the adrenaline crash was immediate, and combined with the lull of the open road, it pulled me under against my will. The next thing I knew, Finn was rousing me.

"Lena." The rumble of his deep voice and his hand on my shoulder woke me. "We're here."

I straightened in my seat, wiping away the tears that

had dried on my cheeks, and peered out the window at the darkened city streets.

The buildings loomed taller than I remembered, shadows pooling darker between them. The streets swarmed with people, a chaotic, restless energy buzzing through the air. Lights glared harsh and blinding.

But God, I'd missed it.

This was home. The city where I grew up, and the place where I'd planned to raise my own daughter. The only place in the world where I felt at peace. Even through the noise and hustle, Manhattan set my soul at ease.

"Did your contact find us a place to stay?" I asked, my voice thick with sleep.

"No need. We've got safehouses throughout the city. But she double-checked security and had some supplies delivered."

There was something in the way he said it—calm and certain. Like Robin was already ten steps ahead, and he trusted her to stay there. I could hear the respect in his voice. The unspoken understanding between them. The quiet confidence that came from counting on someone who never let him down.

A knot pulled tight in my stomach. Robin had her shit together. And me? I was barely keeping my head above water.

"Will I get to meet her?" I swallowed back the jealousy, trying to push its way to the forefront. "She sounds like a good friend."

Finn turned to look at me, his brows raised. "Robin?

She's a great friend. The best I could ask for. But we don't exactly hang out."

"What about us?" The question slipped out before I could stop it.

Maybe it was the leftover adrenaline. Maybe the city. Or maybe I was just tired of holding everything in. Whatever the reason, I didn't take it back.

"Us?" he echoed, his eyes back on the road.

"Yes. You and me. Are we friends yet?"

The shift was immediate. His shoulders went stiff, his breath hitched, and his hands that had been casually resting at ten and two were now strangling the wheel.

"No. And we're never going to be." His voice was flat. Final.

An ache bloomed in the center of my chest, but I reached up and smoothed a hand over my hair like it didn't matter. Like my insides weren't crumbling.

"Yeah. No worries." I forced a quick smile. "I don't want to be your friend anyway."

It was a lie, probably an obvious one, but it gave me something to hide behind. It created a layer of distance I suddenly needed.

He didn't want to be my friend. Fine. But he wasn't just a bodyguard, and he wasn't only a partner in a crime we hadn't committed yet. So what the hell did that make us?

I had no idea where we stood. Where he stood. And that uncertainty—twisted up with the sinking sense that he was hiding something—was dangerous as hell.

We made the rest of the drive in stony silence, his

movements rough and his cold shoulder downright frigid. By the time we made it inside the new safehouse, I was shivering.

Shit. The tremors had started, my pulse was irregular, and my skin crawled. I clenched my hands, willing them to stay steady. It didn't work. My body knew how close I was to slipping back under before I did. How badly I still wanted the escape.

One more bottle. One more pill. That's all it would take.

"I'll take the couch." Finn tossed the keys onto the counter. "You can have the bed."

I didn't even bother looking around. At this point, it didn't matter if we were in a palace or a hole in the wall, as long as I didn't have to spend another second near him.

I turned on my heel and stormed toward the single bedroom. Before I made it there, his hand clamped around my arm, stopping me cold.

His grip was rougher than ever, his dominance unmistakable. God help me, it shouldn't have turned me on to be handled this way.

But it did. Instantly.

Heat surged through me, intense and overwhelming. I shuddered, my breath catching, pulse kicking, and my skin burning under his touch. The full-body tremor that followed wasn't a craving for the drugs. And it wasn't fear.

It was need—deep, pulsing, and undeniable.

A need for him.

"Lena." His voice was a seductive rumble. "I know you didn't mean it."

I swallowed hard, refusing to face him. "Didn't mean what?"

"That you don't want to be friends. I know you do."

"Honestly, Finn, I don't." My voice betrayed me, filled with frustration and the pent-up desire I could barely contain.

And then I was spinning.

He maneuvered me like I was weightless, whirling me to face him and pinning my arm behind my back in one swift move.

A thrill shot through me. And suddenly, I was drowning in him. In his heat, in his scent, his power, and in the way his body caged mine as if he were the only thing keeping me upright.

"Don't lie," he growled. "You can be pissed at me. You can be scared. You can feel whatever the fuck you want. But don't pretend you don't want something more from me. You've been clinging to me since the day I took you out of Rykov's house."

"Well, I wasn't angry before." I lifted my chin, channeling all my irritation into the glare I gave him. "But now? Yeah. Now, I am."

"Good. Get angry for a change. Stand up for yourself. Prove you're not just a victim looking for a goddamn savior."

"You think that's what I want from you? That I'm so

weak and desperate I can't stand on my own?" The words tumbled out, fueled by a courage I didn't recognize. A fire I'd never dared to stoke before.

"No, Lena," he growled. "I think you're a thousand times stronger than you know. And I think if you knew me at all, you'd understand why friendship isn't something I can give you."

"But you're friends with Robin."

"I don't want to fuck Robin." His voice was rough, like the words had clawed their way up his throat.

And they stunned me. My mouth opened, but nothing came out. Was I even still breathing?

He twisted my arm higher up my back, the dull pinch of it reminding me that I was at his mercy. "I can't be your friend. Because every time you get close, it gets harder to hold back. Harder to pretend I'm not about to lose my fucking mind."

His hold loosened, just slightly, like he was about to let me go. But before I could process it, his fingers flexed, and in a swift, merciless motion, he'd wrenched my other arm behind my back, pinning both wrists in one unyielding hand.

"You need something safe. Someone stable. But that's not the kind of man I am. This"—his free hand slid up to wrap around my throat, his fingers pressing into the side of my neck—"is who I am. Not safe. And I'm definitely not fucking stable."

God. Despite the fear, despite the voice in my head screaming to run, heat flooded me, slick and shameless.

He bent closer, his mouth hovering at my ear and his breath rough against my skin. "Because what I want is to tie you up and then take you apart…slowly. Thoroughly. Until you forget every man who ever came before me."

A groan ripped from him, raw enough to scrape my nerves. "I want to ruin you for anyone who isn't me. Then I want to build you back up from the wreckage. Stronger. Fiercer. Like the queen I already see when I look at you."

His fingers tightened around my throat, and my pulse slammed against them. "And then do it again. And again. And a-fucking-gain."

Sweet hell.

A new jolt of heat coursed through me. My body went pliant as I pressed myself to him, my breasts crushing against his chest.

"Fuck." He pulled me even closer, his hand digging into my spine, and I whimpered.

Whatever piece of me he wanted, he could have it. Right here, right now. And any other time he liked.

His head dipped, his lips hovering just over mine, so close I could taste the tension radiating off him. But instead of kissing me, he shifted. His breath ghosted over my skin as he buried his face in the curve of my neck, inhaling deeply. Like he could survive off the scent of me alone.

Another low, guttural groan scraped from somewhere deep in his chest, pained and primal. But he didn't move. Didn't speak. His face stayed pressed against my neck, his breath ragged and his grip on my wrists iron tight.

He breathed me in like he was trying to burn the moment into his memory.

I didn't want memories—I'd had enough of those. Of days spent dreaming and wishing. What I wanted was something solid, grounding me to the here and now. Something beautiful, reckless, and…real.

I wanted him. And I was done acting like I didn't.

Turning my face toward his, I brushed my lips along the shell of his ear. "Finn?" His name was a desperate plea steeped in need and drowning in uncertainty.

He raised his head, his breath skimming my jaw and his deep, stormy ocean gaze meeting mine.

Then I kissed him.

It was soft. Careful. My lips brushed his like a test, my heart thundering and my body strung so tight I thought I might snap.

But he didn't react. He was motionless, an agonizing wall of unyielding restraint.

He was going to leave me unanswered, wasn't he? Untouched, unfulfilled, rejected, and alone.

Again.

Then his control shattered.

Like lightning, he moved. The hand at my throat slid to the back of my head, and his mouth crashed down on mine—hard and hungry, like a man possessed. His tongue swept deep, tasting me as if he had every right, his teeth grazing my bottom lip before catching it.

A gasp tore from me, and he swallowed the sound. Devoured it like it belonged to him.

Like I belonged to him.

His hand clamped tighter around my wrists, holding me captive against him, helpless to anything but the fire racing through my veins. His other hand fisted in my hair, dragging my head back, leaving me no choice but to take everything he gave.

I moaned into his mouth, my body bowing against his, greedy for more.

God, it was like I'd been made to fit him. Like every bit of my being had been waiting for this. For him.

My lips felt bruised and swollen. And I still wanted more.

Was it too much? Too hard? Too fast?

I didn't care.

I needed him. Every dark, dangerous, all-consuming piece.

But suddenly, he was gone.

His mouth tore from mine with a growl of frustration, his hands dropping away like I'd burned him. As though touching me was a sin he hadn't meant to commit.

"I can't," he mumbled, as though talking to himself. "I just fucking can't."

My limbs trembled—nerves shot—but I moved toward him anyway. "Can't what?"

Instead of answering, he paced away, body rigid, movements jerky, the hitch in his stride more pronounced than I'd ever seen. His hand raked through his thick hair, tugging at the ends like he was trying to pull himself back together.

"Finn." I stepped directly into his path, forcing him to stop. "Finn, will you please talk to me? What do you mean you can't? What was so wrong with that?"

He shook his head, turning his back on me.

Frustration clawed at my throat. "Fine. Forget it."

The words were petulant, but I didn't care. I was unraveling. Caught in the whiplash between want and rejection. Scorched by heat one second and gutted by silence the next.

This thing between us wasn't in my head. He wanted me. I'd felt it in every touch, every look. And God help me, I wanted him more than I'd ever let myself want another man.

But he was still holding back, and for the life of me, I couldn't understand why.

"It was a mistake. That's all." His voice was steel.

I blinked, the heat rushing out of me, replaced by a cold pit of emptiness and yearning. "A mistake?"

His gaze met mine, flat and unyielding. No remorse. No softness.

Only conviction.

"Yes. A mistake," he repeated, his features hard. "And it won't happen again."

With my throat and eyes burning, I stared at him, trying and failing to fight the sharp, hollow ache inside me. "So we're not friends, and we're not going to be lovers. That makes me what? A means to an end? A convenient way to kill a man?"

His mouth pinched, his silence stinging more than anything he'd said.

"You're right." I turned away, pushing past the need still clawing at my insides. "This will absolutely never happen again."

CHAPTER
FOURTEEN
FINN

Yelena locked herself in the bathroom, and the moment the door clicked, something dark and ugly settled in my chest.

Not regret over the kiss. No, that had been inevitable. The disastrous pull between us was like gravity or fucking fate. An unavoidable collision of secrets, danger, and want.

It was everything after it that wrecked me. The look on her face when I pulled away. How her body stilled. The way her expression fell, like I'd just taken the last sliver of hope she had left.

I told her it was a mistake. Forced myself to sound hard. Detached. Like it hadn't meant anything. When the truth was, it meant everything.

She meant everything.

But I'd let too much slip. Dropped the mask. Showed her the part of myself I'd kept buried—untouched, untested, and not nearly as dormant as I pretended it was. The part that should terrify her as much as it did me.

That side of me wanted more than she had left to give. More than I had any right to take.

And now she thought I didn't want her at all, that she'd been used and discarded, when all I'd ever tried to do was protect her—from Rykov, from the world, and most of all, from me.

The rush of the shower cut through the silence, dragging me back to the present. But the weight in my chest didn't budge, and my body refused to let go of the hunger.

She was in there, her bare skin slick and glistening under the spray. Water running over every curve and divot, tracing the paths my fingers itched to follow. Warm and pliant. Wet and, if the throaty little moan that had escaped her was any indication, more than willing.

And fuck me, my cock throbbed just thinking about it.

It had been too long. Too long since I'd touched a woman. Since I'd buried myself in slick heat and lost myself in the kind of pleasure that numbed everything else.

But I'd made a promise.

One I was hellbent on keeping, no matter how badly my body begged me to break it. No matter how much I wanted to push her, to see just how long and far I could drag out her pleasure before it snapped.

As much as she might've wanted me, she couldn't handle me. Not with the things I craved.

Not after the hell she'd been through.

Fuck, even if somewhere deep down she carried the same dark hunger, it wouldn't matter. The secrets I was keeping were enough to turn her away. To destroy whatever trust I'd earned.

To lose her completely.

There was no future for us. Not beyond Nikolai Rykov's death. And there was no way in hell I'd risk starting something with her when I already knew how it would end. Because if I had her, I'd want to keep her. Forever.

At any price.

My phone pinged, dragging me back from the brink of insanity. I fished it out of my pocket, my thumb swiping across the screen as I diverted my attention to it.

Another sighting. This time, he wasn't alone.

Robin's text was followed by a blurry photo of Rykov, standing on a crowded street with Sasha Novikoff at his side and two more of his men in the background.

My stomach twisted. What the fuck was this? Another power move? A show of force? Or something more sinister than I could comprehend?

Everything looked normal. As if they hadn't missed a step.

The only difference was Rykov himself. Up to this point, the man had rarely been seen in public. He'd been a ghost since taking over the Bratva, locked away with Yelena, pulling strings from the dark.

But now he was out in the open. Bold. Careless, maybe? And close.

Too fucking close.

My grip tightened around the phone as I fired off a message.

How long ago?

I stared at it, waiting for Robin's reply, seconds dragging into hours as three little dots pulsed on the screen. Until finally her text came through.

Less than an hour ago. The source couldn't give anything more specific.

I swore under my breath. He'd been only a few blocks away, and I'd missed him. Again.

The bathroom door opened. A rush of steam curled into the air, and a wet-haired, fresh-faced goddess walked out in nothing but an oversized T-shirt.

Fuck, it was my shirt. Where had she found it? And why the hell did something so innocent make me so goddamn feral?

Droplets of water still clung to her skin, her cheeks flushed, and eyes dark. And despite whatever damage I'd done, there was still a fire in her. It smoldered low, but it was there—an ember ready to spark into an inferno.

Fucking stunning.

I should've broken the tension. Should've looked away or said something cold to put distance between us. But I just stood there, gawking at her, drowning in the sight of her like a fucking idiot.

"What's wrong?" Her eyes locked with mine.

"Nothing." It was my biggest lie yet. And from the look on her face, she knew it.

She moved closer, every step carrying a quiet determination I couldn't ignore. She was a walking contradiction. Fragile yet unbreakable. Soft but also razor-edged.

And fuck, I wanted her. No matter how hard I pushed against it. No matter how much guilt, shame, and fucking bitterness it brought me. I wanted Yelena Markova.

Lovely little Lena.

"Have you heard from them?" she asked. "Are they safe?"

"Yes." The lie was smooth, instinctual. I hadn't heard from Bodhi and Kira in hours, but the last time I had, they'd been okay. And that had to be enough. For both of us.

"They're safer without us," I repeated, hoping she believed it. Hoping I did, too.

Nodding, she made her way over to me, each step an unintentional seduction. Everything about her caught not only my eye, but my lurid imagination. From the wet fan of her lashes to the pink glow of her cheeks. Hell, even the wet trail of hair over her shoulders gave me wicked ideas.

"What do you think?" she asked, biting her bottom lip.

Fuck, she really didn't want to know what was running through my head. "About what?"

"How did they find us?"

Shit. Here I was, my mind in the gutter, while she was actively trying to solve the problem. "Good fucking question."

"The car?" she pressed. "The one we brought to the cottage. It was stolen, right?"

"Nah. It was too old for GPS, and I swapped the plates. Besides, we'd been in town for what—forty minutes? It's impossible to make the drive from the city that fast. I'm positive they were already in the area."

Her expression shifted. "Could they have tracked me?"

My pulse ticked up. "What do you mean?"

"I don't know. I just…"

She lifted a hand, brushing her fingers over the gold pendant that hung around her neck.

"This." Her voice was barely above a whisper. "It's the only gift he ever gave me. The only time he was ever nice without an agenda." She swallowed hard, her eyes downcast. "He told me to always wear it."

My stomach fucking dropped. "And you have."

Her hands trembled as she fumbled with the clasp at the back of her neck. The thin chain slipped free, the small circular pendant dropping into her palm. She stared at it, unmoving, her breath shallow.

Then, without warning, she flipped her hand and dumped it onto the table, where it landed with a hollow clink.

I picked it up, turning it over, searching for…hell, I didn't even know what.

"I don't know why I did." She ran her fingers over

her throat, as if feeling the absence of the chain. "I mean, I know why I obeyed him while I was with him. But now?" Her head shook. "It became automatic. I'd take it off to sleep, to shower, and the second I was done, I'd put it right back on. Like he still had a hold on me."

My jaw clenched. She'd talked about him before, and it was enough to make me want Rykov dead a dozen different ways. But this? This was worse. This was him still crawling around in her head. Still controlling her, giving her orders.

And she hadn't even realized she was following his command.

Forget a bullet to the head. I was going to tear him apart with my bare fucking hands.

I kept my mouth shut. If I opened it, the rage clawing at my chest would spill out and scorch everything. So, I let her talk. Tried not to buckle under the weight of all the details I didn't know but could vividly fucking imagine.

"What do you think?" she asked again.

Without warning, I dropped the necklace, grabbed the heavy stainless steel pepper grinder, and brought the corner of it down hard, cracking the pendant into the table.

Startled, Yelena's hands flew up to cover her mouth as she stumbled back a step. Her whole body went rigid, frozen in fear.

"Yelena." Lowering my voice, I lifted my hands,

palms open and steady. "You're okay. Everything's okay."

But she wasn't.

Her entire frame was shaking, and I knew—*just fucking knew*—I'd inadvertently triggered something deep. Something ugly. Something that had nothing to do with me and everything to do with the hell she'd already survived.

Her pupils were blown wide, her chest rising and falling too fast, too shallow. Her arms curled tight around herself, like she could fold inward and disappear.

"You're not there anymore." I kept my voice soft and my hands where she could see them. "You're here, with me. Not him. It's just you and me."

She still didn't answer. Fuck, had she even blinked? I wanted to wrap her in my arms, lavish her with care and attention, and take away all her fucking pain.

If only it were that easy.

"Lena," I murmured. "Are you with me?"

That did it. The air rushed out of her in an unsteady breath. Her arms loosened, and her fingers twitched like she wasn't sure what to do with them.

She looked at me then, fight sparking in her eyes. She was dragging herself back, climbing out of whatever pit she'd just fallen into.

"Y-yes. I'm with you. I-I'm okay."

She wasn't. Not really. But she wanted to be, and that was a good start.

I nodded too, offering her a steady smile. "Yeah, you are."

Her gaze flicked to the broken necklace on the table. "Is it…?"

With a heavy exhale, I lifted the pepper shaker, surveying the damage. Not only had I cracked the pendant's outer shell, but I'd crushed part of the chain, breaking it into crumbled pieces.

"Well, I think it's safe to say this isn't pure gold."

I pried at the edge of the pendant, but it was too small for my fingers to get a proper grip. Instead, I pressed around the edges, the metal giving way with a sharp snap. The top half popped off, clattering onto the table, leaving me holding what looked like a miniature circuit board.

"But that?" I turned the exposed device between my fingers, my stomach knotting. "That's a real tracker. And not the cheap kind you buy online."

"Oh my God." She stared, her face pale and jaw slack. "He's been tracking me this entire time."

"Yeah." *Fuck. He's been tracking her the entire fucking time.*

I opened my phone again, studying the photo Robin had sent. Rykov. Sasha Novikoff. Two others. Close. Too fucking close.

It had felt random at first. Like we'd just been unlucky. But now?

Now I had proof of why I should never trust coincidence.

My fingers moved fast as I typed.

Check the area for anything else. They tracked us here. See if there's been movement near any of the other safehouses.

Robin's response was almost instant.

Already on it.

I looked up, catching Yelena's concerned stare. "Grab whatever you can. We need to go. Right fucking now."

Without question or hesitation, she disappeared back into the bathroom.

I moved through the apartment, grabbing only the essentials—cash, weapons, the fake IDs I'd stashed under the floorboard—and left the useless Damon Cullen ID behind.

A few minutes later, Yelena emerged. She was dressed in her own clothes, damp hair pulled back, her face set in stone, and a small fabric bag stuffed with whatever she'd managed to scrounge together clutched in her hand.

With her moment of panic behind us, I led her down the back staircase, avoiding the main exit. The alley was quiet—too quiet for the city that never sleeps—and I didn't trust it.

We had to move.

Slipping through the shadows, we stalked past flickering streetlights, parked cars, and locked doors, on alert and moving fast. But not too fast. Nothing that might catch the eye of anyone watching.

My phone buzzed with another text from Robin just as we rounded the corner.

You were right. There's movement in the area, and around two of the other safehouses. Nothing obvious, but it's them. Be careful.

I already knew it. Had seen the tracker with my own eyes. Held the damn thing in my fucking hand. But seeing it spelled out so plainly turned my stomach all over again.

Rykov wasn't just nearby. Nothing about the sightings had been bad luck or coincidence.

He was coming for us. Corralling us like prey for easy pickings. Biding his time, letting us get comfortable before he made his move.

I reached for Yelena's hand, guiding her into a narrower alley that cut off from the main street.

She followed without question, her steps light but quick, and her breathing tight. She moved like she wasn't afraid, but I could feel her shaking. The thin, sharp edge of panic was humming just beneath her skin, waiting to take hold.

"We need to keep moving," I said, my voice low. "Get somewhere safe and out of sight."

She scanned the darkness around us. "Where do we go?"

I didn't answer right away. The truth was, I didn't fucking know. The safehouses were compromised. Every move we made felt like we were just a single faltering step ahead of an enemy we couldn't outrun.

But we weren't dead yet.

I gripped her hand tighter. "Somewhere they don't know about."

She looked at me then, her eyes locking on mine like she needed something solid to hold on to. "And after that?"

I didn't look away. "We flip the fucking tables. We find Rykov before he finds us and put an end to him just like we planned."

Something shifted in her—sudden, electric—and it made my blood run hot. The fear that was strung around her seemed to loosen. The fire I'd seen in her earlier flickered back to life, breathing hope and determination back into her eyes.

And fuck, it was beautiful.

Even if she was still scared. Even though we had a long way to go. Her resolve to see Nikolai Rykov suffer would help her survive what came next.

And that same fire grounded me, cutting through the noise in my head and forcing me to focus.

This wasn't just my war anymore.

It was ours.

And for the first time, it felt like there was a chance we could actually fucking win.

CHAPTER
FIFTEEN
YELENA

I WAS SHAKING AGAIN. Only this time, it wasn't the drugs. It was raw, unfiltered terror.

Nik had come for me.

Dear God, he could be tailing us even now. Lurking in the shadows. Waiting for the right moment to strike.

My pulse hammered against my ribs and every muscle locked tight, bracing for the inevitable. Every flash of headlights, every unexpected sound set my nerves further on edge.

Were we running into a trap? When would it snap shut around us?

Finn must've noticed the horror on my face. Without a word, his fingers closed around mine and drew me closer, stopping just shy of full contact.

It grounded me. Reassured me that despite the tension between us, despite the reckless, devastating kiss I'd forced into existence, he still had my back.

When he repeated his promise that we'd put an end

to Nik, something inside me cracked open. Hope bloomed, and fear gave way to something darker and more demanding.

A need to watch my tormentor bleed.

Now Finn's calm gaze locked on mine. "Fear is our friend. The adrenaline? That's what keeps us alive. Keeps us moving. Okay?"

I swallowed hard, my throat too tight to answer.

"You still with me?" he urged, his voice low and sure.

"Yes." The word felt weak, but I meant it.

I had to mean it. There was no way in hell I'd let Nik take me again. I might've gone willingly before, but not this time.

Never again.

We kept moving. The streets pulsed with an eerie, restless energy, and I couldn't shake the feeling that somewhere out there, Nik was watching. Waiting.

"Do you have a plan?" I asked, needing to keep my mind on something useful. Something that wouldn't send me back into a panic.

Finn's grip on my hand tightened before he glanced at me. "One thing you should know about me—I always have a plan. Usually more than one." He smirked.

It was just a tiny lift of his lips, but it was there, disarming and impossible to look away from.

Sweet hell. Conviction looked good on him— dangerous but steady.

And right now I needed steady.

I cleared my throat, digging deep for my own confidence. "Okay. So what is it?"

Instead of answering, he pulled me closer, dragging his thumb across my skin. The move was calming yet intimate. And it made my heart stutter.

"Do you still trust me?"

My body hummed. "With my life."

For a moment, he didn't speak. He watched me, his gaze bouncing between my face and our surroundings.

"Good." He nodded, as if he'd made a decision. "Now follow me. Don't stop. Don't ask questions. Just keep moving."

He led us toward the subway entrance, slipping down the worn concrete stairs and past the turnstile, just as a train roared into the station.

His hand pressed to the small of my back as we boarded. The car was nearly empty. Only a few people slumped in their seats, eyes glued to glowing screens and faces dulled by exhaustion or apathy.

The doors slid shut and the train lurched forward, the wheels squealing against the tracks. Normally, the sound would've bothered me, but not this time.

No. This time, I welcomed it.

Because every second, every mile, the noisy subway car carried us further away from Nik.

I drew in a slow, fortifying breath before releasing it, along with the anxiety. We were okay.

For now.

About thirty minutes later, we stepped off the train in Brooklyn. Finn was still moving forward with purpose, charging ahead without looking back. But as we hit the sidewalk, I noticed the falter in his step was more pronounced than before.

Not just his usual limp. His stride was tighter. Heavier. He wasn't injured, but something was definitely off. And whatever it was, he wasn't sharing.

Finn was keeping secrets.

He'd given me plenty of reasons not to trust him. He knew things about me he shouldn't, let it slip, and then lied to cover it up. Not to mention the kiss—the way he'd fallen into it like he was drowning, only to push me away and call it a mistake.

I wanted to believe he'd keep me safe, that I could trust him to get us through this. But standing in the dim glow of the streetlights, in a city that suddenly felt too big and too exposed, something shifted.

Doubt stirred in my chest. It was quiet but persistent. And I couldn't shake the feeling that things were about to go wrong.

Finn didn't give me time to voice my concerns—not that I was brave enough. He veered down a side street, pulling me into a narrow walkway between two buildings that was veiled in darkness and barely wide enough for us to walk side by side.

Apprehension flared, trying to hold me back. But his grip tightened, composed and firm.

We slipped through a gap in a fence, into the rear yard of a brownstone. The grass was trimmed, hedges neatly shaped, and lights strung across a small patio. It was clean, quiet, and lived-in.

This didn't look like another safehouse. It looked like someone's home.

What the heck were we doing here?

"We're going up there." He motioned toward a dark window on the third floor.

I followed his gaze, my stomach knotting. "How exactly?"

His only answer was to step up to the building and yank down the fire escape. It dropped with a screech, rusted metal groaning loud enough to make my pulse stutter. It looked ancient, corroded at the joints—the kind of structure no one had tested in years. A tetanus shot waiting to happen.

And somehow it looked like freedom.

Elation surged through me when my fingers found the first rung and I pulled myself up. Finn's hand settled firmly between my shoulder blades, leaving me no room to fall. No space to second-guess.

He climbed right behind me, close enough that I could hear his breath. Feel it. His presence was a reassuring wall of heat against my spine.

We paused at the first landing while he hauled the ladder up behind us, then kept moving. Higher and higher. Each step felt like we were climbing toward something just out of reach.

Heaven, maybe—if I even believed in it. In fate? Salvation?

Yes. I had to.

Something had kept me standing. Had brought me

this far. And against all odds, it brought me to him. To Finn.

This wildly dangerous man.

My hero. My lifeline.

On the third floor, he moved ahead of me, crouching to fiddle with a window latch. I couldn't see what he did, but within seconds, the window creaked open, and he slipped inside with practiced ease.

I followed, my heart pounding as I swung my legs through the frame and dropped into a dimly lit apartment.

"Whose place is this?" I asked, glancing around as Finn shut the window behind me and drew the heavy curtains closed.

He reached for the lamp and clicked the switch. A soft golden glow spread across the room, carving shadows into the sharp planes of his face. There was still a storm in his eyes, quiet but unmistakable.

"It's mine," he said.

I froze. "Yours? Is this really a good idea? I thought we were avoiding the places Nik might know to check."

"He knows who I am. And once you've got a name, it's not hard to dig deeper. But he won't find this place."

"Why not? If it's yours—"

"It's not in my name," he interrupted, his voice calm and measured.

"Then how is it yours?"

He scrubbed a hand through his hair, his gaze still pinned to mine. "It just is. In all the ways that count."

"Are you trying to be mysterious, or are you just

avoiding the truth?" I arched a brow. "Maybe because we're not friends?"

He shook his head, his hand dropping to his side as dark strands of hair fell across his forehead. "I'm not trying to be evasive, but an explanation might make you uncomfortable. And if I'm being perfectly fucking honest…it's hard for me to talk about."

Hard to talk about?

My stomach dropped. Was it the words or the way he said them—blunt but reluctant—that had my insides twisting?

"You don't have to," I murmured. "I understand."

He studied me for a beat with a tortured look in his gaze. "Yeah, and you're just about the only one who could." His voice dragged, like whatever he was about to say had been weighing on him for far too long.

My lungs burned as I held my breath, waiting.

At last, he broke the silence. "It's my wife's."

Wife?

My world didn't just tilt, it cracked, splitting right down the center, leaving me standing on unsteady ground.

Finn was married.

How the hell could he be married?

The memory of him—his touch, the way he held me up, held me together, and never truly let me go—rushed through me, flooding every nerve, every cell.

Sweet hell, I'd kissed him.

And he'd kissed me back like a man starved. Like I was oxygen. Like I wasn't the only one who was falling.

Now I was drowning in something else. Something colder. Sharper. It was a foreign, unwelcome emotion that crawled up my spine and burrowed deep under my skin.

I'd witnessed many awful things in my life. Let too much happen around me without ever speaking up. Back then, I didn't feel like I had a choice.

But this? Adultery?

It was a deeply personal violation of trust, and I wasn't okay with it.

I forced myself to look at him, but Finn wasn't watching me anymore. His eyes had gone distant, lost in something only he could see. Dark and hollow.

That's when it hit me.

Whatever storm was raging inside me—the tangled mess of confusion, betrayal, and need—it wasn't all about me. Finn had been suffering in silence from the beginning.

And I had a sudden, disturbing feeling I knew why.

"Where is she?"

When he spoke, his voice was raw, scraped down to something jagged. "She's dead." His eyes found mine, and the sorrow in them was so thick I could taste it. "Rykov killed her."

"Fuck," I muttered, and then my knees gave out.

Finn caught me before I hit the floor. His grip was unyielding, and his body held firm against mine. But it didn't stop the cold from seeping in, sinking deep into my bones.

Nik killed her.

Of course he did. Of course it had been him.

He was a monster who'd stolen my life and shattered my reality, making me question whether I even existed beyond the walls he'd built around me. The man had turned me into an addict. Took me from my daughter. My family. The world.

And now I knew I wasn't the only one he'd destroyed.

Finn's hands tightened around me as if he was grounding himself as much as keeping me upright. "Fuck is right."

He walked me to the couch, helping me down to the cushions with so much care it brought tears to my eyes. Then he crouched in front of me, hands warm on my knees and his expression drawn tight with concern.

It was too much. He was too much.

Or maybe it was just the dead wife.

"You okay?"

"I should be asking you that." I bit my lip, forcing back the emotion clawing its way up my throat. "Finn, I know it's none of my business, and you can tell me to go to hell…"

His brow furrowed. "You want to know what happened?"

"Yes. But also, if Nik knows your name, and tracking people is as easy as you say, couldn't he have found hers? Wouldn't it be easy to trace a property she owned?"

"Maybe. But she bought it under her maiden name. After she died, Robin funneled it through a cousin in real estate. It looked like a normal sale, even though the unit never left my hands. No one questioned it."

He swallowed, and a shadow passed over his features. "On paper, someone else owns it, but it's mine. There's no lease, no payments. Nothing tying me to it."

I nodded slowly. "That's…good. I think."

He drank me in, his gaze tracing over my face, soaking in every detail, including the well of tears in my eyes.

Maybe I should've felt exposed under his scrutiny—we were talking about his dead wife after all. I had no right to ask anything. No claim to this part of him.

Instead of shrinking from it, I leaned in.

With every breath, I felt more awake. More alive. As if the space between us had thinned. For the first time, he was letting me in. Not with violence. Not with tension. But with something real. Something profoundly intimate.

Something more than his hatred for Nik.

"What else do you need to know?" His thumbs traced slow, steady circles against the insides of my knees, his hands a quiet tether, grounding me and lending me the strength I desperately needed.

"What was her name?" My voice was barely a whisper.

A faint, sorrowful smile curved his lips. "Emily."

Such a simple, beautiful name. A name that sounded like it belonged to someone gentle and loving. Someone with warmth in her eyes and laughter in her voice.

"And…how exactly did it happen?"

A muscle ticked at the corner of his jaw as he moved to sit beside me. "It's a long story. And you're not going to like it."

The weight in his tone told me everything before he even said it.

"He killed her to get to you, didn't he? To send you a message?"

"She was never supposed to be part of it." His eyes flicked away. "But yeah, it was because of me. And you were there when it happened."

"What?" The air thinned, my chest squeezing tight. "What do you—"

"It was the night he killed your grandfather. The night he took over the Bratva."

There were so many ghosts in my memories. A near-endless stream of nameless people Nik had killed without explanation. Reasons I'd often wondered about but would never have answers for.

Or maybe there'd never been a reason at all.

But amid the sea of carnage, there was one who stood out. One who'd always haunted me.

Emily. A woman I'd only met a handful of times. They'd been brief moments before Nik's men gunned her down.

She'd been trying to help me, to show me a way out of the Bratva and away from my criminal family. Free from Nik's control.

She'd offered me a chance. A path to freedom. But I'd been too scared and too foolish to take it.

And when Nik dragged her in front of me—

bruised, broken, barely standing—he blamed me. Told me it was my fault. That she suffered because of me.

And the worst part? I believed him.

But she never did.

Emily faced him and the wall of armed, trigger-happy loyalists at his back. Never begged. Never cowered. She stood her ground with dignity and courage.

Qualities I'd never been able to find in myself.

"He killed so many innocent people that night," I whispered. "But Emily…your wife…I remember her. She was trying to help me. Nik caught us together, and he took her."

His body went still. Ice filled his eyes, but his grip on me didn't waver.

"I should have done something." My throat closed around the words.

Finn exhaled slowly, his hand shifting to thread his fingers through mine, anchoring me in the moment. "Done what? If you'd tried, he'd have probably killed you too."

The tears burned hot behind my eyes. "I still should have—"

"No," he cut in, his voice low but firm. "You were trying to survive. That's not your fault."

"But I—" I pressed my lips together, holding back a sob.

He cupped my cheek, tilting my face up to his. "It's not your fault."

I stared at him, blinking through the sting of tears, lost in the storm of his eyes. He meant it. Every word.

And somehow that broke me more than all the pain before.

Something fragile and raw passed between us, and suddenly we were too close. His breath warmed my skin. His thumb brushed the edge of my lip. It was barely a touch, but it was enough to make my pulse skyrocket.

For a second, I thought he'd close the distance. That he'd shatter the wall between us.

But he didn't.

We simply hovered there, shallow breaths mingling, gazes locked, the tension thick enough to choke on. My pulse pounded into my fingertips and the hollow of my throat. The space between us felt charged, like an electric current.

Then he blinked, recoiled, and the moment fractured.

"We should get some rest." His voice was rougher than before. His body shifted, and his gaze slid away, putting distance between us. "You can take the bed."

"I think you've spent enough nights on a couch. We can share the bed." The words were bold, but my entire body shook at the thought of another rejection.

His head turned toward the bedroom. His eyes narrowed as he weighed the offer and calculated the risk. And God—the reluctance, the hesitation—refusal was already forming on his lips.

He let out a resigned sigh. "I guess we could."

After a moment of uncertainty, we made our way to the bedroom.

And now? Now it was awkward.

The air felt different in here, heavier somehow. I tried to push it from my mind, tried not to think about how many nights Finn had slept in this bed next to her. *Emily.*

The sheets felt too soft. The mattress too unfamiliar. And the gorgeous four-poster queen suddenly seemed way too small.

I lay rigid beside him, my body tucked close to the edge, my mind anything but quiet. Every time I closed my eyes, I saw Emily's tear-stained face. Heard Nik order her execution. Felt the helplessness crawl under my skin like poison. I didn't want to think about it, but my mind refused to let go.

"You're still awake," Finn murmured, his voice thick with exhaustion.

"So are you."

A small, bitter smile played at his lips, nearly invisible in the dim light of the apartment. "Hard to sleep when the past won't shut the hell up."

I turned onto my side and searched his face. The shadows deepened the lines around his mouth and eyes. Or maybe grief had aged him.

"Tell me about her," I whispered, trying to keep the ache from my voice.

He shifted closer, his presence steady and warm. Reserved yet comforting.

And still completely out of reach.

CHAPTER
SIXTEEN
FINN

WAS I REALLY DOING THIS?

We were in her apartment. Emily's home. The place she'd made her sanctuary. Without me.

I'd spent so many nights here after she was murdered, chasing her ghost. Trying to find a piece of her. Trying to come to terms with the fact that it was my obsession with another woman that had gotten her killed.

My obsession with Yelena.

And now…what? Was I going to share those pieces of Emily with her—the woman who had unknowingly become the pain point in my marriage? The woman Emily had tried to help?

Fuck me.

That little detail had hit like a goddamn sledgehammer.

I'd asked Emily to talk to her once, back when I first

recognized the danger Yelena was in—when I thought there was a chance to get her out.

But Emily never told me she'd kept trying.

It shouldn't have surprised me. That's who Emily was—an advocate who volunteered at hospitals and women's shelters. She'd always given more to others, me included, than she ever gave herself.

And I'd never felt more guilty about it than I did right now.

Because even knowing it didn't change how I felt about Yelena, the woman who, with one look, one breath, one fucking kiss, made me crave something I never thought possible.

Something I'd never had with Emily.

Something visceral. Goddamn dangerous. Deliciously inescapable.

Fuck. I was a despicable asshole. A goddamn traitor to the woman I had once sworn my life to. If ever I needed proof, this was it.

My heart thundered, and my hands clenched into fists.

"Emily was kind." The words sounded bitter and raw. "She was too kind for her own good. And I'm pretty sure that's why she married me. To be kind."

Silence settled between us. Yelena didn't try to fill it, but she didn't need to.

The quiet burrowed under my skin, digging into my conscience, poking at the memories I'd buried and teasing out the secrets I'd hidden. Things I'd held on to for far too long.

Shit I swore I'd never say out loud.

"We weren't happy." The admission clawed its way up my throat, shattering the stillness. "Not for a long time."

Her brows drew together, but she still didn't say anything. Just watched and waited, listening as I spilled my guts.

"Emily moved out six months before she died. This place was bought in her maiden name because she was leaving me." I shook my head, air sawing through my lungs. "She'd already left."

"She left you?" Yelena echoed, her voice was full of the same shock I'd felt when Emily first announced she was leaving.

"Yeah. Only, no one knew. Not our friends, not our families. It was easier that way."

Her gaze held mine, sharp and searching. "Easier for who?"

How could I answer that when I didn't fucking know? Maybe it was easier for Emily. Maybe for me. Maybe for both of us because we were too damn tired of pretending and too scared to actually let go.

"She was kind, but she wanted a life I couldn't give her." I sputtered, nearly choking on the words. "No. Fuck, that's not fair to her—I could have given her what she wanted, if I were a different man."

"Finn…" Yelena's voice was soft, careful. Like she could already sense me cracking.

"She wanted something easy. Simple. Fucking vanilla." The confession turned to gravel in my throat. "And

I tried. I really fucking tried. I told myself it was enough. That I could be what she wanted. That I could be satisfied with what I had."

My lungs burned. My vision blurred. "But it was a lie. And she knew it."

Yelena shifted in the bed, propping herself up on an elbow. Her gaze was intense as she studied me, but she wasn't looking down on me. There was no disdain or condemnation in her expression.

No. What radiated from her was empathy. A glint of something tender in her big doe eyes.

But if she knew that I'd fallen into a world of organized crime—that I'd knowingly stayed there, regardless of my reasoning—would she still look at me like that?

Worse, if I told her that she was the catalyst for it all, would it break her? I was a selfish bastard, but could I really place all of that on her shoulders and expect her not to fracture?

She was still watching me. Still waiting.

For what, I didn't fucking know.

"I let her leave," I said, finally breaking the tension. "I watched her pack her things. Did nothing to stop her. Because I knew letting her go was the right thing. For both of us."

Yelena's lips parted like she was going to say something. Instead, she reached for me.

It was a simple touch, her delicate fingers grazing my arm. A soft stroke of comfort. A small, human gesture.

It was innocent, but her skin against mine felt like a goddamn supernova. Like heat and desire and hunger. An unstoppable force of nature.

I didn't pull away. I fucking should have. But I didn't.

No, I embraced it.

My fingers curled around her wrist, and I pulled her to me. Not fast. Not hard. Just a persistent pressure that urged her closer, until the space between us was nearly nonexistent, and I was wrapped in her familiar, intoxicating scent.

She inhaled deeply, her breath shuddering on the way out. Like this moment, this connection, was something she needed. Something profound.

And fuck, I needed it too. Even if it was a mistake. Even if I couldn't keep it.

"She was too good for me." The words felt stilted. Wrong. Not that they weren't true, but did it even fucking matter anymore? It was too late for confession. Too late to make amends.

But not too late for a warning.

Yelena was too good for me, too. And even though I'd already tried to tell her, I wasn't sure she'd gotten the message.

She started to argue, but I silenced her with a finger pressed to her perfect lips.

Soft. Lush. Tempting as fucking hell.

"It's not up for debate." I forced the words from between gritted teeth. "And if you knew the truth, you'd understand why. Rykov was the one who killed her, but it was my fault. Not yours. Mine."

With firm fingers, she pried my hand away from her mouth. There was no hope of her overpowering me, but I gave in to her all the same.

"You weren't even there, and she was trying to help me. How could that be your fault?"

I shook my head, unwilling or maybe just unable to say more.

"Finn." She moved up on me fast, and her delicate hands framed my face. With uncompromising courage, she forced me to look at her. "Whatever you've done, I can guarantee it's not as bad as you think. Nothing could be as bad as what he did."

"No, what I did was worse. Rykov's despicable, and he's going to pay for that. But I'm the one who made her a promise. A fucking vow."

I swallowed, my voice faltering and my throat trying to close around the words. "She trusted me, Lena. Just like you. And I broke that trust. I fucking walked all over it. She deserved better. And so do you."

Her fingers flexed, and her gaze sharpened. "Did her reason for leaving have anything to do with whatever it is you're too ashamed to tell me? Did she know?"

"Yes," I admitted, exhaling slowly, willing myself to keep my demons in check.

"Then you can't take the blame." Her voice was resolute, like she was refusing to let me carry the weight of it alone.

Refusing to believe I was anything less than worthy.

"Emily made her choice," she said. "She stood up

for herself. She was moving on, without you. And what happened after—what Nik did—that can't be on you."

But it was. And the only way I could make her understand was to give her the truth.

Truth was, I'd wanted Yelena before I even knew her. From the first moment I saw her in a sex club, four years ago. And I'd been ruined ever since.

Maybe it had been the heat in her eyes as she'd stared at the kink on display—a hunger she didn't even seem to recognize in herself. Or maybe it was the way that hunger had been tangled up with fear, with vulnerability so raw it had sliced straight into my goddamn soul.

I told myself I was just concerned. That she was in danger. That she needed someone to look out for her. And as I dug into Rykov and his business, that concern wasn't only solidified, but magnified.

She really was in trouble, and I'd wanted to do something about it. Wanted to get her away from him.

But it wasn't only about keeping her safe.

It was about wanting her. Wanting her in a way I had no right to. Wanting her even though she was a stranger.

Even though I was married.

Even though common fucking sense should have stopped me from chasing the idea of her in the first place—through blood, through violence, and through the wreckage of my own goddamn life.

But none of it had mattered.

I was infatuated with Yelena Markova.

"There was another woman," I finally said, my

fingers wrapping around her wrists, breaking her hold on me and whatever spell we'd been under.

But I hadn't needed to pull her off me because the second the words left my mouth, she bolted upright, pulling away and putting space between us.

Like I was now someone to fear.

"You cheated on her?" She sounded stunned. But also…hurt?

"No. Not exactly."

Her expression hardened. "That's not exactly an answer, Finn."

"You're right." With controlled, measured movements, I sat and looked her in the eyes. "I didn't cheat physically. I never touched the other woman. Never even fucking spoke to her. Not even after Emily left me. Not even after her death."

Yelena's shoulders eased just a fraction, but the intensity of her gaze didn't let up. "Wait…never spoke to her? How was this other woman involved if it wasn't something intimate?"

I could have lied. But the truth would have to come out eventually. It had been eating me alive for so long now. And in the end, didn't Yelena deserve to know? Even if it made her hate me.

Hell, even if she already did.

"Because I was fucking obsessed with her. And it destroyed everything."

Her lips parted slightly, just a breath, her chest rising on a slow inhale, and her body stilling like prey beneath a predator's stare.

The air between us thickened, my skin prickling with something dark and electric. Something that wrapped itself around my throat and squeezed.

"It was you, Lena." I forced my voice steady, but it still sounded like a plea. "You were my obsession, the woman I wanted more than life. It was you. Fuck, it's always been you."

Saying it out loud should have taken some of the weight off. Should have somehow made it possible to breathe. But I was still suffocating.

Because now? Now the power was in her hands. She knew the truth.

What would she do with it?

Her mouth opened on a strangled cry, a mix of disbelief and desperation. "W-what are you talking about? How is that even possible?"

Fractured and raw, her words tore at my already battered heart.

Before I could even form a response, my phone vibrated. The hollow, digital sound echoed through the room, stealing my attention like a thief.

Ignore it. Leave the death and danger until later.

Fuck, I wished I could. I wanted so badly to stay in the moment—right here, right fucking now. Nothing else but Lena and me.

The world outside those four walls didn't give a shit about timing. Our enemy could've been at our door, and as much as I'd have liked to pause and assess her reaction, keeping her safe was a much bigger priority.

Her eyes darted to my phone as I pulled it from my

pocket, the screen lighting up the room with its unnatural glow.

"Is it them?" Her voice was so full of emotion it nearly broke me in two.

"It's Robin." I managed to keep my tone neutral despite the chaos churning inside me.

Call me as soon as you're alone.

Tension coiled at the base of my spine, an old, familiar weight settling into my bones. Robin never bothered with cryptic messages. Asking me to call her? Now? Something was wrong.

My gaze traveled back to Yelena. To the unreadable expression on her lovely face, and the torment of her unwavering gaze.

My fingers closed hard on the phone. I didn't want to move, but I stood anyway, each step away from her an actual ache.

"I have to take this." The words scraped out of me. "Are you going to be okay on your own?"

She was clutching the bedsheets now, her fists shaking with the effort. And fuck me, she was biting her bottom lip so hard there was no way she wasn't tasting blood.

But she nodded. The movement was jerky, uncontrolled, and made the pit in my gut widen. Was it withdrawal? The bag I'd dropped in town had her meds in it. Would she be able to cope without them?

Or was it my confession and our fucked-up situation that was doing her in?

I turned for the door, the weight of my phone heavy

in my palm as it buzzed again, reminding me of Robin's unanswered text.

Before I could take another step, Yelena jumped to follow.

"Wait." Her hand landed on my back. "Don't go."

I exhaled slowly, forcing myself to stay in control. My free hand curled into a fist, my knuckles aching from the pressure.

Just like the first time I saw her, I should have walked away. Should've ignored the quiet edge of need in her voice—the thing coiled around my spine, refusing to let go.

But how could I when the ache in her voice mirrored the pain wedged in my chest, and the tremor of her fingers on my back matched the fragility of my control?

I turned, pulse pounding, until we were face to face and her eyes were locked with mine.

And the look she gave me? It was unapologetic. Bold and goddamn daring.

Her chin tilted up, and her hand pressed to my chest. "Please stay with me."

"Lena." My voice nearly broke over her name, the hunger in my veins pulsing in time with my heartbeat.

With a lump in my throat and staggering pain under my ribs, I moved toward her, drawn to her by a force older than time. I closed what little distance remained between us, our bodies brushing, caught in the same dangerous pull.

"Please, Finn."

That was all it took.

I was past the point of escape, too far gone to fight my way out. The same gravity that pulled me to her now locked me in her orbit. I closed the distance, the air between us crackling with tension.

And then I gave in. To the attraction. To the unmistakable heat in her gaze. To her.

I gave in to the fall.

CHAPTER
SEVENTEEN
YELENA

FINN'S PRESENCE SWALLOWED EVERYTHING. He stood so close I felt the thrum of his heartbeat—steady, thunderous—and dominance poured off him like heat, leaving me suspended in the quiet terror of wanting.

All I could do was stare.

I fixated on the thick cords of his throat as he swallowed, the sharp twitch of his jaw, the haunted tension gathered between his brows like a wound that hadn't quite closed.

"You shouldn't look at me like that." His voice was low, rough around the edges, and vibrating with something dark and barely contained.

"Like what?"

His hand lifted and he dragged a single finger along the curve of my jaw. "Like you still trust me."

The rough pad of his thumb skimmed beneath my bottom lip, igniting a trail of sparks that danced across my skin and settled low in my belly.

"But I do." God help me, I did.

Resisting him wasn't an option. It never had been.

I was already his, and we both knew it.

Was it foolish? Without question. Reckless? One hundred percent.

None of that mattered. Not when I was standing in front of him like this, consumed by the heat of everything neither of us had said out loud.

Nothing had changed. At least nothing about my belief in him or the attraction swelling between us.

A raw, guttural sound tore from his throat, deep and broken and feral. It crashed into me like a live wire, sending heat spiraling through my core and lighting up every nerve with the unshakable knowledge that he wanted me.

Me.

The realization clawed at my insides, and the rush of desire collided with disbelief. He'd been thinking about me, aching for me, before I even knew he existed.

How was that possible?

Emily had died the same night Nik killed my grandfather, seized control of the Bratva, and locked me away in his gilded cage. That was over a year ago. And Finn said she'd left him six months before that.

Because he was obsessed. That was the word he'd used.

Obsessed.

But for how long? God, how deep did this thing go?

He stared at me, his ocean-blue gaze darkening with a look that sent another sharp pang of want curling through me. The intensity of it sent a shiver down my spine.

And yet, he seemed lost. Like his unyielding restraint was fraying at the edges. Like he was waiting for me to break first. To make a move or give him a signal that it was okay to lose control. That it was okay to want me.

And I wanted to give it to him. God, I wanted it. Wanted him.

I was seconds away from doing something fearless —or maybe just plain foolish—when his phone chimed with another notification, breaking the moment.

I flinched, blinking hard, and everything came crashing back. The world. The mission. The reality that danger was still out there.

Nik was out there.

"Is that Robin again?" Urgency laced my tone, the peril of our situation creeping back in. "Is everything okay?"

Finn's brows pulled together as he glanced down again at the device. "I don't know. She asked me to call her, which could mean trouble. Or she might just want to hear my voice for proof of life."

Proof of life.

The phrase sent an uneasy prickle over my skin, and the cold began seeping back into my bones. "Then you should call her."

He shook his head, conflict etched into every line of his face. "We have a code. I'll just..." His fingers hovered for a moment, as though he was thinking of what to say. Then with stiff, agitated movements, he fired off a text and waited, staring at the screen like it had offended him.

Seconds dragged and the silence between us thickened, pressing down with the weight of everything left unsaid.

And still, I trusted him. Craved him. Even with the questions gnawing at me, and no matter the lies he'd told or the truths he'd hidden.

Even with Emily.

Emily, who, despite whatever role I'd played in fracturing her marriage, had tried to help me. Tried to save me from Nik's horrors before it was too late.

Finn was right. She had been kind.

And now here I was, lusting after her husband. The same man who had just admitted he'd been—what? Stalking me? Obsessing over me.

A dark thrill shot through my veins at the thought.

What did it say about me that I liked the idea of it? That I didn't just accept his fixation, but welcomed it?

The thought of Finn fantasizing about me didn't just make me feel wanted. It made me feel chosen. Desired. *Special.*

Finally, his phone buzzed again. The sharp sound cut through the silence, and he let out a slow, relieved breath.

"What is it?" I asked as his thumbs flew over the screen.

"Everything's good. She just wanted an update. To make sure we made it here safely. I forgot to check in."

He glanced up, his gaze pinning me in place. "I guess I was distracted."

"And I guess that's my fault." The words slipped out before I could stop them. Too soft, laced with guilt, and far too revealing.

I dropped my gaze, settling on the slow rise and fall of his chest. The steady rhythm of his breathing was the only calm thing in the room. The only thing that didn't make me feel like I was coming apart.

His finger hooked firmly under my chin. "Eyes up here, Lena." It wasn't a request. It was an order.

And that's all it took to set me on fire all over again.

I lifted my lashes to peek at him, ready to give in. Or maybe just too far gone to stop.

"Do I really need to say it again?" His whole hand slid under my jaw, his fingers pressing just enough to make my pulse skip.

His grip, the heat, and the quiet authority that rolled off him in waves—commanding, dark, impossibly seductive—it should have scared me.

Instead, it made me ache.

My eyes snapped to his, searching for clarity. For confirmation. Was this obsession a thing he'd buried? Or was it still burning beneath the surface, raw and alive?

"You are not to blame." His voice was firm. Unshakable. "For any of it. Okay?"

I nodded, but the movement was restricted by the gentle force of his hand.

And sweet hell, despite the fear and the little voice

at the back of my head warning me to be careful, I wanted to lean into him. To cave to his power. Feel his control. Give myself over, completely.

To let him own me.

"Lena…" His thumb dragged over my bottom lip, pulling it free from my teeth and smoothing back across it in a motion that made my stomach clench.

My thighs pressed together. My world tilted.

His grip shifted, turning to something more reverent, almost adoring. His fingers traced a slow path downward, trailing over my throat until his palm rested under my collarbone like an act of quiet possession.

"There's more I should tell you." His voice faltered, and his brows drew tight. "But I've got to be honest, I'm afraid of what it might do to you. And what it will mean for us."

Us. That single word hit something deep inside me, winding its way through all the dark spaces, lighting me up. Making me burn.

I was shaking now, my pulse pounding as I splayed my fingers over his chest, mirroring his hold on me.

"I'm afraid too," I admitted, my throat thick with tension. "Because you're not the only one with secrets, Finn. My past is littered with so much darkness, I'm afraid I'll never outrun it. Afraid I might not want to."

My fingers clutched his shirt in a move that felt desperate. "I'm afraid because part of me likes dark things, and once you see that—really see me—whatever illusion you've held of me will be shattered."

"Lena—"

"No." I knocked my fist against his chest, urging him to listen. "You're not hearing me. I didn't end up with Nik by accident. I went to him on purpose. I wanted someone who could take control, who didn't shy away from the dark. The danger? I didn't just tolerate it, Finn. I chased it."

The truth burned like acid in my throat. "I wanted a man who could help me take over…" A sudden rush of grief caught me, choking off my words.

"Help you take over what?" Finn's big hand moved to grasp the back of my neck, his intense gaze searching mine.

But I couldn't face him. I squeezed my eyes shut, sending a single tear cascading down my cheek.

And then his mouth was on me. So soft, so gentle, I thought I was imagining it.

His tender lips pressed into the flesh beside my ear, followed by the low hum of his voice. "You don't need to hide from me. I've already seen the darkness in you—all your raw and broken pieces. And just like the rest of you, I think it's beautiful."

My breath went ragged, and my eyes flew open to meet his.

"Tell me what you thought he could do for you. Tell me all the ways he failed. And then let me make it better. Let me be the one to give it to you instead."

Sweet hell.

My core clenched in a way that made my entire body spasm, shooting desire through me like nothing I'd felt before. Urgent and demanding. Like I might die if I didn't fulfill that need right now.

"I wanted him to help me take over the Bratva," I admitted, the words spilling out in a rush of breath.

Finn's gaze burned through me, and his fingers at the back of my neck were now tangled in my hair, clutching me to him in a way that made me feel powerful. Like he needed me as much as I needed him.

Like he was afraid to let go.

"And is that what you still want, little Lena? A Bratva?"

I was melting into him, my body pliant and my mind tangled with lust and longing.

"I don't know." My voice was barely above a whisper. "So much has changed. Back then, it was a childish desire to take something from my sister. Something she didn't care about—didn't even want—but my grandfather was going to hand it to her anyway."

He hummed his understanding, the deep vibration sinking into my bones. His expression remained unreadable yet wholly focused on me.

"Maybe it shouldn't matter to me anymore," I continued. "But it does. Because now I want to take it from him."

"You want retribution." The rumble of his voice and that oh-so-lovely word coiled around me. "To take what's owed."

"Yes." Heat pooled deep inside me, making me feel wild and wicked. "Fuck, yes."

His gaze darkened, approval flickering in the sharp

blue depths of his eyes. "You deserve it. And I'm going to help you get it. That, and so much more."

"Whatever I want?" Wetness coated the insides of my thighs.

"Whatever you want."

"Finn?" I pressed closer, my back arching and my hands grasping his shoulders. "What if what I want more than anything…is you?"

His fingers tightened around my waist, dragging me closer until there was no space left between us—just the crushing weight of heat, unspoken promises, and his erection pressing against my stomach through too many layers of clothes.

"You don't know what you're asking for." His voice was pained, like his restraint was being stretched to the point of breaking.

"Maybe not fully. But you've said enough for me to get the idea. And what you've already shown me…" I leaned in, letting my mouth hover near his. "I want more."

"It should scare you." His breath was hot against my skin.

"But it doesn't. Not even a little. Not when it's you."

A growl rumbled in his chest. It was a feral sound that sent a hot pulse straight through me.

His phone hit the bed with a careless toss, and he was on me. His mouth crashed against mine, brutal and claiming. Nothing soft, nothing sweet—just teeth and heat and possession.

His hand fisted in my hair, yanking my head back

and baring my throat to him. A sharp gasp slipped past my lips, but I didn't try to pull away. I didn't want to.

His lips dragged down the column of my neck, the scrape of his teeth making my pulse hammer against my skin.

"You think you can handle this?" He breathed against my throat, his voice rough. Dangerous. "That you can handle me?"

"Please, Finn." I arched into him, felt the bite of his grip and the weight of his body pinning me exactly where he wanted. "I can handle it. I want whatever you'll give me."

He pulled back, but only enough to meet my eyes. "Careful, little Lena. When you beg so sweetly, I'm tempted to deliver."

He said it like a warning. All I heard was a promise. A vow I hoped he'd never break.

His fingers dug into my sides, but he didn't move. Only stared. Waiting. Like he was giving me one last chance to pull away. To stop this.

We both knew I wouldn't. That I couldn't.

I was lost to him.

Lost to his quiet strength and the unspoken promise of his unyielding command.

He'd told me he wanted to watch me fall apart, to put me back together. And right now, I couldn't think of anything I'd ever wanted more.

"Give me your worst," I murmured. "And I'll savor it."

CHAPTER
EIGHTEEN
FINN

*GIVE ME YOUR WORST, **and I'll savor it.***

I fucking stared. It was all I could do.

The second those bold words escaped her pouty goddamn lips, every rational thought was ripped from me.

I gripped her waist harder—not enough to bruise her, just to make it clear that even though her comfort and safety mattered to me, I was the one in fucking charge.

"You need to understand this isn't a game to me." My voice was low and controlled. "It's not a quick fuck. I don't want to work you out of my system, or rush to get off."

My fingers flexed and my body fucking burned with hunger. "It's going to be slow. Maybe even agonizing. I'm going to wrench every last bit of pleasure from you until you don't know where your ecstasy ends and mine begins."

Dark excitement, and maybe a flash of fear, lit her big doe eyes. "Will it hurt?"

Pain shot through my chest. "It doesn't have to."

"But that's what you want, isn't it? To hurt me?"

"Only in ways that bring you pleasure."

Her brow furrowed, the sweetest look of uncertainty crossing her lovely face.

I cupped her jaw, dragging my thumb over her bottom lip. "Do you still trust me?"

"Yes." There was no hesitation, no fear in her voice. Only pure, unguarded desire.

"Then trust me with this." I traced her throat, feeling the rapid beat of her pulse beneath my palm. "And if I do anything you don't like, or if at any point you don't feel safe, you tell me."

"Do I need a safe word?"

"Your safe word is no. Or stop. Like I said, this isn't a game. You don't want it? Say so, and I'll listen."

Her plump bottom lip disappeared between her teeth, and the ache in my chest slid lower, turning into something dark and primal.

She had no idea how much I was willing to give, as long as she was willing to take.

"We'll start slow and easy. But once we do this, there's no walking away. You're mine, and I'm yours—whether you want me or not."

"Of course I do." Her chest heaved. "I've been trying to show you just how much."

"I've always wanted you." The words ripped from

me, rough and reckless and honest as fuck. "Before I even knew your goddamn name, I wanted you."

A vicious thrum tore through me, excitement, relief, and lust all bleeding into something savage. "Four fucking years, Lena—four years of trying to bury it, choke it down, and pretend I didn't feel it. And it still wasn't enough. I want you more now than ever."

She breathed me in, chest rising hard against mine, and whispered, "Then take me."

Three words. Only three goddamn words, and they detonated inside me. It wasn't just permission.

It was surrender.

How many times had I convinced myself this moment would never happen? Could never happen?

Now that it was here, I felt a desperate need to hold on to it. To drag it out for eternity, just to be sure it was real, to make sure I wouldn't lose her.

That she wouldn't be stolen from me.

"Turn around."

She obeyed instantly, the scent of citrus and lavender wafting from the tail of her silky hair as it brushed my cheek.

"Good girl," I murmured at the shell of her ear.

A shiver rippled through her, and fuck, I wanted to chase it. Wanted to sink my teeth into the delicate flesh of her shoulder and leave my mark there.

Instead, I stepped back, watching. Waiting. "Now take off your clothes."

Her hands trembled as she gripped the hem of her shirt. She dragged the fabric up, inch by inch, revealing smooth, flawless skin, the slope of her spine, and the delicate flare of her waist.

Despite her anxiety and the huge fucking leap of faith she was taking, she didn't pause. Her bra went next, followed by her skirt—the material whispering to the floor like a sacrifice at my feet.

I forced myself not to drop to my knees and devour her on the spot.

"Everything," I urged when she faltered. "Don't make me ask again."

Her spine went rigid.

Fuck. Had I pushed her too far?

Her shoulders squared. Then she hooked a finger around the band of her panties and drew them down her hips, over the perfect globes of her ass, until they slipped down her legs.

"Very good." I stalked around her, my gaze dragging over every bare inch my hands ached to touch.

"Finn…" Doubt crossed her beautiful features, and she moved her hands to cover herself.

"You don't need to hide from me." I grasped her arms and moved them back to her sides. "You're perfect, Lena."

My fingers cupped her breast, my thumb tracing the faint scar that curved across her skin. "Every single bit of you...fucking perfect."

She melted into me, the tension bleeding from her frame, and I let my thumb drift further, flicking lightly over her nipple.

A soft, heady groan slipped from her lips, and I

claimed it with my mouth, swallowing the sound like a man starved.

I didn't just want to feel her pleasure—I wanted to own it. Every gasp. Every broken cry. Every desperate little sound she gave me.

Smiling against her skin, I rolled the tight bud of her nipple between my fingers, relishing the way she arched into my touch. I tugged hard, and a shattered whimper ripped from her throat.

The sound lit a low, brutal fire in my gut.

I let go slowly, not out of mercy, but because I wanted to hear that sound again. Wanted to break her apart piece by piece.

On my mouth. On my hands.

On my fucking terms.

Without warning, I seized her waist and drove her back to the foot of the bed, my body caging hers against the bedpost.

Her hands shot to my chest, fingers curling into my shirt as if she couldn't decide whether to pull me in or shove me away. Her lips parted, maybe to question, maybe to beg. But I didn't give her the chance.

I crushed my mouth to hers. Taking, demanding, owning. I kissed her like I could carve myself into her skin—maybe because breathing her in was the only thing keeping the darkness at bay. My lips ravaged, my tongue invaded, demanding, tasting, and fucking worshiping every inch of her mouth. I pressed her harder against the post until there was no space left between us.

Until she couldn't move without feeling me everywhere.

Her hands were still fisted in my shirt, clinging to me like she didn't trust her own legs to hold her up.

And maybe she couldn't. Not with the way her body trembled against mine, heat bleeding off her like she was seconds away from combusting.

"Give me your hands," I said, tearing my mouth from hers, my voice rough and scraped raw by my thinning restraint.

She blinked up at me, breathless and uncertain. Her grip faltered, but she didn't release me.

"Unless you're ready for this to end?"

Instantly, she let go. Her arms turned pliant as I grabbed them, lifting them above her head and guiding her hands to the carved post of the bed.

"Hold on," I ordered. "Don't move until I say."

Her fingers gripped tight around the post, clutching it like it was now her lifeline.

I let my hands trail down the insides of her delicate wrists, feeling the frantic race of her pulse under my touch. "Don't fucking let go," I repeated.

It was a harsh command, but it didn't scare her. No, it lit something fierce yet fragile inside her. Something that pounded in her chest, shook in her breath, and spilled from her parted lips—raw, aching, and fucking beautiful.

She nodded, silent but resolute, surrendering without pause. She was putting herself in my hands. Daring me to take her apart and trusting me to make her whole again.

I traced down her arms, barely skimming her silken skin, taking my time to tease and watching the way she bloomed with heat. The way she shuddered as I grazed my fingers over the sides of her breasts. And when I flattened my palms over her hips and slid them back to grip her ass, she let out a whimper.

But I didn't rush.

She pushed into me, and I gripped tighter, controlling the movement, loving the way her body begged for more.

Fuck, I wanted to give her so much more. I wanted to give her everything.

Every-fucking-thing.

My gaze roamed over her flushed chest and parted thighs to the spot where my thumbs indented her soft flesh, before I finally met her eyes.

Big. Dark. Wide with need.

"Finn." My name was a whispered plea.

And fuck, I almost gave in. Almost touched her the way I knew she wanted. The way I craved. Instead, my mouth found her throat, licking and biting until she shivered, and her hips jerked forward.

But her hands? They stayed exactly where I'd left them, clutching the post, white-knuckled with restraint despite the strain on her body. Despite any instinct to reach for me.

I'd told her not to let go, and she obeyed.

Such a good fucking girl.

"You want this?" I teased my fingers through the curls at the apex of her thighs, my mouth dragging along her throat.

A broken sound pushed past her lips, and her hips bucked hard against my hand. But still, I didn't give in.

Stepping back, I stripped my hands and mouth away, leaving her squirming, her hands still held fucking high.

"Look at you," I rasped. "So fucking beautiful like this—desperate and needy. Barely touched but ready to fall apart."

"Please," she begged, her body bending toward me, thighs clenching, and hands still locked tight around the post.

I answered with a dark, hungry smile as pleasure licked through me.

Then I dropped to my knees.

She gasped, her body seizing under the sharp, electric snap of tension. She was frozen by the gravity of what was about to happen, and powerless to do anything but submit.

My hands gripped her thighs, rougher now, forcing them apart with possessive intent. And she let me. Opened for me.

Fucking trusted me.

I was going to make damn sure she didn't regret it.

A soft, reverent kiss landed on the inside of her knee. Another found the tender line of her thigh. Then I buried my face between her legs and breathed her in.

Her intoxicating scent hit me, and it short-circuited every rational thought I had left.

A low growl tore from my chest, primal, hungry, and barely contained. Unable to hold back, I turned my head and bit into the delicate flesh of her thigh, reveling in the sharp cry that followed, the sound running straight down my spine like fire.

"Still with me?" I licked over the angry red imprint my teeth had left behind.

A shattered moan slipped from her, and it echoed through me, spurring me on.

"Words, Lena," I demanded, then dragged my tongue higher just to hear her gasp again. "I need to know you'll stop me if it's too much."

"Yes." The word was breathless but clear. "I'm with you. Please…don't stop."

Another low sound rumbled through me—part laugh, part growl, it was thick with the kind of need that left no room for mercy. "I'm not going to stop until you're shaking. Begging. Until the only thing you can say is my fucking name."

The words had barely left my mouth before I dropped my head, flicking my tongue once over her clit. Just a single, ruthless stroke.

She cried out, her head tipping back and her body jolting like I'd shocked her.

Her taste flooded my mouth—sweet, potent, fucking addictive—and it shredded what little control I had left. I descended on her, slicking my mouth against her pussy, feasting like she was my last fucking meal.

And fuck, I was getting off on it. Every soft, wrecked

sound she gave me, every tremor that shook through her, and every desperate clench of her thighs around my head sent a surge of raw pleasure straight through me.

"So fucking good," I mumbled against her clit, too obsessed with the taste of her to pull away.

She rocked against me, wild and mindless, grinding herself against my mouth without a single ounce of restraint.

But her hands stayed up, locked tight around the post. Exactly as I'd ordered.

I slid a hand between her thighs, spreading her wider, wedging in closer until her knee was over my shoulder and I was slipping from the edge of fucking sanity.

Without warning, I thrust two fingers inside her sopping heat. And fuck, despite how drenched she was, she gripped me like a goddamn vice.

The feel of her—hot, tight, and pulsing—sank into my skin, tore through my control, and made my cock throb painfully against my zipper. I drove my fingers deeper, curling them just right and drawing them back against her fluttering walls before sinking in again.

"Finn." My name fell from her lips on a pleading gasp.

"That's it." The words were a broken rumble against her slick, trembling skin. "You're right there, my lovely girl."

A broken sob tore from her throat. "Oh God, Finn… I'm going to come."

I ripped my mouth from her just long enough to growl, "Do it."

Then I was back on her, my lips crashing into her heat, my fingers driving deeper, and my tongue relentless as I sucked her clit hard.

And she did.

She shattered around me, soaking my hand and chanting my name like a fucking prayer.

Her cries echoed through the room, wild and undone, but I didn't stop. Didn't let up. I worked her through every wave, every quake, until she sagged into my hold, shaking and ruined.

Fuck, she came for me like I owned her, still clinging to the post like it was the only thing left holding her together.

And I was just getting started.

CHAPTER
NINETEEN
YELENA

My arms were trembling, my muscles burning from holding them up for so long. But I didn't dare move them until he told me to.

Not out of fear. No. It was because some deep, hidden part of me wanted to submit.

It was a craving for his dominance, and it was stronger than any high. I didn't fully understand it. I also didn't question it. I just gave in.

Pleasing him felt too good to fight.

"Mmm." His satisfied hum rumbled over me as his hands slid up the backs of my thighs, and his mouth, still slick from me, ran over my hip.

"Finn," I whimpered his name again, unable to find any other words.

He stood, his body dragging over mine, the rough friction of his clothes sending new shocks across my skin.

"You can let go of the post now, little Lena," he murmured, his voice low and rich and devastatingly calm. "You did so fucking good."

I complied instantly, my arms dropping to my sides as the blood rushed back in a sharp, tingling wave. It should've been uncomfortable, maybe even painful, but right then, it only fed the delicious ache still pulsing through me.

His hands moved over my arms, kneading gently and coaxing the feeling back into them. Then one at a time, he lifted each hand to his mouth, kissing my sore knuckles while his thumbs traced slow, soothing circles.

It was so tender, I nearly melted.

"You okay?" His gaze swept over me, concern etched into the faint lines at the corners of his eyes.

I nodded, not trusting my voice to hold steady.

"I need words from you. I need to know…" He faltered, like he was grappling with the same crushing tide of emotion I was. The same sense of standing at the edge of something vast.

Immense.

Something I couldn't outrun. Something that should terrify me but didn't.

It was too much, too fast, too tangled in danger, need, and the mess still looming between us. But I didn't want to run or hide. I didn't want to undo any of it.

I only wanted more. Every dark, dangerous, consuming piece of it.

Of him.

"I'm with you." I looked up at him, holding nothing back. "I want to be with you. Always."

His breath caught. It was such a small hitch, it was nearly imperceptible, but I felt it.

God, I felt it. Like a spark against my skin, it turned my already liquid insides molten, lighting me up all over again.

Then he kissed me. Not rough. Not greedy. Just a soft, simple brush of his lips. His mouth met mine with aching reverence—a slow glide of heat and patience that stole the breath from my lungs. Like he needed to savor it. Like my words had undone something in him. Opened something he'd buried long ago.

And set something wild in me free.

The kiss deepened. One hand slid into my hair, and the other cupped my jaw, guiding me in for more. And when his tongue swept across my bottom lip, I opened for him instantly. No fear. No worry.

Just want. A growing, ravenous need.

He tasted like me, my release still fresh on his lips. And somehow, that only made me burn hotter.

I moaned into his mouth, and he fisted my hair tighter, turning the kiss into something feral.

He surged forward, crowding me back until the cold wood of the post bit into my spine. His thigh wedged between mine, the rough material of his jeans dragging hard over my still-sensitive skin.

I cried out, my fingers digging into his shoulders for leverage.

"Say it again," he growled against my mouth.

My heart stuttered. "Always, Finn. I'm with you. Always."

Sweet hell, I meant it. Every hollow part of me had been filled by him.

His lips crashed back to mine, devouring every breath, every thought, every last flicker of doubt. The tenderness was gone. What remained was hunger. Command.

The kind of dominance I'd begged for without ever saying a word.

One hand slid down, his fingers hooking beneath my knee to hike my leg around his hip. The other traced my spine, down over the curve of my ass, until he was gripping me with both hands, grinding me against the hard line of him.

"You're not done yet," he rasped. "Not even close."

And God, despite being wrung out and trembling, he was right.

He kissed me again, brutal in its intensity, then tore his mouth away with a low curse. "Get on the bed."

I moved without thinking, the demand sinking straight into my bloodstream. The moment my knees hit the edge of the mattress, he was behind me, one hand gripping my hip to stop me from moving any farther. The hold was firm, almost punishing, and possessive in a way that told me I wasn't going anywhere unless he allowed it.

A breath later, the slow, harsh rasp of his zipper filled the air, sending a shiver of impatience down my spine.

Then I felt him. Hot, hard, thick, and pressed against me without restraint.

There was nothing subtle about the way he touched me. Nothing careful about the way he crowded my body with his. He felt huge, and the sheer weight of him alone had my core clenching and heat growing low and fast inside me all over again.

"Don't move," he growled. "Stay just like that."

I froze, trembling, every inch of me aware of him. Aware of how close he was and how deeply I already needed him. The heat of his body radiated against my bare skin like a brand I had no desire to escape.

"Fuck, Lena," he muttered, running his fingers down the length of my spine. Demanding yet reverent. Breaking me apart. "You are so fucking perfect. And all fucking mine."

His thumbs spread me open, exposing me completely and eliciting a helpless whimper I couldn't hope to contain.

"So fucking wet," he murmured, his voice low and sinful. "You're dripping for me, Lena. You feel that?"

I nodded, my face burning. But apparently, that wasn't enough.

"Use your words."

"Yes," I breathed. "I feel it."

"Good. You're doing so fucking good. Now feel this."

His thick cock dragged over my pussy, unhurried and heavy, spreading my slick across every swollen, desperate inch. The heat of him made my body arch, my nerves sparking with need. I ached to look back, to see him, to watch the man who could unravel me with nothing more than a touch.

But I didn't dare move. I could only feel. Only want.

When his broad head nudged over my clit once, then again, pleasure shot through me in sharp, electric bursts. I gasped, my hips twitching and my breath snagging in my throat. Every nerve lit up, raw and greedy.

He chuckled—a low, dark sound full of filthy satisfaction. "Now be a good girl and come for me again."

He gripped my hips, positioning me with commanding precision, lining himself up behind me. I expected him to push inside. To take. To finish what we'd started hours ago. But Finn? He wasn't interested in giving me anything that easily.

He dropped down behind me, his tongue trailing over the top of my ass, his fingers gripping hard and spreading me apart. Then he dropped his head further and latched his mouth to my clit like he meant to own it.

Every flick of his tongue was ruthless—circling, sucking, and teasing—just shy of giving me exactly what I needed. Every time I got close, he pulled back. Slowed. Started again. My thighs shook from the effort of holding still.

"Finn," I cried, twisting the sheets in my fists. "Please. Please, I'm so close—"

"That's the idea." He pressed a kiss to the inside of my thigh. "But you don't come until I say."

The tension coiled tighter. Desperate. Maddening.

He slid one thick finger inside me, crooking it just right. Then another. My body clenched around him.

He groaned. "You're ready to break. Fuck, you feel good like this."

"Please," I gasped again. "I need…God, I need you."

"You need to come," he corrected, adding a third finger, stretching me wider, and thrusting with merciless intent. "And you will. Right now."

His mouth returned to my clit. The second his tongue found that rhythm again, everything shattered. Pleasure tore through me in violent waves. I sobbed through it, shaking, my body collapsing forward onto the bed as I came around his fingers and tongue, my thighs twitching with the aftershocks.

But sweet hell, he didn't stop.

He licked me through it, his fingers pumping in perfect rhythm with the aftershocks still ripping through my core. He drew out every last tremor, every helpless spasm, until I was begging him to stop—then begging him not to.

"On your back, Lena," he ordered, his voice rough with restraint. "I want to see your face when I fuck you."

I obeyed, rolling over, chest still heaving, limbs boneless and wrecked from the orgasm he'd torn out of me. My body trembled, ruined in the best possible way.

He loomed above me with his fist wrapped tight around his cock, glistening with precum, his eyes dark and ravenous as they burned over me.

I drank him in. The carved lines of his body were a study in contrast—scars and strength, control and barely leashed need. His abs flexed with every shift, his broad chest gleamed with a sheen of sweat, and the powerful cut of his thighs framed a body built to dominate.

But it was the pale, jagged scar along his leg that held my gaze.

It was evidence of pain, a story of survival etched into his skin. An old wound that was nothing compared to the torment he carried in his heart. And somehow, it made him even more beautiful.

His expression was focused and ferocious. A man not just on the edge of desire but entirely consumed by it.

He gripped my legs and pushed them high, folding me open until my thighs pressed into my chest and my ankles rested over his shoulders. His body aligned with mine, the thick head of his cock dragging through the slick mess he'd already made of me.

The weight of his body, the possessive way he held me, sent a fresh surge of arousal crashing through me.

"You look wrecked already." He leaned forward, his breath spilling over my lips, his voice low and hungry. "Are you ready for more?"

My breath caught somewhere between the pressure of his body and the raw need building inside me. "Yes," I whispered, the sound breaking as it left me. "I want it. I want all of you."

His eyes darkened, and I felt him throb against me, the tension in his body coiling tighter.

"I'm yours, Finn," I breathed. "Take me."

He kissed me again, deeper this time, hungrier. I could taste myself on his tongue, feel the weight of his control in the way he held me—tight, unrelenting, and everywhere all at once.

His hands slid down my arms, gripping just below my elbows, pinning me to the bed. I couldn't move, couldn't reach for him, couldn't do anything but feel.

The thick head of his cock pressed against my entrance, and he paused there, hovering at the edge like he was savoring the tension between wanting and taking.

He didn't take his eyes off me as he started to push in, slow and relentless. The stretch burned in the best way, and a choked gasp slipped from my lips as my body struggled to make room for him. He kept going, inch by inch, until he was buried to the hilt, and I was shaking beneath the weight of him.

"You feel that?" His voice was a guttural rasp. "That stretch? The way your pussy strangles every fucking inch of my cock?"

A moan tore from my throat as my body clenched around him, instinctively holding him tight, like some part of me already understood there was no turning back.

"It's fucking perfect," he growled. "Just like the rest of you."

He drove forward, grinding his hips against me, pushing deeper—so deep it stole the breath from my lungs.

It was overwhelming, and for a heartbeat it bordered on too much.

But beneath the sting, beneath the pressure of being split wide around him, there was heat. Blistering, unbearable pleasure that made my muscles melt and my vision blur.

God, he felt incredible.

But all too soon, he was pulling out, leaving me empty, trembling, and desperate. The sudden absence coaxed a broken sound from my lips before I could stop it.

I didn't care how wrecked I sounded. I needed him.

He waited just long enough for my body to start begging on its own, then slammed back into me with one savage thrust that drove me straight into oblivion.

I cried out, my head tipping back as the force of it shattered what little control I had left.

"Mine," he growled, the word vibrating through me like it was another thrust.

He pulled out again, only to surge forward again. Harder this time. Deeper.

"Say it, Lena." His pace didn't slow. His grip didn't soften. "Fucking say it."

"Yours," I gasped, the word ripping from my throat without thought, without hesitation. "All yours."

A sound tore from his chest—raw, savage—then he drove into me again, more brutal than before. He didn't hold back. He filled me completely, every thrust stretching me wide, forcing my body to take him again and again. There was no patience, no mercy, just the relentless rhythm of him owning me from the inside out.

He fucked me like he had something to prove. Like he was branding me, claiming me, making sure I never forgot who I belonged to. Every stroke was punishing yet perfect, and all I could do was take it—held down, pinned open, and entirely his.

Each thrust came harder, sharper, like he was chasing something. But not his own release. No. He was building another in me. Like making me come again was the only thing that would satisfy the wildfire inside him.

He shifted his angle, wedging one hand between our bodies. His fingers found the place where we were joined, slick and aching, and a groan tore from his throat at the feel of it.

"Fuck, Lena," he breathed, his voice wrecked. "Do you feel what you do to me?"

His thumb circled my clit once, and I shattered.

The orgasm hit me like a violent surge, stealing my breath as my body locked around him. My cry echoed sharp and broken through the room, while my muscles seized, pulsing around his cock in frantic waves.

He groaned, his rhythm faltering. "Fucking hell, Lena—"

With a final, desperate thrust, he buried himself deep and came with a raw, guttural sound, spilling into me as he collapsed over my body.

Still inside me, he moved just enough to ease the strain on my legs, lowering them from where they'd been pinned to my chest. My thighs fell open around him, trembling and sated, draping loosely over his hips.

We stayed like that, panting and shaking, with our bodies locked together as the aftershocks rippled between us. His weight pressed me into the mattress, grounding me even as everything inside still spun.

His breath warmed the curve of my throat, each exhale unsteady. My hands slid into his hair, fingers tangling in the soft strands, savoring the contrast—tenderness after something so fierce, so consuming.

He pulled back, brushing my hair from my face, his thumb grazing my cheek. "You good?"

What I saw in his face went beyond softness—it was stripped bare, achingly intense, and unguarded. Like something had cracked open between us, and neither of us could pretend it hadn't.

"I don't think I've ever been this good in my entire life."

His gaze shifted, reverence etched into every hard line of his features, tempered only by the quiet glow of satisfaction. But beneath it, something stirred. Tension, maybe. Or restraint. Like he wanted this more than he should. Like he didn't trust what it meant.

Maybe I didn't either. Maybe that was the pull—the rush that hit too fast, too strong, like the first taste of something I already knew could ruin me.

I smiled up at him anyway. "What about you?"

The look he gave me said he already knew exactly what this was. How deep it ran. How dangerous it could become. For both of us.

But there was no doubt in his eyes. No sign of retreat. Only certainty and a quiet, unwavering devotion that wrapped around me like armor.

"Always," he murmured.

And then he kissed me—slow, deep, claiming—with his cock still inside me, and the whole damn world narrowing to just the two of us.

CHAPTER
TWENTY
FINN

THERE WAS nothing that stood out about the warehouse. And that was the point.

It blended in, plain and forgettable, just another slab of concrete in a stretch of industrial decay near the docks. Its walls were weathered by salt and time, the steel doors streaked with rust, and the surrounding asphalt fractured with years of wear.

Even the security cameras mounted at every corner looked standard—just enough to suggest someone cared, but not enough to invite a second glance.

Nothing that happened here was innocent.

Owned and operated by Rykov's Bratva, it held secrets most either couldn't stomach or wouldn't dare believe.

For Yelena, this place held the blood-soaked memories she was still healing from. A living nightmare she'd once numbed with drugs to survive.

For me, it was a previously unsolved mystery. The place where my wife was murdered.

Now I knew the truth. Rykov hadn't just killed Emily here—he'd made Yelena watch. He'd chained her to him through fear and spectacle, a display of power that left her helpless as her grandfather was executed the same night.

The ghosts in this place weren't imagined. For us, they were real.

But we hadn't come to exorcise them. We'd come to watch the living. To track Sasha, Rykov's second in command, and spy on the men who still moved in and out of this place, like it didn't reek of blood and betrayal. To figure out a way to take our enemy down.

For the third day, I watched the warehouse through binoculars, crouched on the edge of a rooftop a block over. Beside me, Yelena sat cross-legged on the gravel, field-stripping the Glock I'd given her with practiced ease. No wasted motion. No uncertainty. Like her hands had done this a thousand times, and her mind was already on the kill.

She hadn't spoken much since we'd started coming here. Not a word since we'd climbed onto this roof hours ago. Her shoulders were tight, her jaw was locked, and any trace of softness was buried.

She was using the weapon to ground herself. Something clean and mechanical. Her hands moved with clinical precision, but I knew what it was costing her to be here. I understood the old triggers this place unearthed from the dark.

I fucking hated bringing her back, but she'd been determined to face it. And there was no way in hell I was leaving her behind.

She handed the 9mm to me without a word so I could check her work—perfect, again.

"You sure you've never touched a gun before?" I checked the chamber out of habit, even though I already knew it was flawless.

Yelena shrugged, her mouth twitching. "Just the ones aimed at me."

That earned her a sharp look, and the briefest flare of something primal in my gut. I didn't like her answer. Not because it shocked me, but because I could picture it all too easily.

"Not funny," I muttered, setting the gun down.

She arched a delicate brow. "A little funny."

I leaned in, close enough that her smile faltered. "You keep learning at this pace, and you'll be outmaneuvering me in no time."

"I'm trying." Her voice softened, turning compliant, and making my pulse hitch. "You're a good teacher."

"Careful." I brushed my fingers over her jaw. "Say that like you mean it, and I'll make you repeat the lesson in private."

"Maybe I'd like that." Her bottom lip disappeared between her teeth in a teasing, challenging little bite.

Fuck me.

Every instinct warred between dragging her into my lap to take what I craved and shielding her from the hell we were about to walk into. Instead, I reached past her and slipped the Glock back into her holster, my fingers lingering on her thigh.

"Come on." I rose from my crouch and jerked my chin toward the roof access door.

The sun was relentless against the exposed metal, and we'd been up here long enough to feel it searing through our clothes.

She slung her bag over one shoulder and fell in behind me, silent. I scanned the landing below, made sure it was clear, then led us down the rusted stairwell with practiced caution.

We descended into the skeletal remains of what used to be a packing floor. The air cooled instantly, and shadows swallowed the noise from outside.

Cracked concrete. Splintered beams. Broken glass underfoot. We were too far to keep eyes on the target—not that it mattered. We'd spent days watching from the rooftop with nothing to show for it.

"Stance." I motioned her forward.

She dropped her bag and squared up, lifting her weapon into both hands. Her form was solid and focused, but still too tight through the shoulders.

"Relax." I moved in behind her, setting my hand at the base of her neck. "You don't need to strangle it."

She huffed. "You're the one who told me to grip it like I mean it."

"I did. But tension and control aren't the same thing." My hands slid down her arms to her wrists, adjusting her grip as I went. "You're strong," I murmured in her ear. "Let the weapon feel that. Don't force it."

Her breath caught, but the tightness in her frame softened.

"Good." My hand settled just above her hip. "Now show me again. Smooth and controlled."

She lowered the gun, shook out her arms, then reset her stance—steady, fluid, and exactly as I'd taught her.

Silence stretched between us, charging the narrow space with more than heat. It pulsed with something sharper, both electric and volatile. A current that ran soul deep.

My voice dropped low as I leaned in, rumbling from my chest to her spine. "Still want that private lesson?"

"Isn't that what we're doing now?" Her tone dripped with sass, but her body told another story. She arched toward me, her thighs shifting with restless urgency, like she was already reaching for me, aching for more.

With my hand clamped on her waist, I forced her still. "Now turn and point it at me."

She dropped her aim with a jolt. "What?"

"You heard me." I stepped in front of her, slow and calculated, until we stood face to face. "Raise the gun and point it at my chest. Like you mean it."

"Finn." Her lips parted around my name, soft and uncertain. Like she was caught between defiance and the urge to please me.

"Do it."

Doubt crossed her beautiful features, and a tremor passed through her hands.

"It's not loaded. You know that. I know that. But you still need to feel what it's like to aim at someone. To hold that power."

Her gaze filled with steely resolve, and with a sharp nod, she raised the 9mm as though she'd done it a million times. Shoulders squared. Grip firm. Eyes locked on mine. She aimed her weapon at my chest, squeezed the trigger, and pierced my fucking heart. No ammunition required.

I held still for a moment, letting her sit with the aftermath of the choice she'd just made. Watching as the weight of it settled into her bones. Until a tiny smirk of satisfaction crooked the corner of her lips.

Then I moved.

I snapped one hand to her wrist, wrenching it wide, while the other pried the Glock from her grip and dropped it to her bag on the floor. It hit the canvas with a dull thud that echoed through the hollow space like a warning.

She gasped, mouth dropping open. Before she could steady herself, I spun her around and bent her over an old packing table, her cheek meeting scarred wood. I grabbed both wrists and pinned them behind her back in one hand, locking her in place.

"No weapon in the world," I rasped against her neck, "is going to make you stronger than me."

"I-I wasn't trying—"

"I know." I flexed my fingers around her wrists, firm and unyielding. "It's a fucking lesson, Lena. One you need to remember."

I ground my hips against her ass, the hard line of my cock pressing along the seam of her jeans. She moaned, helpless and wanton, and the sound hit me like gasoline thrown on an open flame.

"You want to be dangerous?" I reached around to pop the button on her pants, then shoved them down, baring her to the cool air. "Learn this…"

My fingers slid between her thighs, finding her slick and hot, just like I knew she'd be.

"Anyone can aim a gun," I murmured, teasing slow circles over her clit. "Anyone can pull a trigger. But only you can outplay him. Out-survive him."

"Yes," she gasped, her voice rough with need. "Yes."

I tore my hand away, already aching to feel her from the inside. My zipper came down with a quick drag of teeth, and I freed myself, fisting the base of my cock to stave off the edge.

Fuck control, it could wait.

What I needed more than anything was to feel her come apart.

Still holding her wrists tight, I dropped over her, my mouth at her ear and my cock notched at her entrance. "You don't need a weapon, Lena. You are one."

I drove into her, claiming every inch.

She cried out and bucked, her head snapping back and hips tilting as far as my grip would allow.

Fuck, she was already close. I could feel it in every quiver, every desperate clench.

I pounded into her without mercy, fucking her like

she belonged to me—to break, to worship, to remake—proving it with filthy, punishing thrusts.

"You feel that?" I rasped, palming her ass, pulling her back into every stroke. "That's your body begging for me. It fucking knows who it belongs to."

She whimpered something unintelligible, too far gone to speak, too wrecked to pretend she wasn't already mine.

"Give it to me," I growled. "Let me feel it."

Her whole body locked up, her muscles clenching so hard I nearly lost it with her. A cry tore from her throat —part moan, part broken sob—as the orgasm slammed into her. She came apart around me, pulsing and trembling, every inch of her slick with heat and surrender.

I fucked her through it, dragging out every spasm, every shiver, until she collapsed against the table, spent.

Finally, I let go of her wrists, grabbed her hips, and drove into her one last time, chasing the edge that threatened to snap me. My balls tightened, my release rushing up hard and fast.

"Fuck, Lena."

I pulled out at the last second, my cock slick and twitching. One hand kept her bent over, her ass arched just right as I stroked myself, needing to see it.

Needing her marked.

I came hard, spilling across her lower back and the curve of her ass—hot, messy, perfect. Chest heaving and my cock still pulsing in my palm, I stood and watched my cum drip down her skin.

Mine. All fucking mine.

She looked back over her shoulder, eyes wet, tears streaking silently down her cheeks. Not sobbing or panicked—steady and raw, like something had cracked open inside her, and I hadn't noticed until it was already bleeding.

The rush in my veins turned cold.

"Lena." I was already moving, already tucking myself back into my jeans and reaching for her. Gently. So fucking gently.

She flinched when I touched her—not a full recoil, but enough to gut me.

"I'm sorry." My voice was hoarse. "Was it too much?"

She wiped her face with the back of her hand and shook her head. "No…it's not that."

Fuck. Why didn't I believe her?

Maybe because I couldn't stand seeing her like this. Not after everything I'd promised.

I brushed her hair back from her face. "Talk to me."

She only shook her head again, fingers still scrubbing at her cheeks, smearing the wetness but never quite stopping it.

"Did I hurt you?"

"No. You didn't hurt me," she whispered, her lips trembling. "I just...I don't know. It hit me all at once."

An ache spread deep in my chest. Fuck, I'd been so caught up in how good she felt, how much I wanted her, I hadn't stopped to ask if she could handle it. Especially here, like this—with ghosts still clinging to every shadow around us.

I pulled her into my arms, still half-dressed and shaking. I held her as though my touch could fix whatever damage I'd done. Like I could shield her from the fucked-up mess I'd created.

"I've got you," I murmured into her hair. "You're safe. You hear me?"

She nodded against my chest, her breath finally slowing and the tremble in her limbs fading little by little. But I kept my arms wrapped around her, my body still tense with the weight of what I'd done.

What we'd done.

When she finally pulled back, it was just enough to look up at me. "I'm not used to…receiving."

The words hit low in my gut, stoking the rage that was always there, waiting.

She swallowed, her eyes flicking away. "I think I've always believed sex meant I had to give something. My body. My silence. My approval. Whatever it took to be wanted. To not feel so fucking alone…"

Her voice trailed off, but it wasn't fear or doubt holding her back. It was a quiet gathering of courage.

She straightened her shoulders, curled her fingers against my chest, and looked me in the eyes. "You don't take from me, Finn. You give. Even when you're rough. Even when it's too much. You give until I forget what it felt like to be nothing."

A hard, hollow ache opened under my ribs.

I wrapped my hand around the back of her neck, anchoring us together. "I see you, Lena. Every bruised, battered, and broken piece. Even the parts you think you've lost." Forehead to hers, I breathed, "You're not nothing. You never were. And I'll keep giving until you believe it. Until you can't forget it, even if you try."

Silence settled between us again. This time, it wasn't sharp or fragile. It was full. Real.

And I held on to it with both fucking hands.

When I tugged my shirt off over my head, she blinked up at me, confused. Then I dropped to my knees behind her and started wiping her down. Gentle and methodical, not a trace of shame in it.

She stayed quiet while I cleaned the mess off her skin. Some part of her seemed to understand this wasn't about fixing anything. It was about care. About giving her a reason to trust me.

When I was done, I pressed a kiss to the small of her back and stood.

"I've got a clean shirt in the van," I said, already zipping up. "Stay here for a second."

She nodded, tugging up her pants without a word.

By the time I returned, she was strapping a holster to her thigh like nothing had happened. But the way she looked at me—like I'd given her something she didn't know she needed—said otherwise.

"You ready for more?" I asked, motioning to her weapon.

A relieved smile graced her perfect lips.

I helped her back into position, working her through her stance again—feet apart, shoulders down, and elbows soft but steady.

"You're still gripping too high," I murmured, stepping behind her to adjust her hands. "Don't strangle it. Own it."

She smirked. "That sounds kinky."

"Damn right," I said with a laugh.

I showed her how I'd disarmed her earlier. This time, I did it slowly, guiding her wrist, showing her where she'd left herself open and how to shift out of it.

She watched every move with laser focus, her body tense and breath measured.

We ran it a few more times, and she improved with each pass, leaning into it like she was born to do this.

And then, without needing to say anything, we both turned and walked back up to the roof. Back to the surveillance. Back to waiting for Rykov's men to show.

The heat outside was just as heavy—oil, rust, and something darker humming in the air. But this time, the silence between us wasn't strained.

It was focused. United.

She spotted the movement before I did.

"Two cars," she said, pointing toward the east gate. "Blacked-out SUVs, same make Sasha's crew drives."

I raised the binoculars again. "Shit. You're right."

She was already reaching for the camera, adjusting the zoom with practiced ease. No hesitation. No emotion. Like the heat between us, the tears, the brutal fuck in that empty warehouse had all been sealed away and stored someplace safe.

What remained in her was sharp, calm, and deadly.

It was power.

And fuck, it made me smile.

She clicked a few shots, clean and steady. "Got plates on the second one."

"You're not shaken," I said.

"Should I be?" The question wasn't rhetorical. It wasn't exactly innocent either.

I studied her—the way the light kissed her cheekbone, the set of her mouth, the determination in her eyes. It didn't look like adrenaline. It looked like purpose.

"You ever think maybe you're too good at this?"

She turned to me with an unreadable gaze. "Are you worried I'm becoming like them?"

"No. I'm worried I'm getting too used to having you with me."

Because I was. And because some part of me—maybe the part that had already fallen fast and fucking hard—still couldn't tell if letting her get close to Sasha was a brilliant strategy or an insane gamble I'd live to regret.

CHAPTER
TWENTY-ONE
YELENA

THE NIGHT AIR was cooler than before, but the silence between us felt heavier. I sat cross-legged near the rooftop ledge, binoculars clutched tight in my hands, tracking the movement around the warehouse below.

We were at the same building, with the same vantage point, but everything felt different tonight.

Yesterday had shifted something between us—not just the physical, though that alone had left its marks. No, this was something deeper. Unspoken but undeniable.

A new, raw thing had been unearthed between us, and now we were both pretending we hadn't seen it.

Finn hadn't said much since we got into position, but he didn't need to. The tension coming off him was thick enough to feel across the space between us. Was it because of what we were watching, or what we weren't saying?

Just after midnight, two SUVs pulled in, their

engines humming low as they rolled toward the east entrance. Men spilled out with practiced precision, moving like they'd done it a hundred times before.

They obviously weren't afraid to be seen.

I zeroed in on the loading dock. Wooden crates stacked beside the open bay door. No obvious labels. Just quiet, methodical movement and the occasional nod passed between men.

It was too smooth. Too careful.

I couldn't shake the feeling that we were only watching the surface of something that was a heck of a lot more dangerous than it seemed. Which was terrifying, since we were already assuming it was deadly.

"This doesn't look like one of Sasha's usual drops."

"No." A dark expression crossed Finn's features. "And that's not his usual crew. I don't recognize any of these guys."

Neither did I, and that unsettled me more than I wanted to admit.

Even during the year Nik kept me under his thumb, he never hid his operations from me. No, he flaunted it. Bragged about every deal, every shipment, every loyal soldier he had at his back.

As if reminding me of his power would not only keep me in line but was somehow its own form of seduction.

A series of sharp clicks cut through the silence as Finn snapped photos with the rooftop camera. He focused on one of the men who unlatched a crate and lifted the lid just enough to shine a flashlight inside.

"Can you see what's in it?" I asked.

"Not from this angle."

He reached for his phone, wasting no time as he pulled up his most recent contact. His jaw hardened as he waited for the line to connect.

Robin's voice crackled through the speaker, sharp and alert. "I'm here. Talk to me."

"I'm sending images. We've got crates going into the Bratva warehouse. The men on-site aren't familiar. Can you run them?"

"On it. Hold on."

There was a pause as the files went through, followed by the rhythmic clatter of keystrokes on her end.

The tension between Finn and me narrowed as we waited. It was pulled tight by silence, both of us watching the warehouse like it might give up all its secrets if we stared long enough.

"That's a no," Robin said, finally. "Facial recognition came up blank. No known affiliations. No flags. Whoever these men are, they're ghosts."

"Shit." Finn dragged a hand over the back of his neck, tension bleeding through the motion. "Okay. Keep me posted."

"Wait," Robin cut in before he could hang up. "I've been hearing chatter. Bowen Alexander's been expanding. He's been doing it quietly, but aggressively. Bringing in new guys with no paper trails. If they're not Bratva, they might be his."

Finn went still beside me.

"Bowen Alexander?" It was a name I knew too well. "You mean the man who bankrolled Nik's takeover of the Bratva? The guy who played kingmaker while pretending to be nothing more than a bored billionaire with a power complex?"

Finn's head snapped toward me, the look in his eyes letting me know I'd shocked him.

His expression also said there was more to the story. A lot more. And whatever it was, he wasn't sharing it with me.

"Yeah, he's a rich prick. A dangerous one." Robin's voice cut through the moment of uneasy silence. "Finn, you still have that contact. The one who used to run security for Bowen. If anyone knows these guys, it's him."

Finn sat like a statue, his face a mask of fury and... was that fear?

"Who's she talking about?" I asked, my stomach sinking.

"Law," Robin answered when Finn didn't.

His fingers flexed tighter around the phone. Finally, he muttered, "I haven't spoken to him in more than a year."

"That doesn't mean he won't pick up," Robin said. "He's still tied to Bowen. Might even be your fastest way to confirm the connection."

"Or he tells Bowen I'm sniffing around."

"He won't." Robin's tone grew gentle, balancing Finn's hard edges. "If something's happening with Rykov, he'll know. And you need to know too."

Finn ended the call with a sharp flick of his thumb.

Questions pressed at the edges of my mind, but I didn't ask. Whatever history he had with this Law person felt too raw, too complicated to touch.

Fifteen minutes later, Finn's phone lit up with an incoming call. He stared at the screen for a moment longer than usual, then answered with a sigh, putting it on speaker. "Yeah."

"Didn't think I'd ever hear from you again," a man replied, his voice like gravel. "Did you finally run out of options?"

"Nice to hear from you, too, Law."

A deep chuckle reverberated over the speaker. "What do you want?"

"I'm sending you some photos. I need names or affiliations. Whatever you can give me."

"Since when do you need my help?"

Finn hit send. "Since guys I've never seen before showed up at Rykov's warehouse."

The silence that followed cut clean and cold, like the moment before a storm.

When Law finally came back, his voice was tight and wary-sounding. "Yeah, they're Bowen's men. New hires—mercs, and one or two ex-military. No records, no real questionable history. Nothing that would draw the kind of attention we like to avoid. I didn't know what Bowen brought them in for…until now."

Finn's voice dropped. "So it's real. Bowen and Rykov."

"Looks like it," Law said. "But we both knew this was coming."

They knew—what? I'd never felt more in the dark.

Finn nodded, calm and unreadable, like none of it surprised him at all.

"Guess Bowen's not just backing Rykov anymore," Law continued. "Looks like he's stepping into full partnership. And together? They've got the means for Cartel-level reach—trafficking, weapons, whatever. They can take over the whole city."

Finn let out a slow breath, the weight of it dragging the word from his mouth. "Shit."

"I warned you," Law said. "Told you chasing Rykov was trouble."

"You did."

"Be careful," Law added, his voice dropping with something that sounded a heck of a lot like concern. "If Bowen's all in, this isn't just a Bratva war anymore. It's consolidation. And you know what that means."

"No witnesses." Finn's knuckles had gone white, gripping the phone like he was ready to break it.

"Don't get yourself killed, Decker."

The call ended without another word. No goodbye. No reassurances. Just the cold confirmation that the threat was real—even if we still didn't know what it meant for us, how far it would reach, or how it might derail our plan.

The warehouse below had gone quiet again. The SUVs were gone. Crates sealed inside. Shadows back in place.

"We're running out of time, aren't we?" I asked, a prickle crawling across my skin.

"No. This changes nothing. We stick to the plan—cozy up to Sasha, pretend you're looking for a way back in. Find out what the hell they're up to, if we can. Burn Rykov to the fucking ground."

But his denial didn't ease my anxiety. Especially not when the look in his eyes contradicted every ferocious word.

We made our way back to the van in silence, like two soldiers trying to hold the line against something already too big to stop.

The quiet between us wasn't just tactical. It felt really damn personal.

Because while the truth about Bowen had hit hard, it wasn't the only thing gnawing at me. The interaction with Law proved Finn had a history I didn't know about. Connections he still hadn't bothered to share.

Secrets he hadn't trusted me with.

Maybe it shouldn't have mattered—not with everything we were facing, and not when the physical bond we shared was so real. So solid.

But it did.

If we were really in this together, then why did it still feel like he was holding something back? And why did his secrets feel more dangerous than what was waiting for us inside that warehouse?

As we drove back toward the apartment, the weight in my chest didn't ease. If anything, it deepened. Not because of the new men we'd seen tonight.

It was because of the man beside me.

Headlights and neon signs streaked past outside, the city a blur of light and shadows, but inside the van, the air was thick with everything we hadn't said.

Finn's grip on the wheel stayed iron-tight, his jaw locked in a way that said he wasn't just focused, he was waiting for me to say something. Ask the questions he hadn't answered. Demand the truth he wasn't offering.

"You're not going to tell me about him, are you?"

His eyes kept focused on the road. "About who?"

"Law."

The silence that followed spoke louder than any answer he could've given me.

"He sounded rough." I willed my voice to hold steady, despite the pain lancing through it. "But not heartless. He didn't have to warn you about Bowen. Right?"

Finn's dry laugh was brittle at the edges. "He warned me a long time ago. Told me I was taking unnecessary risks. That it would all catch up with me someday."

"And I'm guessing you didn't listen?"

"Of course I didn't fucking listen. I let my pride win, and I didn't stop until it was too fucking late." He flexed his fingers over the wheel. "He and I were close once. But he wanted money and a spot at Bowen's side. All I wanted was you."

My breath caught, something fragile and aching opening wide in my chest.

"And now?" I turned toward him, not fully sure

what I was asking. Maybe where he stood with Law. Or maybe, how he felt about me.

He'd made it clear he wanted me. Had obsessed over me. But now he had me, and I still had no clue what it meant to him. Did his feelings run even half as deep as mine?

He'd said once we started, we'd be together. But did that just mean I was a bigger part of the plan now? Or were we something more?

"Now I'm dragging you through the same fire he tried to warn me away from." His voice didn't waver, and he didn't even glance my way.

Despite the words, he was cool and calm, as always.

I turned to the view out my window, hiding the pressure that squeezed around my middle.

He must've known I wasn't just asking about Law. But instead of bridging the gap between us, he deflected. Offered logic instead of feeling. More distance instead of clarity.

"He knew who those men were. That must count for something," I said, pushing hard against the fear that was trying to drag me under.

"It does," he agreed. "It means Rykov's not just rebuilding his empire. He's evolving it. Turning it into something more dangerous than any of us have seen before."

"And Law? Do you trust him?"

"I don't know whose side he's on, but he called. And after all the shit he and I have been through, it's more than I expected."

I leaned my head against the glass and watched the streetlights race past. "Seems like everyone's got ghosts," I murmured.

"Yeah." Finn reached across the console, found my hand, and laced our fingers together.

Even with fear and doubt clawing at my insides—despite the fracture in my trust—I held on.

And I didn't let go.

CHAPTER
TWENTY-TWO
YELENA

THE CITY FELT different without Finn beside me. It was quieter, less vibrant, somehow.

But not safer. No, this was the farthest thing from safe. Every step echoed with risk. Every shadow tugged at my nerves. I felt eyes burning through me with every slow-moving car and every glance that lingered too long.

I kept moving anyway.

This wasn't just a test. I was proving to myself that I could move through the world without Finn at my side. That I could stand on my own if I ever had to.

He said we were in this together. Made me promise him *always*. And I believed him. I did.

But belief didn't erase every flicker of doubt. There were still too many unanswered questions—things that hadn't been said out loud. Secrets he was holding on to that coiled like knots in my stomach.

And I still kept going.

If I were going to walk into that warehouse and into Sasha's circle—if I had any hope of luring Nik into our trap—I couldn't afford the slightest hesitation. I had to be ready. Not just to follow Finn, but to stand beside him.

Even if I had to get there on my own.

The sun was barely over the horizon, and the last traces of starlight clung to the fading edge of night. It was both comforting and unnerving to know the sky would be fully lit by the time I reached my destination. I wouldn't have to fear what lurked in the shadows, but I'd also lose the safety of disappearing into them.

My steps faltered at the thought, but only for a moment. Now wasn't the time to lose focus. The longer I waited, the longer it would take to put our plan into motion. And every delay meant more time away from Anya.

More time with Nik out there, breathing free.

With new urgency driving me, I picked up my pace, jogging the final block to where we'd parked the van. It started easily, and I didn't think twice as I pulled into early morning traffic, heading toward the Red Hook docks.

Yes, this was undeniably dangerous. Maybe even a bit foolish. But the closer I got, the more confidence surged in me.

It was almost terrifying how good it felt to move through the city, not as a captive or a liability, but as someone with purpose. Someone with a burgeoning power that was all her own.

Parking a few streets away, I walked the last stretch, hood up and a bottle of water in hand. I picked a spot on a nearby bench and watched. Waited.

The longer I pretended to be a casual observer, the higher my pulse climbed, not with panic but with anticipation. If this worked—if I could get close to Sasha without tipping my hand—it would be the first real move in a game I'd been forced to play blind for far too long. This time, the board would be mine.

For once, I wasn't playing to survive the threat.

I was becoming one.

My line of sight to the east gate of the warehouse was clear. Nothing moved. The lot was mostly bare, just a rusty truck and a few shipping crates stacked along the fence. No blacked-out SUVs. No men lingering in the shadows.

But I wasn't naïve enough to think it was empty.

I didn't have Finn's training. Didn't have his instincts, his discipline, or that lethal calm he wore like a second skin. But I'd spent days watching him work. Weeks observing him move around the forest like danger couldn't touch him.

It had taught me more than I expected. How to look without being seen. How to notice what wasn't happening as much as what was. When to move. When to wait. When to call in backup.

And there was something I hadn't dared admit, even to myself.

I knew this world. I always had.

Maybe even better than Finn.

Years at Nik's side had trained me in ways I hadn't fully understood until now. Even before that, growing up in the Bratva, born into power but kept just outside its reach, I'd absorbed everything. The silent language of danger. The codes spoken with and without words. The difference between a man on a smoke break and one keeping watch.

It was already inside me, buried beneath years of fear and abuse, straining to surface. And that scared me.

Not because I didn't know what to do with it.

Because I did.

Movement caught my eye near the far end of the lot. A figure stepped out from behind one of the loading bays, head high, shoulders squared. I was too far away to make out his face, but I recognized the walk—that arrogant, unhurried gait, moving like the world should make way for him.

Sasha.

I straightened without thinking. My breath snagged, and my gaze narrowed.

He didn't linger. He was already moving for the back gate when a black SUV eased in, as if they'd timed it. Had he been in there all night?

If so, what the hell had he been doing?

The back door opened before he reached it, and he slid inside with ease. A second later, the SUV pulled away, vanishing into the waking city.

I kept staring long after it disappeared.

So the intel had been right. He really was here, still running things from the spot where everything had been torn apart. Where loved ones had died, and my free will had been stolen.

It didn't surprise me. If anything, it etched the plan deeper into my bones. We weren't guessing anymore. This was real.

I could do this.

Even with Bowen Alexander's new men in the mix. Even with fear still crawling under my skin like an old scar that refused to fade.

I was done hiding in shadows. Done cowering. I'd made it this far.

And I'd done it alone.

With every passing minute, that fragile new confidence began to calcify into something stronger. Not just readiness. Resolve.

Still watching the spot where Sasha's SUV disappeared, I heard a car pull up behind me. I didn't have to turn around to know it was Finn.

The engine cut. A door opened. Slow, measured footsteps approached.

He said nothing as he moved to stand beside my bench, outrage radiating off him in heavy, silent waves.

"Nice morning for a drive," I said, keeping my eyes fixed ahead and my voice casual, even as my pulse raced.

Silence stretched, and my neck prickled.

Maybe realizing I wasn't going to cave, he growled, "You want to tell me what the fuck you think you're doing?"

I took a slow sip of my water before answering, "Testing myself."

"Are you fucking kidding me?"

"What?" I said with a shrug. "I came here to watch. It was going great until now."

"You didn't even bring a goddamn weapon."

"I wasn't planning to need one."

He moved closer, crowding me with his anger. "You came back to the warehouse where Nik took everything from you. Where Sasha's crew still operates. Alone. No backup. No warning. That's not a test, Yelena. That's a fucking death wish."

I stood, my newfound confidence rising to meet his displeasure. "I wasn't trying to be reckless or cut you out. I just needed to know I could handle it. That I could walk the same streets Nik walks without falling apart."

His ocean-blue eyes searched mine for a long, tense moment. I had no clue what he was looking for or whether he'd found it. He simply turned and started back toward the car.

With my conviction still intact, I chose to follow.

The door slammed shut behind me, sealing us in— the air charged with heat, secrets, and fury.

He didn't look at me. Jaw flexing, he shoved the car into gear and pulled away, the sharp turn making the tires groan.

Only after we'd cleared the block did he speak again, his voice low and tight. "What if Sasha had been there? What if he'd seen you?"

"He was there," I said, watching the flicker of surprise cross his face. "And he didn't notice me."

"But he could have."

I clenched my fists, holding back my sudden temper. "I'm not your burden, Finn. You don't get to keep me out of this because it makes you feel better."

"You are part of this," he snapped. "That's the fucking problem. Because now I have to worry that the person I'm relying on is going to blow our whole operation just to prove she doesn't need me."

I leaned toward him, close enough to feel the heat coming off him as my seatbelt pulled uncomfortably across my chest. "Don't pretend this is just about the plan."

His gaze darted toward me. "It's not."

The space between us stilled, thick with frustration and something darker. Something needier.

"You're scared," I whispered, the realization hitting hard.

"No, Lena. I'm fucking furious. I honestly thought you were done being self-destructive."

"It's not like that at all." My voice broke before I could stop it. "I'm trying to become someone who can survive this. Someone who can fight."

"You think I don't see that?" His expression tightened. Was it anger or pain? "You think I haven't watched you claw your way back from hell?" He stared out the windshield, his hands flexing around the wheel like he wanted to wrap them around someone's neck. "I've seen it, Lena. Every fucking step. And it kills me that you've had to go through that." He swallowed hard. "Because I keep thinking, what if I'm the one who breaks you next? What if I push you too far, or don't pull you back when I should? What if letting you walk into that warehouse is the thing that gets you killed?"

The words landed like a heavy fist, and for a long moment I could only stare at him, stunned by the rawness he usually kept buried under all that quiet control.

"You're not the one who broke me, Finn," I said when I could finally speak again. "And you're not going to be the one who saves me either."

He sucked in a sharp breath, his gaze locking on mine, intense and unguarded.

"I don't need saving. I just need you to trust me."

He reached out, slipped his hand to my nape, threaded his fingers into my hair, and drew me toward him. Not rough. Not demanding. Just real.

He pressed his lips to my forehead and held me until I relaxed, my head resting on his shoulder.

I closed my eyes, letting the silence hold us both. Letting him hold me.

"Next time," he murmured, "you take me with you."

A smile stole across my lips. "Next time, don't try to stop me."

CHAPTER
TWENTY-THREE
FINN

THE PLAN WAS RISKY. Manipulative as hell. But it would work.

Fuck, it had to work. If it didn't…

No. I couldn't let my mind go there. Not after this morning. Not after watching her stand her ground with fire in her eyes and defiance in her voice, refusing to be protected or sidelined.

She didn't want to be saved. She wanted in.

And I wanted her that way. Dangerous and determined. Capable of walking into the fire and coming out scorched but alive.

She'd told me to trust her, and I did.

God fucking help me, I do.

But trust didn't silence the voice in my head that tracked her every move, wondering if I'd pushed her too fast. If throwing her back into the fire so soon would be the thing that finally broke her. Or got her killed.

She sat across from me at the table, legs tucked

under her, hair still damp from a rushed shower, and eyes locked on the laptop screen like it owed her answers. Pure, sharpened focus.

She wasn't the woman I'd pulled out of Rykov's prison. Hell, she wasn't even the woman I bent over that warehouse table two days ago. She was steel now.

And every part of her demanded to be reckoned with.

I watched her work as Robin's voice came through the speaker, smooth and detached. "I can bounce the signal through six or seven dead accounts, ghost the IP trail so it looks like it's coming from a secure Bratva channel. Rykov will think someone in his network is feeding him intel."

"And the message?" Yelena asked, already typing.

"That's on you," Robin said. "It should be bait without sounding like it is. Something desperate enough to seem real. Tempting enough to hook him."

I nodded. "Make him think you're ready to come back. That you're scared. Or cornered."

Yelena didn't blink as her fingers flew over the keyboard. "He always did prefer me weak."

"You sure you're okay to do this?" Robin asked, voicing my unspoken concern.

The keyboard went silent as Yelena's fingers hovered in midair. Her bottom lip disappeared between her teeth, but only for a moment. It slipped out clean—no more habitual biting or intentional self-mutilation. She was in control.

And fuck, it looked good on her.

"It won't be the first lie he wanted to believe about me." Her brows drew together. "Trust me, this is the easy part."

Easy. Was that bravery or trauma talking?

Either way, I believed her.

If the pause on the other end of the line was any indication, so did Robin. When she finally spoke again, her tone shifted to something quieter, laced with awe. "You know him better than any of us, Yelena. You'll get it right."

Her words twisted deep in my gut.

Robin was right. Yelena did know him—intimately. She could weaponize their history, every keystroke carrying the weight of her past.

I hated that we had to use it. That we had to use her. Fuck, if we weren't careful, this whole mission could jeopardize all her progress.

But there was no other way.

We worked the rest of the afternoon, building our trap and the trail that would lead Rykov into it. We walked through every layer of the plan, dissecting it from all sides, anticipating every possible complication and every variable that could throw it off.

Robin worked on Yelena's fabricated message, embedding metadata and layering just enough digital noise to make it convincing.

"Message is out," Robin confirmed.

There was no dramatic fanfare. No explosion of fireworks or code-red alarms. Just silence and the sun dipping behind buildings as the sky turned to dusk.

Yelena stood and crossed to the window, her arms folded and her profile etched in the last streaks of sunlight. She didn't look scared or even worried. She looked composed. Like she was gathering her strength and preparing to step into the fight.

This wasn't a bluff. It was a war cry.

And we'd just fired the first shot.

Robin's voice came through the speaker again, quieter this time. "How's she doing? Really."

I reached for the phone, lifting it from the table and taking her off speaker, my gaze still locked on Yelena's silhouette. "Hold on."

With one last glance, I stepped into the hallway, moving far enough away that Yelena wouldn't overhear the things Robin was about to ask.

"She's steady," I murmured once I was sure we were alone. "Sharp. Focused."

"Right. And you?"

I only grunted. Not because I didn't know what to say, but because admitting it out loud felt dangerous. Like naming it would make it real.

What would be the point anyway? Robin already knew the fucking answer.

She sighed. "You sound like hell."

"Comes with the territory."

Finally, she steered the conversation where I'd known it was headed all along. "If this doesn't land the way we need it to—if things start to slide—you sure you don't want to call in Law?"

"No." My grip tightened around the phone.

"Finn—"

"It's been a year. Since Emily died. Since I left without a fucking word to him about it."

"I know."

"We were on the same crew." I paced down the hall and back again, but the motion didn't ease the tension in my spine. "Ate shit together. Bled together. Got our hands dirty for Bowen. He covered me more times than I can count, and I did the same for him."

"So call him." Her voice was quiet but firm.

"He's still in it. Still working for Bowen. Still neck-deep in that world."

"So were you." There was no judgment from her, only truth.

"But I got out," I argued. "He didn't. And if this goes sideways? If we misstep even once, Law won't have the luxury of picking sides. He'll protect Bowen the same way I used to."

"You think he'd sell you out?"

"I think he'd survive. That's always been his priority. And fuck, I can't blame him for that."

"He might surprise you."

She didn't get it. Or maybe she was just a hell of a lot more optimistic about this world and the people in it than I was.

"Yeah. Or he might cut my throat just to prove he hasn't gone soft."

Robin's answering sigh was equal parts frustration and weariness. "Just be careful, please. You've already lost too much. We both have."

The line went dead, and for a moment I just stood, silence pressing in like the guilt and rage I could never outrun.

By the time I stepped back into the apartment, the sun had vanished, dusk settling as long shadows bled across the room.

Yelena was still at the window, framed by the glow of the streetlights. I stepped in behind her, sliding my arms around her waist, and she leaned into me like she'd been waiting for my touch the entire time.

"We just told him where to find me," she whispered.

"No." My lips found her temple, the warmth of her skin anchoring me. "We're going to him with a loaded deck. Yes, it's risky. He might see through it. We might light ourselves up just by getting close. But Robin's covering our tracks. And all we need is for him to poke his head out."

She turned in my arms, lifting her gaze to mine. "Do you think we're ready?"

"You are."

Her brows drew together, a flicker of concern tightening her beautiful expression. "What about you?"

"I won't let him touch you." It wasn't much of an answer, but it was all I could give without letting the utter fucking terror claw its way out of me.

I kissed her forehead first. Then her cheek. Then the soft corner of her mouth. Each one, a gentle reminder of what we were doing this for.

What we stood to lose.

Her eyes stayed on mine, steady and unflinching,

holding something raw and resolute in their depths. And when I leaned in again, finding her mouth with mine, the kiss we shared was slow and grounding. Lingering. Like we had time to waste, like we hadn't just struck a match and set the world around us on fire.

She kissed me back with quiet desperation. Measured but full of all the things I felt—gratitude, fear, want. And something deeper that I couldn't say out loud.

At least not until I knew we were in the clear. Not until Rykov was dead and fucking buried and I knew I wouldn't lose her.

But for now, I could show her.

My hands slid up her back, under the hem of her shirt, my palms flattening against her warm skin. She breathed in sharply when I pressed her closer, her body molding to mine like it was the only place she belonged.

The kiss deepened. Still unhurried, but heavier now. Weighted with certainty and need.

Her fingers gripped around the back of my neck, as if staying pressed together might stop time, might spare us from what came next.

I wished that it could. Wished we could stay in this moment together for-fucking-ever. But if there was a chance this was all we had—all we'd ever get—I wouldn't waste it.

Her fingers trailed down, soft against my chest, curling in the fabric of my shirt. My hands held her steady, my thumbs tracing slow, thoughtless circles across her bare skin.

The world beyond the windows kept moving. A car passed. Distant voices echoed. The city turned over. But here, everything felt still. Suspended. Poised on the edge of something that couldn't be undone.

Our mouths broke contact as I slid my hands down to the backs of her thighs and lifted her in one smooth motion. She wrapped her legs around my waist like it was instinct, her arms tightening around my shoulders as her mouth found mine again.

By the time I reached the couch and lowered her onto the cushions, we were already breathing hard, clawing closer like we couldn't get enough. Her hips rolled up to meet mine, and I groaned into her mouth, grinding against the heat between her legs—still separated by too many damn layers.

I tugged her shirt up and over her head, baring skin I already knew by heart but could never get enough of. She arched beneath me, her breath catching as my mouth trailed down her neck, slow and open-mouthed, then lower.

Her fingers tangled in my hair, gripping tight.

When I reached the waistband of her skirt, I hooked my thumbs beneath the elastic and dragged it down, taking her panties with it. She lifted for me without a word, offering herself up as I stripped her bare.

I paused just long enough to drink her in. Flushed cheeks. Swollen lips. Eyes dark and wide with want.

In one fluid motion, I shifted us, sitting back on the couch with her still clinging to me, her legs wrapping around my waist as she landed in my lap.

She blinked, her breath stuttering, but she wasn't afraid. Fuck, she was never afraid of me. And that stunned me. It all did. How quickly the world had narrowed to this.

To us.

I reached for my belt, the leather sliding free with a slow, deliberate hiss. Her eyes tracked the motion, wide and dark, and I felt the shiver run through her when she realized what was coming.

"Hold still," I murmured against her ear as I caught her hands, gently drawing them behind her back and then looping the belt around her wrists.

Her breath caught as I cinched it into place, the look on her face nearly doing me in.

"You like this." It wasn't a question but a rough-edged truth, turning my voice to something jagged.

How many times had I told myself she wasn't ready? That what I wanted would scare her, break her, or leave her flinching from my touch? That the parts of me I kept buried were too dark for someone like her?

Someone delicate and breakable—a woman who'd already been broken once.

And yet, here she was, tied and waiting. Wanting.

I closed the distance, claiming her mouth in a kiss that didn't ask. It devoured.

She gave in instantly, melting against me like this was exactly where she belonged. Thighs locked around my hips, wrists bound behind her, and shoulders drawn back just enough to leave her off-balance and exposed.

Stunning as hell, and all mine.

As I slid my hands over her thighs, I traced slow, possessive paths up the curve of her ass and gripped hard. She rocked into me, chasing the friction, the soaked heat of her dragging against the rough denim of my jeans. The sound she made—half gasp, half broken moan—lit me up like a live wire.

I caught her hips in both hands, holding her still. "You're not ready for that yet," I murmured, even as my cock throbbed for her.

One hand slid between her legs, my fingers gliding through slick, bare heat. No barriers. No resistance. Just the pulse of her clit trembling under my touch.

She jolted at the contact, her jaw clenched tight and breath catching hard in her throat.

Fuck, just a few fast flicks of my fingers and she was already twitching with need. Her body was desperate, writhing, and begging without words. And despite wanting nothing more than to draw this out—to make her really, truly beg for it—I was too goddamn greedy to wait.

My zipper tore open with a loud rasp. I freed myself, clamping my hands to her hips again, and dragged her over my cock, coating me in her wet heat.

"Fuck, Lena. You feel so good. I can't wait to be inside you."

Breathless and with her eyes pinned on mine, she smirked. "Then don't wait."

With a strangled groan, I pulled her onto me, sinking deep in a single, brutal thrust. And it was the best goddamn feeling on this planet.

Her whole body locked around me, a ragged cry ripping from her throat as her forehead dropped to my shoulder. She tried to breathe through it, fighting to hold on without the use of her hands.

I didn't give her the chance to figure it out.

Relentless and clinging to control, I pulled her up, savoring the slick glide of her pussy. Locking her in place, I slammed up into her, pumping my hips hard enough to knock the air from her lungs. Again. And again. And a-fucking-gain.

Her wrists stayed pinned behind her, bound by the looped leather, her body helpless to do anything but take what I gave her.

And fuck, she took it, like a goddamn queen.

Gasping my name, her thighs trembled as she bounced on every thrust as if my cock was the only thing anchoring her to the world.

Her orgasm started to rise, building inside her like a live thing ready to tear loose.

"You gonna come for me?" I growled. "Like this? Tied up and at my mercy?"

"Yes," she cried, high and frantic.

And then she broke apart.

Her whole body tensed, her back arching and walls pulsing around my cock in tight, relentless waves. Her orgasm tore through her like a scream without sound. A surrender that felt like goddamn salvation.

I held her through it, still driving into her with everything I had, chasing the edge that had burned in me from the moment she climbed into my lap. One final thrust buried me deep, and I came with a low snarl. My release tore through me, hot and savage, fierce enough to scramble my senses.

She clenched around me, tighter with every beat of it, her body milking the last surges from mine as her thighs trembled against my hips, her breath coming out in short, shuddering bursts.

I didn't let go.

One hand fisted at her nape while the other locked around her bound wrists, holding her to me, caging her against my chest like the weight of my body might be enough to ground us both. Like the wreckage we'd just made was the only thing still holding us together.

Her breaths slowed first, then mine. Our hearts still pounded in sync, wild and unsteady, but the desperation had ebbed. What was left was quieter. Heavier.

I eased the belt free. The leather slid loose with a soft clink of the buckle. She sighed, content, as I drew her arms forward and rubbed slow circles into her skin.

A faint mark lingered where the strap had held her. Not deep or angry, but it was proof.

Of trust. Of surrender. Of how far she'd let me take her.

"You okay?" I wasn't doubting her, not with the way she'd come apart in my arms, but I still needed to hear her say it.

She nodded, then lowered her forehead to mine. "I am." The words were soft, steady, and came without pause.

Something eased in me at the sound of them, low and quiet but solid enough to hold on to.

She folded into my chest, still straddling my lap, her skin warm and damp, and her breath steady where it brushed over my throat. Her heartbeat slowed against mine, her body no longer trembling, only pliant now. Calm and safe.

And I held her the way you hold something you've nearly lost.

The way you hold something that's yours.

We stayed like that, wrapped in silence, sweat, and held by something too big for words. The chaos beyond our walls—the blood, the betrayal, and the war we were walking into—slipped away.

Death could wait. Destruction could wait. So could the rest of the goddamn world.

For now, she was in my arms.

Exactly where she was meant to be.

CHAPTER
TWENTY-FOUR
YELENA

THE SHARP BUZZ of Finn's phone cut through the quiet, pulling me from a restless sleep.

I'd been dreaming again. But this time, it wasn't a nightmare. It was the kind of dream that left a flush on my skin and a slow, aching throb between my thighs. And Finn had the starring role.

He groaned as he rolled to the edge of the mattress, still half asleep, his muscles stretching as he reached for the phone on the nightstand.

But the second he pulled it into view, everything in him shifted. He snapped upright, his spine going rigid and tension coiling tight across his shoulders. Whatever remnants of sleep had lingered vanished in an instant.

"Bodhi?" His voice was rough but alert.

I sat up, my heart already racing, and a cold rush of fear took hold before I even understood why.

He didn't say anything else, only listened with his

features tight and gaze locked on the wall. Away from me.

Something was wrong. He didn't need to say it. I could feel it in my bones.

Finn's grip on the phone tightened, his knuckles straining white as he turned to me and put the phone on speaker. "Say it again so Yelena can hear."

"I'm so fucking sorry." Bodhi's usual steady, carefree tone was now rushed and jagged. "It's Anya. She's gone. We don't know how—there was no sound, no forced entry, nothing. One second she was there and the next…"

The world fell away. I couldn't breathe. My hands curled into fists, my nails biting into my palms. My throat burned, and my heart felt like it was collapsing in on itself. Everything tilted, spinning, spiraling out of control.

"She was supposed to be safe." My voice didn't even sound like mine. It was something foreign and detached from my body. From reality.

Finn sat frozen at the edge of the bed. Not moving. Not even blinking.

Bodhi kept talking, maybe to soothe me, but he only stirred up more terror. "We've searched the whole area and we're calling in every emergency contact. Kira's losing it. Sunny's trying to—"

I didn't hear the rest. My mind was already gone, pulled to the darkest depths of hell. Back to the one place I'd hoped to never return.

Nik. This was him. It had to be.

My baby hadn't wandered off on her own. She'd been taken. There was no other reasonable explanation.

I bolted out of bed and started dressing. It didn't matter that my hands were shaking. Or that my vision was blurred by tears.

"Keep looking," Finn growled into the phone before abruptly ending the call.

"She's with him. Nik has her." God, saying it out loud made me want to scream.

Abandoning the phone on the bed, he turned to me, his hands raised like he was trying to calm a wild animal. "We don't know that for sure. And even if he does, he could have her anywhere."

"I'm going to the warehouse," I said, zipping up my pants and slipping on my shoes.

He moved in front of me, blocking the path to the gear bag and my gun. "No, you're not."

"It's the only place we know his men are still active." I held his gaze as fear and fury clashed inside me. "The one place I can get a message to him directly. No more hoping. No more guessing."

"And that's exactly why we can't be reckless," he growled. "This is what Nik wants, Lena. He's baiting you. Trying to draw you out."

"So what am I supposed to do, sit here and wait for his next move? Until it's too late?"

"No. But we need to re-evaluate our plan. We need to stick together." He crowded close, dropping his hands to cup my shoulders. "I need you in this. With me. If you leave now, you're walking straight into a trap."

If my heart wasn't already crushed, it would've broken all over again with the look he gave me. It was a look I'd seen before. A look that was equal parts protectiveness and fear. Only this time, that look said something else.

He still didn't trust me.

Not really. Not when it mattered most. And if he couldn't trust me…

Then I couldn't count on him.

I forced my body to relax. My breath eased out in a practiced surrender. I even gave him a nod. "Okay. You're right."

His eyes searched mine, narrowed with suspicion, as if waiting for a bigger argument.

But then his phone buzzed from its spot on the bed, and he moved to grab it. "It's Robin."

"Answer it." I kept my voice even. Kept the hurt and terror buried. "I just need a minute."

He threw a final look of doubt my way before answering. "Robin, tell me what you know."

He paced toward the window, Robin's voice drifting through the speaker, the conversation already pulling him into strategy mode.

I crossed the room with calm, purposeful strides toward the bathroom. At the door, I yanked it open and shut it again, loud enough for Finn to think I'd gone in.

Instead, I flattened myself against the wall with my breath steady and my feet rooted to the hardwood like I wasn't about to do something impossible.

Last time I slipped out, it had been a test. Proof that

I could face the fear without folding. That I could move through this world on my own terms. Not just as a survivor, but as someone with agency. Someone free.

This time was different. This wasn't about proving anything. This was a mission. Maybe the most important thing I'd ever do.

Forget the gear bag. Forget the gun. I was dressed, focused, and alive with purpose.

And that was all I needed.

When I was sure he wouldn't catch me, I snuck out of the room, slipped out the living room window, down the fire escape, and into the night.

And I didn't look back.

Not when I stepped outside. Not when the cold air hit my face like a slap. Not even when I walked down the street and slid into the driver's seat of the van, pulling the door shut behind me.

The sound echoed too loud, like it might wake the whole damn city.

But no one followed. There were no alarms or shouts, just the rumble of the engine and a rising throb in my chest.

By the time I reached the docks, my fear wasn't gone, but it wasn't in control either. I was doing the one thing Finn had always told me to do. I was using it.

Fear is my friend.

With my adrenaline harnessed, I parked three blocks away and walked the rest. No disguise. No backup. Just the weight of a mother's rage held tight inside me like a fist ready to strike.

The warehouse hadn't changed. It was the same rusting shell at the edge of the docks, disguised as just another forgotten building. But I knew better. I knew exactly what kind of corruption lived behind those walls.

And now I was walking back in. Alone.

Two guards waited just inside the entrance, but I didn't recognize them. Maybe they were new. Maybe Nik had already rebuilt. Or maybe they weren't his men at all.

One of them stopped me long enough to ask who I was. I gave him my name and waited while another gave me a half-hearted pat-down, grunted something under his breath, and waved me through as if I wasn't worth the trouble.

What they saw was a woman with no weapon and nowhere else to go. I was wrecked and raw, clinging to whatever scrap of loyalty I might have left. I wasn't a threat.

At least that's what I wanted them to see.

Inside, the place was quieter than I remembered. Not abandoned, just…hollow.

It had been stripped of the grime, scrubbed down like someone had tried to erase the violence from its walls and blood from the floor. But I could still feel it. Beneath the bleach and fresh paint, the memories were still there. The horrors were still fresh.

Sasha sat at the same desk Nik used to lounge behind, back when he was my grandfather's golden boy. Nik always looked like a bored king in that chair, drunk on power and completely untouchable. Sasha, by contrast, looked like an exhausted middleman, trying to make it through another shift.

He looked up. A flicker of emotion crossed his face, then vanished behind the same smug indifference he'd always worn like armor.

"So the princess returns." His voice held its usual edge, but it didn't land the way it used to. There was something frayed beneath the mockery—defensiveness, maybe even guilt. "What's the matter, Yelena? Did you get tired of slumming it with the Decker twins?"

"I need to talk to him." Fear crawled up my throat and choked my words, but I didn't care. I was too raw for pretenses. Too scared to put on a performance. "Please. Can you help me get a message to Nik?"

"What makes you think Nik wants to hear from you now? After you vanished for weeks?" He sneered. "Loyalty clearly doesn't run deep in your family. Tell me, does Kira still pretend Bodhi was worth it?"

I didn't rise to the bait. He could rot in that bitterness for eternity for all I cared.

With tears in my eyes, I met his stare and gave him the bare, ugly truth. "Nik took Anya."

He jerked forward, something volatile rising in him. "What are you talking about?"

"He has her. I don't know where. I don't know why. But I know she's gone, and I know he's the one who took her."

"You expect me to believe Nik would hurt his own daughter?"

My heart raced, but still I held his gaze. "Wouldn't he?"

He didn't answer right away. I watched the flicker of doubt cross his face, brief but unmistakable.

"You don't know what you're talking about. He wouldn't touch her. No matter what else he's done. That kid…" His hands balled to fists, and he swallowed hard. "She's his blood."

"I know what she is." I forced back the tears, willing my voice to remain steady. "And I also know what he's capable of."

His eyes flicked away, uncertainty creasing his brow.

But God, what did it mean? Would he help me?

"You know he'd do anything to get me back. Anything." My voice cracked, fear squeezing around my ribs. "He can have me, Sasha. I don't care what it takes, I just want my daughter safe."

When his gaze met mine again, it was unreadable. "You're either very brave or very stupid. Maybe both."

Silence stretched between us as he continued watching me. Testing me, maybe. Or waiting for me to back down.

But I wouldn't. No, I couldn't. Not with Anya's life on the line.

Finally, he let out a heavy sigh, the fight seeming to drain from him. "You really shouldn't be here." He shook his head, and something in his expression shifted.

It was something that looked a hell of a lot like pity.

"He doesn't have her, Yelena. You're giving yourself up for nothing."

Doubt slammed into me. Maybe Nik didn't take her after all. Maybe Finn was right, and I should've waited. Should've planned instead of charging in blind and reckless, throwing myself into danger like a fool.

But if Nik didn't have her, where the hell was my daughter?

The cold edge of terror crawled over me, poking at the back of my neck and whispering of unfathomable horrors I was too afraid to face. What if she were hurt? Scared? Needed me?

Worse, what if I never saw her again?

My mind tumbled into chaos, but Sasha didn't move. He didn't call the guards. Didn't reach for a weapon or try to send me away. He just kept staring.

Then it hit me. A familiar, sweet, suffocating smell.

The unmistakable stench of imported cigars curled through the room, a cold finger down my spine. It wrapped around my throat, sending my body into instant, silent panic.

"You always did have a flair for the dramatic." Nik's slick, cold voice slithered in from behind me. "Wandering in all alone. No one to hold your leash. What's the matter, darling? Did your savior get tired of you already?"

I turned on a gasp to face him. "Nik." I didn't drop my gaze, but I didn't challenge him either. There was no point. Not with the stakes this high.

A venomous smile spread across his face—the same

smile that had once charmed me. And for a heartbeat, I felt the old pull. Not to him, but to the role I used to play. The woman he'd twisted into something small and compliant.

The one who obeyed no matter the cost.

He stepped closer, hands in his pockets, and polished shoes tapping against the concrete. "So," he drawled. "To what do I owe the pleasure? Regret? Desperation? Or maybe just a flare of nostalgia?"

"Anya's missing." The words caught in my throat, heavy and raw. "Did you take her?"

For a moment he said nothing—the cruel smile still playing on his lips and amusement dancing in his eyes —and my resolve nearly crumbled.

"That's quite the accusation," he said, finally.

"Please, Nik. I just need to know if you have her. I'll do anything. Whatever it takes. Whatever you want. I swear—"

His harsh laughter cut me off. "You're a terrible liar."

He circled me, and I shifted with him, refusing to let him out of my sight.

"Isn't she?" He glanced at his second as he moved closer.

Sasha nodded, face unreadable.

"That used to be one of the things I liked about her." Nik met my gaze as he talked about me like I wasn't there. "She was always so easy to read. So predictable."

"You know I'd do anything for her," I said.

But God, what if he really didn't have her? How the hell would I get out of here to find her?

"You'd do anything for her." His voice turned sharp, slicing through me. "But what about me, Yelena? You want so much, but what do you give? What can you even offer now that you've been tainted by Finn Decker?" He crowded into my space, his breath reeking of cigars. "You think I don't know what happened while you were gone? What kind of little games you and your white knight were playing?" He hovered too close, his eyes gleaming with malice. "I know he touched you. I know you let him, you little whore. And I know you liked it."

I didn't breathe. Didn't move.

He reached into his pocket, pulled out a familiar bottle—orange plastic, white cap, no label—and held it up between two fingers like a prize.

"I bet it got confusing, wanting him but needing me." He shook the bottle, rattling the little white pills inside. "Needing these. How long did you last without them, darling? Two days? Three? Aren't these the real reasons you've come crawling back?"

I stared at the bottle. Not because I wanted a pill, but because I remembered what they'd done to me. How he'd used them to control me. The way he'd offered relief like a gift and then tightened the noose the second I reached for it. And for one terrible second, I could feel it again—the hum under my skin, the promise of numbness.

But I didn't give in.

I let the silence stretch. Let my fingers twitch, just enough to sell the lie. Like I might lunge for it. Like I was seconds from breaking.

Then I met his eyes, masking the fire inside with something softer. Something fragile and pleading.

"I don't know what's real anymore," I whispered, feeding his need for power. "I just want her back. That's all."

He smiled. That same sick, indulgent smile. "That's better. That's my darling girl."

The bottle vanished into his pocket, and I shivered. Not from fear. Not from withdrawal. But from the rush of control, however fleeting, at making him believe me.

"If you want another chance, you'll need to prove it." His repugnant smile stretched even wider. "On your knees."

Oh God. I hadn't planned for this. Hadn't thought far enough ahead. Of course he'd want a show of loyalty. Of submission. Of ownership.

He'd want to humiliate me. Use me. Remind me I was his to torture however he liked.

Sasha shifted beside him, like he wasn't sure if he still belonged in the room, but he didn't dare leave without permission.

When I didn't move, Nik's expression twisted. "Did you forget how this works? Or maybe—" He dug into his pocket again. "You just need a little incentive."

Only this time, he didn't bring out pills. He pulled out a phone, tapped the screen once, and turned it toward me.

Everything in me collapsed.

Anya. My sweet, beautiful angel was there on the screen. Alone and huddled in the corner of a room that could have been in this building. She was pale and silent, with tears staining her little face.

Nik didn't even glance at the screen. At the distress he was causing his own daughter. Instead, he watched me, drinking in the devastation.

High on my agony.

"She didn't even hesitate to come with me. Funny what kids do when their mothers abandon them." He moved even closer, the phone still glowing between us. "You should've known better."

My knees buckled, and I dropped to the floor, willing to do whatever he asked. Give whatever piece of myself he wanted. All of me, if that's what he demanded. Anything to keep Anya safe.

His eyes flared as sick satisfaction spread across his face. The smugness didn't vanish, it evolved, hardening into something sharper. Crueler.

"Well…" His voice was thick with lust as he ran a hand over the top of my head. "Maybe there's hope for you yet."

He slipped the phone back into his pocket, then bent low, his fingers fisting hard in my hair. The sudden, vicious pull wrenched my head back, forcing my eyes up to meet his.

That's when the door behind me opened.

Finn.

His presence crashed over me like a wave—furious,

unyielding, and all-consuming. And I welcomed it. That dark, simmering menace. The rage he barely held in check. The protective force that filled the room and sent a wild rush of relief tearing through me.

Nik felt it, too. His grip on my hair tightened, and his body locked, tension rippling through him. "Looks like we've got ourselves a reunion. Your precious white knight has come to save the day."

But he didn't look at Finn. His eyes stayed fixed on mine as his awful, twisted smile spread.

"Should we give him a show?" His voice echoed through the room. "Do you think he'd enjoy watching you choke on my cock?"

Finn's answering growl rumbled low, his fury barely caged.

Sasha flinched, taking a cautious step back, not fleeing but clearly wanting no part of what was about to happen.

Nik released my hair and straightened, every movement precise and deliberate. He held out his hand, palm up.

Without question, Sasha handed over his gun.

"Mr. Decker," Nik called, his gaze still fixed on me like I was the trophy in some sick game of chicken. "So nice of you to join us."

Finn didn't answer, but I felt him draw closer.

And I knew, whatever happened next, someone was about to die.

CHAPTER
TWENTY-FIVE
FINN

I WALKED in like I owned the place. No guards. No resistance. That meant only one thing.

They were expecting me.

Waiting, watching, letting me get closer because this was exactly how Rykov wanted it to go. I was walking into his trap.

And I didn't give one single fuck.

The plan was already in pieces. It had shattered the second Yelena slipped out on her own. Now I was doing the one thing I'd sworn not to—charging into enemy territory without backup, without a strategy, and without her beside me.

There hadn't been time to think, plan, or calculate. When I realized she was gone, I moved. Fast. Blind. Running on fury and instinct, I walked straight into the viper's den. And my only armor was rage.

After more than a year of hunting this bastard, living

with his name like a poison running through my blood, I thought I knew what to expect. An army with guns. Chaos. A bullet with my name on it. I thought I would walk into hell.

But this? Fuck. I hadn't been ready for this.

Yelena was on her knees, with his fucking hand in her hair, dragged back into the role he'd once forced her to play—his possession. Rykov murmured filth in her ear, threatening to make her suck his dick in front of me, as though it was poetry. And Sasha watched it all with a blank, unreadable stare.

My rage flared so hot it nearly blinded me.

I knew what Rykov was doing. This wasn't just about power or punishment. It was a message. One meant for me. He wanted me to see her like this. To lose my nerve and unravel. To doubt the bond Yelena and I shared.

Except the fucker had miscalculated.

What I saw in her wasn't weakness. It was strength. The kind that survives and adapts.

The kind that lures a monster into thinking he still has control, then slits his throat the moment he turns his back.

And fuck, I loved her even more for it.

Rykov didn't even glance at me. His gaze stayed locked on Yelena, full of sick amusement as he extended a hand toward Sasha with lazy, expectant authority.

Sasha didn't blink. He placed his gun in Rykov's hand like it belonged there.

The moment the weapon was in his grasp, I raised mine. Steady and centered, I aimed straight for the bastard's head.

"Mr. Decker." Rykov's stare was fixed on Yelena, like I was nothing more than background noise. "So nice of you to join us."

His tone was casual. Almost bored. Like we were two old acquaintances forced to interact, instead of two men circling the inevitability of death.

Finally, he looked at me with a smug smile curling his lips. "I must admit, when I killed your wife, I didn't expect you to replace her quite so quickly. But then…" His gaze slid back to Yelena. "She does have a certain flavor, doesn't she?"

My finger twitched on the trigger. I wanted to put a bullet through his conceited fucking face. Wanted to watch it blow out the back of his skull and stain the wall.

I held, tamped down the rage, and forced myself to focus.

This wasn't the endgame. It was the opening move in a trap laid with surgical precision. I couldn't see them, but I felt Rykov's men in the dark—tucked behind crates, posted above us—itching to kill me. Or waiting for the signal to shoot Yelena.

She was still too close, kneeling at his feet, neck craned up, fingers curled into fists.

Every nerve in my body screamed for vengeance. For justice.

But I couldn't pull the trigger. Not with her in the

crossfire. One twitch in the wrong direction and she'd be dead.

I hadn't come this far to watch her die. Not after everything she'd survived.

Not when she was mine.

"She's broken in all the right ways, isn't she?" Rykov trailed the barrel of the gun along the side of her head. "Damaged enough to stay loyal. Beautiful enough to be lethal."

Yelena didn't flinch or make a sound.

Rykov's eyes gleamed with cruel calculation. "You're not the first man to fall for that illusion. But don't worry, Finn. We all think we're the exception. Until darling Yelena looks at us and sees opportunity instead of love."

I wanted to rip the sneer right off his face, tear his throat out, and make him choke on her name the next time he dared to speak it.

Instead, I moved to the right, slow and methodical, bringing Yelena's profile into view. She barely moved, but when her doe-eyed gaze met mine, the will to fight still burned in them.

She was down, but she wasn't out.

My gaze shifted to our enemy. "Emily died with more dignity than you'll ever earn. And you know nothing about Yelena—you don't get to speak for her. Face it, Rykov, you've already lost. You lost her."

His smile didn't falter. If anything, it sharpened. "To you? Bowen Alexander's bootlicker? I don't think so."

At the mention of the name, Yelena's attention

snapped to him. Her breath hitched, and she bit her bottom lip.

"Oh, Yelena." His voice filled with fake empathy as he circled her. "I can tell from your reaction you have no idea what I'm talking about, do you?"

Her eyes darted back to mine, and what I saw nearly gutted me. Hurt. Fear. A flicker of something uncertain.

"Your Finn wasn't always a noble savior. Before all this,"—he gestured carelessly between us—"he worked for Bowen. Personal security, at first. Then he moved to clean-up. Quiet threats. Disappearances. A loyal soldier who was well-rewarded." He traced his gun along her shoulder in a slow, possessive move. "And he was good at it. Not because he had to be. No. Because he liked it. The violence. The thrill."

Sasha moved in my periphery. It was a subtle repositioning of his weight, his arms unfolding as his stance loosened, like he was preparing for something.

And still, Rykov droned on, too drunk on the sound of his own voice to recognize the subtle shift in the room around him.

"And you know what else?" His vicious smile widened. "While he was working under Bowen's roof, he started snooping. Little by little. Digging into my business. Using Bowen's access to sniff around places he didn't belong. Finn wasn't in it for the money or the power. He did it for you, it seems." The words slipped from his mouth like a knife dipped in honey. "All that loyalty, all that bloodshed…and you were the prize waiting at the end of it."

Finally, he turned to me, a glint of victory in his gaze. "So tell me, Finn, when exactly did your conscience kick in? Was it before or after you started fucking her?"

My jaw flexed hard, my teeth grinding with the effort it took to stay silent through his bullshit. Not because I wasn't angry—I'd been burning from the moment I saw his hands on her.

No. I wouldn't react because that's what he wanted. This was all just a fucked-up game to him. And he expected me to play along. To feed his ego.

Fuck that.

I was here for Yelena. All that mattered was getting her the hell out of this.

"I never lied about who I am." I held her stare, willing her to understand. To believe. To trust. "Yes, I left out the bloodier details of how I got here, but you know me, Lena. You know the kind of man I am, and what I'm willing to do."

My focus moved to Rykov, my aim still at his head. "I might like the rush. Maybe even the violence. We're alike in that way, I guess. But I don't get off on exploiting the people who trust me. The people I love. And unlike you, *Nik*, I don't mistake silence for weakness."

The victorious gleam in his eyes faltered. He turned back to Yelena, the mask of smug control slipping into something colder. Crueler.

His hand shot out, and he yanked her up by the arm,

making her stumble. "No more pretending. You want back in? Prove it."

She caught her balance but didn't try to pull away.

"I've got your pills, darling. I've got your little girl. Everything you care about, everything you need, runs through me." With a touch so calm it looked obscene, he pressed the gun into her hand. "Kill him, and I'll give Anya back to you."

My gut twisted as Yelena finally broke. There was no screaming, crying, or begging for mercy. No defiance or attempted self-sacrifice. There was simply surrender. A quiet collapse of hope.

He had her cornered, pills in one hand, her daughter in the other. And I was the blood price he demanded. The cost of her betrayal laid bare at his feet.

I dropped my aim, the gravity of the situation settling deep as I lowered the barrel.

This was her nightmare, alive and breathing. A madman stood at her back, directing the gun in her hand, and her daughter's life was on the line if she didn't follow through.

And me? I was just the body between her and the exit. A man she hardly knew. One who'd lied to her, tried to use her, and dragged her out of one hell just to thrust her back into another.

She looked at me but I couldn't fucking read her.

Was she stalling? Strategizing? Falling apart?

I had no fucking idea what she'd do. But I knew what she needed from me. What I had to give her.

I met her gaze, poured everything I had into one

look—every ounce of love, regret, and devotion—and gave her the only thing I could.

My trust.

"It's okay." My voice was low, calm, and meant just for her. "I understand."

Her breath caught, and her grip faltered.

"You're strong, Lena. You've always been strong. Always." My body tensed, bracing for what would come. "You can do this. Right now. Set yourself and Anya free."

This wasn't about me. Not anymore. This was about her daughter. Her pain. Her goddamn freedom. And if that meant dying here? If it meant being the final weight she had to cut loose? So be it.

I'd burn for her. I'd die a thousand deaths. Anything she needed was hers.

For a moment, the world fell away. Rykov and his despicable, gloating sneer. Sasha's impassive stare. The watching eyes of the men surrounding us. Even the crushing weight of my past lifted.

All I saw was her.

My lovely little Lena. Torment in her gaze. My heart, battered and bloody, resting in the palm of her hand.

As she stared at me, something shifted behind her eyes. Grief cracked and splintered, giving way to something lethal. Not fear. Not pain.

No. It was rage. Pure and fucking deadly.

It rose in her like the summer sun—brilliant, blinding, and blazing hot. It seared through her expression, burning away every trace of doubt until all that remained was intent. The calm confidence of a woman on the edge of greatness.

Rykov moved behind her, still too close, still so fucking sure of himself. He didn't see the shift. Didn't recognize the birth of a monarch.

Her shoulders squared, focus sharpened, and her grip shifted, just like I'd taught her. Then she moved. No warning. No scream. Fast and agile, she spun and fired the gun.

With one sharp, deafening crack, she put a bullet straight through Nikolai Rykov's chest.

He staggered, eyes wide, hands grasping at the bloom of red spreading across his ribs.

Another shot followed, lower this time. Then a third.

He dropped to his knees, a string of gurgling noises spilling out of him as blood bubbled from his lips. His face was a contorted mask of panic, pain, and disbelief.

And then he was nothing. Just a heap of flesh and bone, bleeding out across the concrete floor.

For a moment, no one moved. Even Sasha stood frozen, his eyes locked on Yelena like he was seeing her for the first time.

Yelena stood over Rykov, her weapon still aimed and her breath tearing in and out of her lungs in sharp, uneven bursts. There was no triumph on her face.

She stared at his body as if she couldn't quite process it, some part of her still expecting him to lurch back to life. The man who'd broken her. Controlled her. Who'd carved himself into every corner of her mind.

Now he was bleeding out at her feet, and she was the one who'd put him there.

The shock of it clung to her, cold and silent. Rykov was dead and she'd pulled the trigger. She'd just killed a man.

And thank fuck, it wasn't me.

CHAPTER
TWENTY-SIX
YELENA

I DIDN'T FEEL the gun fall from my hand, or hear it hit the floor. The ringing in my ears was too loud. Endless. It wound its way into my skull and hollowed me out from the inside.

Nik lay sprawled on the ground, his blood soaking onto the floor around him. His wide eyes stared up at me, empty.

I'd done that. I'd pulled the trigger.

Three times.

He was dead because of me.

My breath came in short, shallow, almost frantic gasps, but the world around me had slowed. My chest burned like I'd been running for miles, yet I hadn't moved. Not an inch. I couldn't. My feet were cemented in place, rooted in the ash of everything he'd taken from me. Stuck in a feeling I couldn't name.

God, what was this feeling?

It wasn't guilt, regret, or even fear. It was something

wild and unruly. Something that buzzed beneath my skin and tasted a little like…

Freedom.

The realization clicked into place, and I let it in. Let it fill me. Let myself breathe. Even as chaos rose around me.

Men shouted. Boots pounded the floor. Sasha yelled in Russian. It all washed over me, distant echoes reverberating through my mind.

"Lena!" Finn's voice cracked through the fog like a whip, snapping me back to my senses.

Suddenly I was in the middle of a war.

Finn's strong, unyielding arms wrapped around me, and he became a force of nature cutting through the chaos. He yanked me back from Nik's body, dragging me out of the path of the oncoming storm. My feet left the ground, and for a breathless moment the world tilted.

Gunfire exploded behind us. I flinched, twisting on instinct, but Finn's grip only tightened, one arm locked around my waist, the other raised and firing blindly behind us.

"Stay down." His voice was rough and ragged in my ear.

The scent of him—mint, sweat, and leather—cut through my confusion, anchoring me to something solid. Something real.

And somehow, even as everything came apart around us, I felt safe. Grounded. Because in his arms, backed by his strength and defended by his fury, I could do anything. Survive anything. Be anything.

Maybe even a queen.

Another burst of gunfire rang out, cutting through the shouts. The screams. The sound of bodies hitting the ground.

Finn moved fast, carrying me with him, shielding me with his body as we cut across the floor. His chest pressed tight to my back, a solid wall of muscle and heat. And every time his gun fired, the recoil vibrated through my spine like a second, brutal heartbeat.

We dropped behind a crate, landing hard. Finn kept me low, his body still covering mine, his weapon raised as he fired into the fray.

My heart hammered. My ears rang. But I wasn't afraid.

I shoved out from under him and scrambled toward the Glock lying a few feet away. It was slick with blood, still warm from someone else's hand—no doubt the corpse beside it.

My fingers curled around the grip. I pulled it to me and crawled back toward Finn, sliding in beside him just as another shot ricocheted off the metal edge of the container above us.

His gaze cut to mine and something fierce passed between us. Something deeper than fear, louder than survival. It was a look of devotion forged in fire, and it flooded me with heat and purpose.

I raised the weapon, braced my arms, and aimed.

We fired together.

The first shot cracked like thunder, echoing through the smoke-filled room. Then another. And another.

My shoulder kicked with each pull of the trigger, the force vibrating through my bones. I couldn't tell which bullets came from me and which from him. It didn't matter.

We moved in sync, not just beside each other but as extensions of the same will. I drew their fire, and Finn carved through the chaos with lethal precision.

Shells clattered to the ground. Sparks flashed. The air turned sharp and bitter with the burn of gunpowder. But I kept going, my breath steady and vision clear.

I felt him behind me, anchoring me, and for the first time in my life, I understood what it meant to be matched. To be seen.

To be unstoppable.

Another man dropped ahead of us, collapsing into the haze, and a sharp breath escaped me—not from fear, but from revelation. This wasn't about surviving anymore. This was about choice. Power and ownership.

I was choosing this. Choosing to fight. To finish it.

Finn moved like a storm—cold, fast, and efficient. He swept through the room with terrifying control, covering angles I hadn't even seen.

But even storms break.

It happened fast. A pivot, a clean kill, and then a loud crack from the shadows.

"Finn!"

He jerked sideways, a raw grunt tearing from his chest as he staggered back behind a crate. Blood spread across his side, dark and fast. The sight of it nearly stopped my heart.

He didn't go down. God, he'd barely missed a beat.

He turned and aimed at the man who'd shot him, striking him down with a single shot.

Across the room, Sasha bolted. He was limping but still agile, slipping between columns and vanishing toward the exit.

"Fuck, no. No!" Finn pushed off the crate, nearly losing his balance, then staggered forward. "I'll go after him."

"Finn, you're hit!"

He didn't slow. Didn't even look at me.

I sprinted after him, grabbed his arm, and tried to hold him back. But he wrenched away, blood streaming from the wound and his jaw clenched like the pain didn't matter.

"I said I've got him," he snapped, his eyes burning with rage. But his words didn't have the same punch to them. His face didn't have the same color.

"You'll bleed out before you get to the door."

Still, he kept moving.

I raced in front of him, shoved both hands to his chest, and forced him back with everything I had. "Stop. He's gone."

He stared at me, wild-eyed and feral, like letting go of this moment meant the whole damn mission would unravel.

"He's the last one." His voice was low, almost desperate. "He's the last fucking thread, Lena."

"I don't care." My voice broke over the words. "He's not important. Not right now. Anya's still here, somewhere in this building, and I need to find her. She's the only one who matters."

His jaw flexed, eyes locking on mine, a war still waging in them.

"You're right." He reached for me with a blood-slicked hand, touching my face like it might be the last time. "Go. I've got this. I'll cover the doors. I'll be right here when you come back."

I faltered. One beat. Two.

Then I ran.

Not because I didn't love him. Because I did. But if anything happened to Anya, I'd never forgive myself.

I tore through the main room like a woman possessed, crashing toward the smoke-stained hallway, shoving past empty crates and rusted beams.

My heart thundered so loud it swallowed the fading gunfire.

"Anya. Anya, it's Mama. I'm here." I called it again and again until my throat burned.

Every breath was a blade in my chest, but also a plea. Not for vengeance. For her.

Always, for her.

Panic curled my gut as I moved from room to room, the silence stretching into something ominous.

A breakroom with half-eaten food and mismatched chairs. A supply room with crates pushed to the walls, a spilled box of wires and tools littering the floor. An office reeking of sweat and cologne, and a cigarette still smoldering in an ashtray on the corner.

But no sign of her.

I moved faster. My boot slipped on something slick near a doorway, and I hit the frame with a grunt, catching myself before I went down. Pain flared along my ribs, sharp and immediate, but I shoved it down. The air stung with smoke and metal, a cloying scent of spent adrenaline and blood, but I didn't slow.

I turned the next corner and found a hallway, narrower than the others. At the end, a door stood slightly ajar, and soft light glowed from inside.

Something shifted in my chest. I rushed forward and eased the door open.

It wasn't a cell. Not exactly. But it had that feeling—cold, controlled, and impersonal. There was a chair in the corner. A folded blanket on a cot. And tucked into the far corner of the room beside a storage cabinet, barely visible in the low light…

"Anya?"

She was curled in the corner, her knees pulled to her chest, thumb in her mouth, and her other hand clutching the hem of her shirt. Her eyes met mine, wide and glassy. Her cheeks were stained with tears. But she was breathing. She was alive.

Oh, thank God, she's alive.

A sob of relief tore from my throat, and tears flowed freely. "Anya."

I crossed the room in two steps and dropped to my knees. "It's me, angel. It's Mama."

She didn't react at first, but when I reached for her, she launched herself into my arms. Her small body collided with mine, and she wrapped her arms around my neck, shaking, clinging so tightly I thought I might break in half from the relief.

"Mama," her sweet voice whispered in my ear.

"I've got you." I closed my eyes and held her tighter. "I've got you, angel. I'm never letting go."

The sound of footsteps behind me sent a jolt down my spine. I turned, one arm still wrapped tight around Anya, ready to fight whoever had followed.

Until I saw him.

Finn.

He stood in the doorway, his breath shallow, one hand braced against the frame and the other pressed tight to his side. Blood had soaked through the fabric of his shirt. His forearm was slick with it, too, like he'd tried to stop the bleeding with whatever he could grab. He looked like hell. Pale and unsteady.

But his eyes were locked on me. On us.

The corner of his mouth hitched into a pained smile. "She found you."

Heat pricked behind my eyes, tears spilling hot and sudden. Because he was talking to me. Finding myself had brought Anya back to me, just like he'd predicted.

She peeked at him, her small body still trembling, but she managed a smile. Not her usual mischief, it was just a delicate, uncertain flicker. But it was real.

Finn's expression broke, and all his hard edges softened. "Think maybe we should get out of here?"

I nodded, the lump in my throat too big to speak around.

He pushed off the wall, hand pressed to his side. Wounded and bleeding, he still kept his eyes on us—not on the blood on my knees or the dirt in Anya's curls.

Just us.

"Come on," he said. "Let's go."

CHAPTER
TWENTY-SEVEN
FINN

THERE WAS A TIME, not that long ago, when I would've sworn Rykov's death needed to come by my hand and my hand alone. I'd imagined it in every way a man could. Slow. Brutal. Personal as fucking hell.

But when Yelena pulled the trigger? I hadn't felt cheated.

I'd felt peace.

Not the clean kind. Not the kind that made my chest lighter and my thoughts quiet. No, this was a jagged, blood-slicked kind of peace. Something earned, not granted. The end of something violent and vile.

The only ending that had ever made sense—Yelena with steel in her spine, taking back her freedom by taking the monster's life.

Her eyes had been glassy, her hands steady. And the moment the bullet left the barrel, everything shifted. Maybe not in the world, but in me.

At that moment, I realized the revenge had never been mine to take. It had always been hers.

I might've been the one who first pulled her out of Rykov's clutches, but it was her confidence, her will to pull the trigger that finally dragged her out of hell for good.

Fuck. She'd been stunning in her moment of glory.

Later, when I'd found her with Anya, I'd stood in the doorway and let the warmth of seeing them together —alive and unharmed—wash over me like the first light after a long, dark night. I let the feeling of love sink deep. Because I did. I loved her.

I loved them both.

Not in the way I'd ever loved before. Not the way I'd clung to Emily out of duty, guilt, or some fractured idea of who I was supposed to be. This was different. Fierce and certain.

In that moment, nothing else mattered. Not the bodies in the warehouse. Not the blood on Yelena's clothes. Not even the guilt I'd been carrying—over Emily's death, my lies, or the man I'd become.

None of it held any weight compared to this.

Yelena had stood trembling, shaking from exhaustion, her hair a wild tangle, and her face streaked with blood, dirt, and tears. And Anya? She'd clung to her like she'd never been gone. Like some part of her had always known who her mother was.

The kid was tough, tougher than most adults I'd met, and still the sweetest damn thing. She'd looked up at me with tearstained cheeks and swollen eyes, managing a crooked little smile that nearly brought me to my knees.

"Mama," she'd whispered, like it was the only word she remembered. The only one that mattered.

Yelena had whispered it back again and again, her voice low and raw as we moved. She'd clutched Anya to her chest, murmuring promises, and telling her she was safe now. That Mama had her. That everything was okay.

We'd made it out slowly, every step cautious. My side had been on fire, each breath cutting like broken glass, but I'd led the way, clearing the path ahead. Making sure no threats remained. That there was no one left to hurt them.

When we'd stepped outside, the early morning air had wrapped around us, thick with the heat of late summer. Beyond the lot, the city had murmured with life—distant engines, the steady lap of water against the dock, and the groan of shifting cargo containers.

Familiar, grounding sounds. It was strange how normal it had all felt, like the warehouse behind us hadn't been littered with bodies. Like none of it had ever happened.

The city hadn't noticed. Hadn't cared.

Nikolai Rykov was dead, and the world kept turning.

Now, days later, I sat on the edge of an Airbnb mattress with a bandage wrapped tight around my middle and a burner phone pressed to my ear.

The room was simple. Plain white walls, beige decor, and a single window cracked just enough to let in the hum of traffic below. Somewhere above, footsteps moved across another unit, followed by the faint clink of dishes.

Life continuing.

It wasn't a dump. Not luxury either. But it was clean, quiet, and tucked above a bookstore in Queens with no doorman and no working intercom. The kind of place you could disappear into for a while. The kind of place where no one asked questions as long as the neighbors stayed quiet and the rent cleared.

On the other end of the phone line, Robin's voice was clipped but steady. "Bodhi and Kira are safe. They've gone back upstate for a while, somewhere new. Sunny's home and already back at work. She said not to call unless it's about stitches or trauma codes."

I smiled faintly. That was Sunny, always putting herself last. Always running headfirst into someone else's mess just to drag them out. Hardheaded as hell, worked too much, cared too much, and never asked for a damn thing in return. She'd patch someone up while telling them off, then walk away like none of it touched her.

But it did. It always did.

She carried everything, quietly and stubbornly. The same way she'd carried Bodhi through his injuries. The way she'd helped Yelena overcome her addiction. And the way she'd held me up during the worst of my grief.

And yet, somehow, she'd managed to avoid getting caught in the middle of this. The danger I'd brought to her doorstep hadn't touched her.

Thank fuck for that.

"What about us?" I asked, needing to be sure. "Are we safe?"

Robin paused. Only for a second, but it twisted my gut. She never hesitated. Not unless something worse waited behind the curtain.

"Cops are calling it a gang war," she said finally. "Nice and tidy. Case closed. But I don't buy it. Not with how deep this went. Feels like the feds are circling now. They're quiet, but I bet they're watching."

Pain surged in my side as my body tensed. "Are you in trouble?"

"Not yet," she said. "But if they start pulling threads and follow one back to me, I might need to disappear for a bit. But if I go dark…"

Neither of us rushed to finish the thought. We both knew what it would mean if Robin pulled the plug on her operation. People would die.

But not the ones who deserved it.

She sighed. "That's not even the part that's got me on edge."

"What is?"

"There's movement." She paused again, her silence broken only by the sound of typing. Fuck, she was still working, even now. "Remnants of the Bratva are trying to organize. A few are still loyal to Sasha, although no one seems to know where he is. The rest are grasping for control. You tore a hole straight through the center of their world, Finn. And holes like that don't stay empty for long."

"They'll try to fill it," I agreed.

"And it won't be with someone better. They'll fall in line behind the loudest voice, the biggest threat. Whoever makes the kind of promises that taste like power."

"Let them."

"You sure?" Her voice wavered. "Because if you don't take the next swing, they might come after you. You're a threat now. One they'll want to erase."

"I'm done." I exhaled like I'd been holding my breath for the entirety of the last fucking year.

"But Finn—"

"I said I'm done, Robin."

I leaned back against the wall, feeling the dull throb of my wound as I shifted, and allowed the silence to stretch between us.

The mattress beneath me was firm but thin, one of those cheap kinds that made every pain feel sharper. My ribs ached with every breath, and still, I let myself sink into it. Let the ache settle in. Let the weight of everything I'd done, everything we'd survived, begin to pull me under.

Not into sleep, not quite. Just into stillness.

"You sound like a man who's got it all figured out." Robin's voice was soft. "Like you finally have what you want."

"I do," I murmured. "And it's not blood—I don't need it. Not anymore."

Her answering silence might've been agreement, but

it felt more like the beginning of a goodbye. Was this where things ended between us?

Robin had been with me from the start. Before the plan had taken shape. Before I even knew what I needed from it. For the last year, she was the one who called me out when I got reckless, the one voice that could cut through the noise and keep me grounded.

She'd had my back like no one else. Not even Bodhi. Not when it came to this.

But now Rykov was gone. The mission was over.

What was left?

"Law got in touch," she said at last, and the words stabbed into my ribs. "He said killing Rykov tipped the balance. Bowen's already shifting. He's lining up tighter with the Irish. Looks like he's using it—your work. He's claiming the win and using it to solidify control. His empire just got a whole lot stronger overnight."

I let out a low grunt, not because I disagreed, but because it figured. That's how our world worked. One man's vengeance was another man's leverage. One body on the ground became someone else's throne.

It sounded like trouble. A fight I had no interest in throwing my weight into. Not anymore.

Robin continued, "He also said not to get any ideas. Just because you did him a favor doesn't mean there's a seat waiting for you. He said you should stay gone."

A low laugh rumbled through me. Of course he had. That was Law—cool as ice, even when he gave a damn. But the warning wasn't necessary.

"I'm not going back," I said, the decision already made. "I've got everything I need."

"I'm happy for you Finn, really." Her words were tender, but her voice strained. "Just…please be careful. Both of you."

The call ended, the screen going dark as the phone slid from my fingers to the floor. My chest ached with every breath, the tension from the last few weeks—hell, from the last goddamn year—still lodged deep in my bones.

Beneath it all was something quieter. Something closer to stillness than I'd felt in years. Not quite the peace I'd imagined, but something close enough to believe in.

Footsteps moved across the floor just outside the door. Yelena's were measured and steady. Anya's followed close behind, light and uneven, the soft shuffle of her bare feet brushing over the old hardwood. I could hear Yelena murmuring to her, gentle and low, the way someone spoke when they were trying to build something fragile.

A moment later, Anya let out a quiet giggle, the sound small but bright, and it reached into a part of me I hadn't realized was still locked tight.

The part of me that had never really known what it was missing.

I used to think I wasn't made to have a family of my own. That some men just weren't wired that way. I'd convinced myself I didn't want kids, didn't need them, and told myself I was doing the world a favor by keeping that door closed.

But that was before her. Before one tiny girl with big eyes and a brave heart cracked something open in me, something I didn't know I was capable of feeling.

Now I couldn't imagine a world without her in it. She'd carved out a space inside me so deep, so permanent, that life before her barely felt real.

And watching her with Yelena—watching the two of them move through each new day together—was like witnessing something being made from the inside out. They were finding their rhythm together. A mother and daughter rebuilding something that had been stolen from them.

Not perfect. Not easy. But real.

I let my eyes close, just for a second, and let the sound of them settle into the space inside me that had never stopped hunting for vengeance. That place didn't feel quite so raw anymore. Not with them just beyond that door. Not with the world finally quiet.

Let them come. Let the Bratva scramble for a new king. Let Bowen build his empire one corpse at a time. Let the city face the sunlight without ever knowing what happened in the dark.

We'd already won.

And if someone came to tear it apart—if anyone dared to touch what we'd fought so hard for—I'd bury them. No holding back. No remorse.

Because this? This was mine now. And I'd burn down the world to keep it.

To keep them.

THEY ACTED like they were still waiting for someone else to walk through the door and take control. Someone older. Someone male.

As if I was just keeping the seat warm until the next alpha rose up and claimed the throne.

Three men sat around the table, all former lieutenants of Nik's. Men who'd once bowed to my grandfather. And then to the man who'd murdered him.

These men had trafficked weapons, drugs, and women—all without flinching. They'd carved power from suffering and called it strategy. Had worn obedience like armor, convincing themselves it wasn't their hands doing the damage, it was just the orders they followed.

They weren't speaking up now either. None of them had raised their eyes or their voices.

Not yet.

At my feet, Anya sat cross-legged on the floor, carefully stacking coasters into a crooked little tower. Her concentration was fierce, and her small hands worked with a kind of precision that seemed far too advanced for a child her age. Until she'd knock the whole thing down to start over.

Every few seconds, she peeked up at me. Just a quick glance. Like she needed confirmation I was still here. Still solid. Still hers.

It had been almost a week since the rescue, and she hadn't let me out of her sight for more than a breath. She followed me from room to room. Slept curled against my side. Clung to me like she was afraid I'd disappear if she blinked.

And I let her.

I wanted her close. Needed it, even. I knew that feeling—the ache of separation so sharp it felt like abandonment. A bone-deep fear that whispered the people I loved most would vanish the second I let go.

Even as I held her and reassured her with soft words and quiet touches, I burned with the knowledge that she'd been changed by all of this. That she'd been marked by her father's malignancy.

It didn't matter that I'd pulled her out or that I was keeping her close. The fact that she'd ever needed saving at all made something primal rise in me.

And the men at the table? They were part of that brutal history.

They might not have laid a hand on her, but they'd upheld the structure that allowed it. Their compliance fed Nik, turned him into a god—at least in his mind.

"I'm not here to debate legacy." I kept my chin lifted and my tone even. "I'm not here to avenge my grandfather or finish what he started."

Pavel shifted in his seat, his broad shoulders rolling like he was readying for a fight. The thick cords of his neck flexed beneath his collar, and his eyes held no emotion, only calculation. The other two stayed still, more patient, more careful. But no less dangerous.

"I'm here to end what Nikolai turned this organization into," I said. "Starting with the trafficking."

One of them sucked in an audible breath, and I could see the muscle in Viktor's jaw twitching. Still, none of them spoke.

"Those operations are finished." My hand sliced through the air. "As of right now, they're done."

The silence held, but it wasn't because of obedience. It was tension—that brief flicker of restraint before a fight breaks loose.

Viktor leaned forward, his hand landing in a fist on the edge of the table. Not hard enough to cause a scene or scare anyone, just enough to make a point. "And if someone doesn't agree with this new direction?"

I met his stare. "Then they're free to leave."

Pavel scoffed, loud enough to draw attention. His lip curled as he leaned back in his chair, his arms crossing over his chest like he was settling in for a show. "Just like that? No punishment? No blood?"

"Just like that," I said. "Walk away and I won't come after you. But if you leave, you don't just leave the Bratva, you leave the city."

Someone choked out a sound of disagreement, but I didn't back down. "If you stay—and gentlemen, I hope you all do—you follow my rules."

"Your rules," Viktor echoed, more thoughtful than mocking.

"That's right." I offered a tight smile.

Pavel let out a snort. "And what happens when the Albanians or the Irish start knocking? When they smell weakness and decide to take a bite?"

"They're welcome to try." My voice didn't waver. "But they'll find I bite back."

That earned a slow chuckle from Oleg. He was the oldest, the quietest, and the one I watched most closely. Men like him didn't survive this long without learning to wait. To listen. "You sound like him," he drawled, his eyes fixed on mine.

My spine snapped straight. "Don't confuse me with Nikolai. I'm nothing like him."

Oleg didn't bang his fist like Viktor had. He didn't challenge me with a sneer like Pavel. Instead, he eased back in his chair with the slow confidence of a man who'd survived too much to waste energy on posturing.

His gaze held mine. "I wasn't talking about Nikolai," he said. "I meant your grandfather. Ilya."

The other men went silent.

So did I.

Oleg gave a slight nod, as if to confirm the comparison wasn't made lightly. "He cleaned up his share of blood too. Never did it for greed. Just control. Order. You sound like him now."

"Good." My voice held steady, even as my heart crawled into my throat. "Because that's exactly how I plan to run things."

At my feet, Anya let out a soft giggle as her tower gave way. The coasters clattered to the floor, forgotten. I didn't turn, just caught the movement from the corner of my eye as she pushed them aside and clambered up into the chair beside me.

She didn't say a word. Her quiet, determined presence was its own kind of power.

God, she really was going to rule one day. Maybe not the whole world…but her own.

The room stilled. All three men watched her, tracking every one of her small movements. Their postures eased, their gazes softened, and whatever resistance they'd brought into this room faded in the space of a breath.

It wasn't fear that kept them quiet. And it sure as hell wasn't loyalty.

It was shame.

They wore it differently—some more deeply than others—but I could see it on each of their faces. Could feel it in the silence, heavy with the things none of them dared to say.

I let them sit with it for a while before I spoke again.

"We've all lost something. Some more than others. And Nikolai left this organization in pieces." My gaze travelled around the table, looking them each in the eyes. "But we can rebuild it. It won't be easy, and I'm telling you now, I won't tolerate the old ways. From this point on, we give more than we take. We make some-thing better."

I turned toward Anya, giving her a soft smile. "For the future."

A long moment passed before Viktor stood. "I'll fall in line," he said, giving me a short decisive nod, then turned and left.

Pavel followed. He was slower, stiffer. His mouth was tight, but he kept it shut.

Oleg didn't offer a speech or any pledges, just a knowing look before the scrape of his chair broke the silence and he walked out.

They didn't trust me yet. Not fully. But they hadn't challenged me either. Trust would come with time—once they saw me stand by my word and realized there was more power in cooperation than control.

For now it was a start.

I turned to Anya and lifted her into my arms, her small body curling against mine like she'd always been there. Her cheek was warm against my neck, her thumb already in her mouth. One tiny hand clutched the collar of my shirt.

We stayed like that, rocking gently in the quiet as the last of the day's fight slowly drained from my body.

Then I heard the soft clearing of a throat behind me.

I turned to find Kira standing in the doorway, arms crossed, spine straight, expression unreadable—guarded in a way that made my chest tighten.

"You know…" She took a single measured step into the room, her eyes cast toward the ground. "I thought

I'd lost you." She let out a quiet, breathless laugh, shaking her head. "Not when Robin called to say you'd gone after Nikolai alone. Not even when he first took you."

My brows drew together as I moved toward her, but I didn't rush. Didn't interrupt. I gave her space to say what she needed to, on her own terms.

"It was after." Her voice dropped to something small and fragile. Something unfamiliar for my bold and brash sister. "After we got you out and you were safe. When you looked me in the eye and told me you'd gone with him willingly. That you chose him. That you'd do it again…" Her voice broke over the words. "That was the moment I thought you were gone for good."

"I didn't choose him." I adjusted Anya in my arms, her warmth anchoring me in the here and now. "I chose her. I stayed because I didn't know how to leave. And I thought if I played by his rules, she'd survive."

"I know that now." Kira's gaze drifted past me to the open room—to the table where I'd held my first Bratva meeting, the empty chairs, and the scattered coasters on the ground. "And after seeing this? I understand why."

She closed the distance, lifting a hand to gently smooth a lock of hair from Anya's forehead. "I heard what Oleg said," she murmured. "He's right. You do sound like our grandfather, Batya. He'd have been proud. Not just because you survived, but because you took it back. All of it."

Our eyes met—hers bright with unshed tears, mine

still searching. Needing connection. Needing to know we were still on the same side.

"Are you angry I've done it?" I asked, my voice low. "That I stepped into the role he always wanted for you?"

"No." She answered without pause. "Because I never wanted it. Not then. And not now."

"Not even a little?" The corner of my mouth quirked up. "Maybe just to boss Pavel around?"

Her bark of laughter was so sudden it startled Anya. Kira's eyes widened and she clapped a hand over her mouth as Anya settled again.

The levity faded as quickly as it came, leaving something quieter in its wake—something honest.

"I'm not a leader, Yelena. I never have been. I did what I had to. Protected who I could. But this?" She stared into the empty room. "This life—the power, the decisions, the weight of it—it was never meant for me. I'm glad it's you. You're stronger than I ever was."

Emotion pressed sharp against the back of my throat. I tried to swallow it down, but it stuck. "I don't want you to feel like you're being forced to walk away. There's a place for you here, if you want it."

"I don't," she said with a smile. "I'll always have your back. But I'm done fighting for a place in a world I didn't choose. And so is Bodhi."

I studied her face—the softness there, the quiet peace that hadn't been present in years. For the first time, she looked like someone who wasn't running.

She'd made her choice. Fought her battle. And now, finally, she was laying down her gloves.

"We've been talking." Her voice lightened. "About starting a business. Something that can help people in tough situations…but who knows. Maybe we'll run away to a farm."

"A farm?" I snorted. "I cannot picture that."

"Yeah, me neither." She smiled.

"Well, whatever you decide, you deserve a little peace and happiness. Both of you."

"So do you," she replied. "And maybe this is your way of finding it."

In my arms, Anya stirred again. "Mama…" Her voice was soft and drowsy, like a thought spilling out of a dream.

Kira smiled, slow and warm. "Happiness is all that ever mattered."

I pulled Anya closer. Her breath was steady against my neck, her fingers still curled into my shirt. With my sister beside me—still standing, still whole—I wasn't clinging to the broken bits of my past. I was laying the first stones in the path of something new.

Only one piece was missing.

"What about Finn?" Kira asked as though reading my mind.

I hesitated, my fingers brushing lightly over Anya's back. "He's still recovering."

The wound hadn't been as fatal as it first looked, but it would take time before he was whole again. Physically, he was doing better than I'd expected and getting stronger every day. But mentally? I wasn't sure.

Kira tilted her head. "That's not what I was asking."

"I don't know. So much of my focus has been on Anya. On this." I motioned to the room behind me. "We haven't really talked since…everything happened."

"But you care about him." It wasn't a question.

Kira might not have shared my experiences or understood how they'd shaped me, but she still knew me. We shared something deeper than blood. A connection forged in trauma and loss but anchored by something stronger.

Hope.

It was hope that kept us tethered when everything else pulled us under. I'd lost sight of it for a long time, but Kira had helped me find it again.

So had Finn.

He didn't just show me the way back, he reached into the storm and pulled me from the wreckage. Lifted me above the waves, even as he drowned.

"I do care about him. More than he probably knows," I admitted, my gaze going soft. "But this isn't exactly what he signed up for." And I wasn't going to hold him to promises he'd made in the heat of passion.

She shot me a skeptical glance. "Did any of us?"

"No. But everything feels different now." I sighed, but it didn't release the tension. "With Nik gone, I don't know where that leaves us. I don't know how he feels."

"Maybe it's time to find out."

She didn't push the point any further. She didn't need to.

Because she was right.

Finn had helped me reclaim my strength, piece by piece. He'd believed in me long before I believed in myself. And if I wanted to hold on to him—really hold on—I had to show him I could do the same. Not with fear, but with courage.

With choice.

CHAPTER
TWENTY-NINE
FINN

THE WORLD LOOKED different now that the war was over. Not calmer or even safer. Just clearer. Like the haze had lifted, and I could finally see beyond the mission. Beyond the secrets, lies, and the trail of bodies we'd left behind.

For the first time in a year, my focus wasn't narrowed to a single ruthless objective, and the path ahead didn't end in violence. It opened into something else.

Something that looked a hell of a lot like possibility. A future with a love that—if she still wanted me—could redefine the kind of man I'd become.

Yelena stood in the doorway of what had once been her grandfather's office, before Rykov had stolen it with blood and deception. Now, like the rest of the properties they'd owned, it was back in her family's hands.

The room was all heavy shadows and old-world power—dark wood, hand-carved furniture, and the faint smell of cigars still lingering in the air. She hadn't changed any of it. Not the desk. Not the shelves lined with aging ledgers. Not even the heavy curtains that blocked the light.

None of it suited her, and yet she looked like she belonged here. Like she owned not only the room, but the leadership that went with it.

Her stance was loose, almost casual, and nothing about her was uncertain. She filled the space with calm and confidence. But her authority didn't come from fear. And it sure as hell wasn't borrowed.

This strength was all her own.

Anya tore past her with a shriek of laughter, chasing a scuffed plastic truck across the floor. It bumped into my boot and spun in a lazy circle before tipping over.

She looked up at me with wide eyes and a grin that took up half her face. "Finn!"

I crouched to greet her. "Hi there, little animal."

She launched into me like a rocket, all wild limbs and delighted giggles, her arms wrapping around my neck with a force that nearly knocked me off balance.

A flash of pain sparked in my side, shooting up under my ribs. Sharp and quick, it was enough to remind me I wasn't fully healed. The stitches still pulled when I moved too fast, and the bruising ran deep—my muscles and bones were still tender beneath the surface. But it was better than it had been, and it was getting better every day.

Anya leaned back and patted my cheek with tiny fingers that were warm and clumsy. Her eyes searched my face, wide and curious, and her brow was drawn in quiet concentration. Almost like she was memorizing me.

"Up?" she asked.

I lifted her into my arms, settling her against my non-injured side. She melted into me and tucked her head beneath my chin, one hand fisting in the too-long hair at the base of my skull.

Something in me cracked open.

Yelena watched from the doorway, her gaze drifting over the two of us, soft yet impossible to read—the small smile on her lips trembling.

Fuck. Was that happiness? Did she look at us and see a new beginning?

Or was it regret? Maybe what she saw was something she planned to end. A goodbye already forming.

"She's doing better." Her voice was quiet but strong and gave no hint of what she was thinking.

"I can tell." I looked down at Anya, still curled into me like I was something worth holding on to.

When I met Yelena's eyes again, the distance between us was unbearable. It fucking hurt. Worse than the goddamn gunshot.

Anya squirmed in my arms, pointing to the window. "Look." She waved her hands and kicked her feet. "I go look. Look."

Despite the tension in my limbs and the lump in my throat, I laughed. She was a demanding little thing. She was also fucking adorable and impossible to resist. I carried her to the window and pushed the curtain aside so she could look out. Together, we watched two men carry crates toward an idling van.

The world was still turning, just on new terms. Rebuilding, restructuring, reimagining. The Bratva wasn't crumbling, it was evolving.

And Yelena was the reason.

She moved up beside me, close enough that I could feel her warmth. Not quite touching, but still filling the space around me.

Her presence had always filled the room in a way no one else ever could.

"You shouldn't be up," she said after a moment, her voice lower now. "Not this soon."

"I'm fine." Not entirely true, but I'd survived worse.

Lying in that bed, alone, knowing she was out here rebuilding without me, had nearly broken me. I needed to see her like this. On her feet. In charge. Standing in the place where her nightmares had lived and turning it into something she could own.

"You're still healing."

"So are you," I murmured. "Just in different ways."

She didn't argue.

We stood there in the quiet—me with her daughter in my arms, her with the Bratva at her back—and for the first time in days, I didn't feel like a ghost hovering at the edge of her life. I felt like maybe, just fucking maybe, I still had a place in it.

"I planned to kill a man." My voice was low. Honest. "I thought if I ended him, I could finally put Emily to rest. Bury the guilt with him and walk away clean." I turned toward her, and the pull of my stitches created an ache that mirrored the one in my chest. "But I didn't kill him. You did."

Her expression remained calm, impossible to decipher. "Do you resent that?"

"I should." I forced the words to stay steady through the banging of my heart. "But I don't. Watching you do it…it felt right. Like every loss, every choice that led us here, happened so you could be the one to pull that trigger."

She moved closer, her hand brushing lightly over Anya's back. "I didn't know I was going to do it," she said softly. "Not until the moment came. And when it did, there was no reluctance. No fear. I knew it had to be done."

"Because it was always supposed to be you."

Her gaze lifted to mine. "It changed something. Not just in me. Between us."

"Yeah. It did." Fuck, had it ever.

Watching her take back what was stolen, watching her end it, had changed everything for me. It didn't just cement my feelings for her. It gave me something I hadn't even realized I'd been chasing. Something stronger than retribution. More enduring than redemption.

It gave me love.

Not the kind that comes clean or easy, but one that's forged in fire and scar tissue. The kind I could've only ever found with her—the woman who'd clawed her way out of hell. Who chose blood and rebirth over quiet survival. The mother who fought like a soldier, who led like she was born for it.

The woman who showed me there could still be light within darkness.

"I sold Emily's place," I said.

Surprise flickered across her beautiful face. "You did?"

"Robin and her cousin handled it. Quietly. A legit purchase agreement went through this morning."

I swallowed hard, then let the truth tumble out of me. "It didn't feel right to hold on to something that was never really mine. It belonged to Emily. She bought it to get away from me. It was time to let it go. Let her go."

Yelena's throat bobbed as she swallowed, her eyes glossing with tears that didn't fall.

Still, I couldn't read her. Couldn't tell if she was drawing closer or pulling further away.

"This isn't just about survival anymore." The words scraped up my throat, my voice rough-edged and wavering. "I need to know what comes next. I can't keep pretending I've got nothing to lose. But if you're on a different path now—if you need time or space or don't want me—I'll let you go too."

She jolted back, like the words had landed a physical blow. "Wait. Are you saying you don't want this anymore?"

"No." I closed the gap between us and grabbed her hand. Not just to reassure her, but because I needed the contact. I needed to feel her skin against mine. To feel like I had some semblance of control. "I want this. I want you, Lena. More than anything. But not because we clawed our way through hell together. And not because of promises we made in the dark. I want you because even after all of it, you're the one who lights me up. The one I want to spend my time with. Grow old with. You're the one I choose."

I swallowed hard. "I need to know you're choosing me too."

She stared at me. Her spine held strong, but her gaze…fuck, her expression cracked wide open. Hurt, hope, and unspoken need came pouring through.

"God, Finn…" The words caught in her throat.

And then she was in my arms, wrapping herself around me like she'd been holding herself back for far too long.

My free hand slid to the back of her neck, my fingers threading through her hair as I pressed a kiss to her forehead. Relief crashed through me, sharp and grounding.

Anya squealed, gleeful and unbothered, wiggling between us with all the enthusiasm of a child who didn't know she'd just witnessed something life-altering.

I breathed a laugh into Yelena's hair, kissed her again, then leaned back to look at both of them. "I'm all in," I said. "You, me, and this little animal glued to my side."

Anya made a pleased little hum and burrowed in deeper, her thumb already back in her mouth like she was claiming her territory.

Yelena laughed softly. The sound was low and rich,

and it curled somewhere deep in my chest. "She really is, isn't she?"

I kissed Anya's temple, then looked back at Yelena. "What about you?"

"Me?"

"Are you all in?"

Her body answered first, leaning into mine. Her head tucked under my chin like it belonged there, and her fingers stroked over my back. She whispered, "I'm all yours."

And just like that, I let myself believe the fight might really be over. I let go of the past, finally looking forward.

I glanced down at Anya, her head tipping against my chest, lashes heavy. "You getting sleepy, little animal?"

She blinked up at me, drowsy but stubborn, then wriggled hard enough to make my side throb. Her eyes were already locked on the scuffed plastic truck resting a few feet away.

I grunted softly and crouched to set her down. "Go on then."

With a quiet little squeal, she ran off, plopping onto the floor beside the truck. She pushed it in a crooked line across the rug as her thumb snuck back into her mouth.

When I rose, Yelena was watching me. She hadn't moved from her spot, leaning against the windowsill with her arms loose at her sides, but her pouty bottom lip was caught between her teeth, and her eyes were molten.

"You look like you want something." I moved in close, crowding her back against the glass. Close enough, there was no room for doubt.

Her chin lifted, slow and deliberate. "Are you offering?"

My hand found her hip, my fingers skimming the hem of her shirt—light, teasing, and in control. "I've been patient, letting you find your footing. Giving you time to claim your crown."

Her lips parted, but I didn't let her speak. I leaned in, brushing my mouth over hers. It was barely a touch, but the air sparked between us, and my cock took notice.

"But if you keep looking at me like that," I whispered, "I'll tie you up and remind you what surrender feels like. Not to chaos. Not to fear. To me."

Her cheeks flushed, and her hands curled into the front of my shirt as if by muscle memory.

I kissed the corner of her mouth. Just a soft graze, but it felt like a promise. "I'm going to worship every delectable inch of your body until you're dripping, begging, screaming for me…"

I drew back, letting the tension hang between us, taut and electric.

"Later." My voice was quiet but firm. "Once she's down."

She gave the smallest nod, her throat working and her eyes locked on mine.

I let my thumb trace the curve of her plump bottom lip, slow and teasing. "I love you."

Her chest hitched like I'd ripped the air from her lungs. She didn't speak, but she didn't need to. Her silence was everything.

It wasn't absence. Or doubt. It was breathless wonder. An unspoken promise. Fucking devotion.

And it was enough.

I stepped back, my heart pounding, because what she gave me wasn't surrender. It was trust.

Yes, she'd given it before.

This time, it felt like I'd earned it.

THREE WEEKS LATER
YELENA

Finn crawled over me. The look on his face was that of a man possessed.

I was naked. So was he.

My hands and feet were bound, the delicious bite of rope digging into my skin, each loop meticulously placed.

He'd taken his time with the shibari, his hands both reverent and ruthless as they worked, weaving knots that weren't just meant to restrain but to worship. The pattern across my body felt like his signature, painted in tension and control. Like a work of art that would put me at his mercy and bring me to ruinous bliss.

By the time he'd secured the final wrap at my ankles, I was trembling. Desperate. The ache between my legs was sharp and constant, and tears already blurred my vision. Not from pain, but from the exquisite torment of anticipation.

He knelt above me, his eyes tracing the lines of rope

like a map he'd drawn. His thumb dragged lightly down my sternum, over the point where two bands crossed between my breasts, making me shiver in the restraints.

"Look at you," he murmured, his voice low and rough with awe. "So lovely, all tied up. Every inch of you mine."

"Finn." My voice cracked. I didn't know if I was begging or warning. Maybe both.

His mouth curled with a dark, wicked smile. "I know you're aching, Lena. And I promise I'll give you release. But not until I say."

He reached between my thighs, ghosting his fingers over my soaked flesh. I bucked without meaning to, frustration and need colliding. But the ropes held, and that only made it worse.

He leaned down, dragging his lips along the underside of my jaw. "You don't get to come," he whispered, "until I break you with it."

His fingers pressed harder, stroking me slow and precise, never fast enough to give relief, just enough to make me gasp. To make me plead. His other hand gripped my hip to keep me still while he watched every reaction with razor focus. Like each moan and whimper was a prayer he intended to memorize.

But then he stopped.

I sobbed his name.

And he kissed the sound right off my mouth.

"You're doing so good," he breathed against my lips. "But not yet."

He moved, but not to fuck me like I wanted. Instead,

he circled me like a beast deciding where to sink his teeth. His hands roamed, gripping, teasing, and squeezing until I was writhing in the ropes, a knot of tension and hunger so sharp I could barely breathe.

"You want release?" he asked, low and dangerous.

"Yes," I choked. "Please."

"You want to show me how pretty you are when you come for me?"

"Yes—"

"Then you wait." He bent down and slid his tongue over me, slow, deep, and merciless. My whole body jerked. My moan was a cry. The tears came harder now, leaking down into my hair.

He didn't stop. He licked. He sucked. He worshipped me. Until I was falling apart, every nerve ending on fire.

But just when the orgasm was about to peak, he pulled back.

"No," I whimpered.

"Yes." His voice was silk-wrapped steel. "You're going to come when I tell you. And when you do, it'll feel like fucking ecstasy." He kissed the inside of my thigh, teasing.

And then he started again.

It was impossible to tell how long it went on—I lost all sense of time. Finn edged me over and over, until the need burned hotter than pain. Until I was shaking, my entire body slick with sweat and trembling against the ropes.

Every time I got close, he'd stop. Then he'd drag me

back. Sometimes with his fingers. Sometimes with his mouth. Sometimes with nothing but a quiet, devastating command in my ear.

"Not yet."

"Hold."

"You'll beg me for mercy before I let you break."

And I did. Sweet hell, I begged.

"Finn," I gasped, my chest heaving and hips writhing helplessly. "Please…I can't—"

"You can," he whispered, pressing a kiss to the center of my chest, right over my heart. "You will."

He slid two fingers deep and flicked his tongue over my clit in a pattern that felt like sin. And this time, he didn't stop.

My body locked. The pressure snapped tight. And just as I was hitting my climax—just as a scream ripped from my throat—he rose over me, lined himself up, and thrust deep.

I shattered around him. The orgasm tore through me like fire, fury, and grace. My scream was swallowed by his mouth as he kissed me, as he moved inside me with a desperation that bordered on frenzy.

"Fuck, Lena," he growled into my skin. "I've got you. I've fucking got you."

The feel of him—thick, relentless, and buried so deep it felt like he reached into something more than just my body—drew out every last tremor.

Then he broke. With a curse and a groan that sounded half-worship, half-surrender, he pulsed inside me, burying his face in my neck as he spilled everything he had. Every ounce of restraint, of control, of need.

When it was over, he didn't move. Instead, he wrapped his arms around me, his body trembling from release, and his breath hot against my shoulder.

Eventually, he pulled back, loosening the ropes with careful precision. Unwinding me like a gift. His hands were steady, but reverent. Slow and tender. When the last knot gave way, he pulled me into him, letting me curl against his chest as we lay back on the soft blanket beneath us.

I melted against him, my body wrecked, my heart still racing, and my soul settled.

His hand stroked down my spine, his fingers trailing the path of the indents left by the rope. "You okay?"

I nodded, still breathless. Too overwhelmed to speak.

He pressed a kiss to my temple. "You were perfect."

I reached for his hand, placing it over my heart. "So were you. I'm always amazed at how much you give, even when you take."

His ocean-blue gaze met mine, still dark and dangerous, but now threaded with something gentler. Something that felt like safety. "It's not hard to give to you, Lena. It feels like I'm bleeding out all the parts of me that never made sense. It's like I'm exorcising every fucking demon one stroke at a time."

"Really?" I huffed a laugh. "That's all it took?"

"Need me to prove it again?" His brow arched with a challenge.

I smirked, even as my body still trembled. "You are obsessed with me."

"No, Lena. It's more than that…" His breath caught. "I'm in love with you."

He'd said it before. Many times. And I'd said it back. But this time?

God, this time…

Maybe it was the afterglow still clinging to my skin, or the way his voice cracked as he said it. Maybe it was everything that led us here. Every scar, bruise, and battle. Every broken piece that somehow fit together.

Whatever it was, this time when he gave me those words, I felt them bone deep. It was a blistering yet beautiful feeling. The highest of highs.

One I never wanted to come down from.

"I love you too," I murmured, curling into him.

We lay like that, tangled and undone, silence stretching warm and deep between us. And in it, I felt the truth of it settle around us.

It wasn't just release. Not just devotion. It was love, in its rawest, most ruinous form.

It was happiness.

And it was ours.

EIGHT WEEKS LATER

FINN

THE MESSAGE CAME through while Yelena was rearranging the spice cabinet. She was barefoot, her hair twisted into a loose knot, and sleeves pushed to her elbows as she sorted jars into meticulous rows, each one labeled in her perfect handwriting.

Paprika, cumin, coriander.

Her movements were calm and deliberate, like the rest of the world didn't exist.

It was almost laughable that the woman working in the kitchen—humming under her breath, focused on spices—was the same woman who'd taken control of the Bratva without blinking. The one who'd dismantled an empire built on trafficking, forced three dangerous and stubborn men to fall in line, and made it clear she wasn't inheriting anything. She was remaking it.

The same woman who was carrying my child.

She was the most amazing woman I'd ever met—a goddamn queen—and she was pregnant with my kid.

I was the luckiest son of a bitch in Manhattan.

My phone buzzed with a text from Robin.

Still no sign of Sasha. Maybe he's moved on? Left the city?

I stared at the screen a little too long. Let the words settle. He hadn't moved on. Not a chance in hell. Men like Sasha didn't vanish—they circled. Waited. Changed masks and picked new, easier targets. Found friends in lower places.

Robin wanted to believe the silence meant safety. But I'd lived in this world too long to mistake quiet for peace.

Yelena looked over, catching the shift in my posture. "You okay?"

I slid the phone back into my pocket with a nod. "Yeah. Just Robin being Robin."

Her brow arched. She didn't believe me. But she didn't push either. That was the thing about her now—she didn't need every detail to feel steady. She trusted me to tell her when it mattered.

"You sure it's not a vampire sighting?" she asked, deadpan.

"If it is, I hope it stays the hell out of our city."

"Or at least waits until after the baby's born. I'm too tired to fight any more bloodsuckers."

That earned a small smile from me, the tension easing just a little.

She crossed the room—her belly just starting to round beneath the soft sweater she wore—and slipped her hand into mine. "Come on," she murmured, lighting my soul on fire. "She's finally down."

We padded through the penthouse on quiet feet, the late afternoon sunlight casting long golden streaks across the floors. The city outside pulsed with life, but in here, everything was still.

We stopped outside Anya's room. The door was cracked just enough to see her—arms splayed, mouth open in that deep, slack-limbed sleep only toddlers managed. A stuffed bunny was tucked under one arm. Her cheeks were flushed, and her hair stuck to her forehead.

Yelena rested her head against my shoulder, her fingers looping with mine. "She won't nap like this forever. One day she'll fight us at every turn."

"She already does. She tried to negotiate more blueberries at breakfast like she was brokering a peace treaty."

Yelena laughed, her breath warm against my skin. Then her hand slid down, resting over the curve of her stomach. "Are we ready for another one?"

"Fuck no."

She elbowed me, and I grinned.

"But we'll figure it out," I said, turning toward her and catching her face in my hands.

Her pouty bottom lip disappeared behind her teeth, and I knew damn well she did it to mess with me.

"We should take advantage of this time while we have it." Her smile curved with heat and mischief.

That look in her eyes—tired, amused, and full of hunger—shredded the last thread of my restraint. I kissed her hard and fast, pulling her close until there was no space between us. Her arms looped around my neck, her mouth warm and eager, answering every press of mine with more.

I walked her backward, my breath tangled with hers, until we reached the bedroom door. She reached behind her blindly, found the handle, and pushed it open.

Our clothes hit the floor, and with them, the tension I'd been carrying.

It didn't crash out of me, it eased, pouring slow and steady until I was consumed by nothing but her. Her skin. Her breath. Her trust.

I made love to her sweetly—no ropes, toys, or leather straps. Just the two of us in a slow, aching build of passion and release.

Her nails bit into my back, her mouth whispered my name like a vow, and I gave her every inch of myself, over and over, until neither of us could breathe without the other.

And later, when her body tucked up against mine and her breathing turned soft and even, I watched the gentle rise and fall of her belly and made a promise I didn't need to say aloud.

If Sasha ever came near her, I'd bury him so deep even the devil wouldn't find him.

But tonight wasn't about threats or vengeance. Tonight was for love.

Tomorrow could fucking wait.

ABOUT THE AUTHOR

Kimberly is a contemporary romance author, born procrastinator, and lover of morally gray heroes. She enjoys lively conversations, usually with imaginary people, and can often be found daydreaming at work.

She writes gritty, messy, dangerous romances, featuring beautifully flawed characters, pursuing love at all costs. It's romance with rough edges.

When she's not busy writing, you can find her with a coffee in hand, dog at her side, and exploring the wilds of her hometown in Ontario, Canada… Or on her couch, getting lost in a good story.

Subscribe to her newsletter https://kimberlyquinn. myflodesk.com/newslettersignup, visit her website https://www.kimberleyquinnbooks.com, and follow her on Goodreads https://www.goodreads.com/author/show/ 27348216.Kimberly_Quinn

- instagram.com/kimberlyquinn.books
- amazon.com/stores/Kimberly-Quinn/author/B0B-V18S35M
- bookbub.com/profile/kimberly-quinn
- threads.com/@kimberlyquinn.books
- tiktok.com/@kimberlyquinn.books

ABOUT THE PUBLISHER

Harbor Lane Books, LLC is a US-based independent digital publisher of commercial fiction, non-fiction, and poetry.

Connect with Harbor Lane Books on their website (www.harborlanebooks.com) and social media.